SCARE ME

SCARE ME

TERI TERRY

HODDER CHILDREN'S BOOKS

First published in Great Britain in 2023 by Hodder & Stoughton

1 3 5 7 9 10 8 6 4 2

Text copyright © Teri Terry, 2023

The moral rights of the author have been asserted.

A CIP catalogue record for this book
is available from the British Library.

ISBN 978 1 444 96272 7

Typeset in Bembo Infant by Avon DataSet Ltd,
Alcester, Warwickshire

Printed and bound in Great Britain by Clays Ltd, Elcograf S.p.A.

The paper and board used in this book
are made from wood from responsible sources.

Hodder Children's Books
An imprint of Hachette Children's Group
Part of Hodder & Stoughton Limited
Carmelite House
50 Victoria Embankment
London, EC4Y 0DZ

An Hachette UK Company
www.hachette.co.uk

www.hachettechildrens.co.uk

1

Echo

I try to stop myself getting on the train.

I've been at Victoria all day. Leaning on a wall, pacing, sometimes on a bench. Ignored or avoided by commuters, then students and waves of tourists. Now and then, just for fun, I stare and almost catch someone's eye; they look uncomfortable before turning away. A lone teenage boy – one that looks like me? – they don't want to engage.

Then the students and commuters come again, and finally the evening crowd. Still I watch the departures board for each train to Brighton, willing myself not to go. I was here yesterday, the day before too. Each day it is harder to stop myself.

The last train will go soon. I've almost made it, but even as I'm congratulating myself and heading for the exit my feet turn me around in the wrong direction, towards the train and not away from it. I'm fighting to stop, to turn, each step of the way.

I reach the ticket barrier and don't even pause to look around and choose a likely moment: hands up on either side of the gate, I vault over to the platform. Maybe a guard will see, give chase? But there are no cries of stop, wait, no rushing footsteps.

No such luck.

Platform eighteen. The train is already here. People are running to catch it, out of breath as they go through the doors.

1

This is it; this is the moment. Stop agonising; either get on the freaking train, or don't.

Who am I kidding?

I step on just as the doors start to close. The whistle sounds and now it's too late to change my mind. I'm committed.

I follow a group of gasping, giggling students down the aisle. There are more students already in seats, some drunks. A few people with laptops and suits. Enough empty seats this late for me to avoid them all and find a row to myself, and I sit down, lean against the window.

Why am I doing this?

It's almost a year since Mum died. There's nothing I can do to change what happened, but I can't leave it alone.

They thought I couldn't hear the whispers – that it couldn't have been an accident, not when she pointed her car at the cliff's edge, hit the accelerator, hurtled down and crashed into the sea. They think she did that, on purpose, with me in the car? I'll never believe it.

And it kills me that I can't remember. Somehow I must have opened the passenger door, jumped out. Hit my head. When I woke up, I didn't know what had happened – it was amnesia from the trauma, or the head injury, or both. I'd hoped my memory would come back, but it never did. The last thing that I remember before the crash is getting in the car; the next is waking up on the side of the road, lost, confused and alone.

When I opened my eyes I didn't even know that my mother was dead.

It's all a blur from that point. The inquest, with its open verdict; the funeral. The few relatives who turned up – like my dad's parents – who grudgingly took me home to London with them. It was all like it happened to someone else, as if I saw the funeral – my mother lying in her coffin, still and cold – through a fog.

But now the closer the anniversary of that day gets, the more stark and painfully clear everything becomes. There's no point in fighting it because there is nothing else I can do. As much as I never, ever want to go there, where it happened, I have to do it. I have to see if being there will make me remember.

And if the memory still won't come, there is another way – to return to the moment. To live the nightmare again.

I flinch inside to even consider it, but the closer the train gets to Brighton, the more the darkness calls.

2

Liv

'Can you jump it?' I say.

Bowie eyes the distance between the window and ground below. One floor up, grass to land on.

'Yeah. No problem. Where are my . . .'

We hold our breath as floorboards creak on the stairs.

'. . . trainers,' he whispers, finishing the sentence.

I find one and after a minute he finds the other on the floor, under his jacket. He pulls them on and bends to tie the laces.

One step, two . . . past my door. Pipes grumble and water splashes in the bath two doors down.

Thank God.

'I know this doesn't look good, but is she really that scary?'

I shrug, preferring not to answer. Mum's reaction if she finds Bowie in my bedroom at – I glance at the clock – almost 1 a.m. doesn't bear thinking about.

He straightens up, pulls on his jacket. Leans on the windowsill and smiles. Framed in moonlight. His blond hair is tousled, his eyes still sleepy from our unplanned nap over our English homework. They seem to be staring into mine. My mouth goes dry and my stomach flips.

'Away you go, then,' I say.

'Kiss me first.'

'What?'

'Kiss me, or I'll tell everyone we slept together.'

'You wouldn't dare!'

He laughs. 'You can't deny it: it's true.'

'Ssssh.'

'OK, you're right; I wouldn't dare,' he says, his voice lower. 'But kiss me anyhow. Please?' He holds out his hands and smiles again.

Moonlight *and* dimples. My feet seem to have plans of their own, and step forward. He catches my hand in one of his. Bends – when did he get so tall? – and slips his other hand around the side of my face, my neck. My skin comes alive, vibrates with the warm touch of his.

I shiver. 'This is weird.'

'Shut up.' He leans down, and there is mint and soft lips and some earthy smell all his own and I'm melting, inside, until all that is left of me is where his hands and lips hold me still, unable to breathe, to move, to do anything but kiss him.

All too soon he pulls away.

'Bye, Liv.'

He pushes the window open wide, sits on the ledge. Starts to swing his legs around, but then my bedroom door opens.

'Livia Brogan Flynn! What on earth is going on in here?'

Bowie freezes.

I spin round, heat rushing up my neck, my face.

Mum. Still dressed – thank God for small miracles – and looking very amused.

She is across the room to Bowie before I can blink.

'Hi, I'm Liv's mum.'

'Ah . . .'

5

'Don't worry. I won't bite.'

'Hi, Mrs Flynn. I'm Bowie.'

'It's Ms, but call me Lexi.'

He has one leg hanging out the window and one in, looking from me to her, holding on to the window ledge with his hands like he'll fall off if he lets go. Sort of how you feel I guess when you are expecting the parent of a not-quite-sixteen-year-old girl to react in a hysterical fashion, and instead you get a Lexi.

Mum laughs. 'You can jump if you want to, but now that I've caught you sneaking out of my daughter's room you might as well use the front door.'

He swings his other leg back in the room.

'Stay for tea? Or a beer,' Mum says.

'Ah, sure?' He's hesitant, a bit shocked. I'm guessing his parents don't offer beer to the underaged.

'Mum, the bath?' I say.

'Oh!' And she dashes out of the room to turn off the water.

'Run,' I hiss at Bowie.

'What?'

'I mean it. Go!'

But he is too slow, only half across the room when she reappears in the door.

'Come on, you two miscreants. Downstairs.'

'He's cute,' she stage whispers as she follows behind. Then she adds, 'It's about time.'

I wish very hard I could melt like the wicked witch of the west into a puddle and disappear.

No such luck.

She puts the kettle on for us and hands Bowie a beer, and I

make myself small on a chair. Bowie's eyes follow her. I told her that dress was too tight before she left on her date.

'Don't you need to get home, Bowie?' I say. 'Won't your parents be worried?'

'Nah. They're not bothered on a Saturday night.'

I look daggers. He's too busy looking at Mum's cleavage as she bends to pour the tea to notice.

She puts the cups on a tray. 'Follow me,' she says, and crosses the hall. I groan. The sitting room. I *hate* anyone going in there.

'So, where have you been hiding your young man?' she says to me. 'Apart from in your bedroom after midnight.'

I cringe. 'He's not my *young man*, whatever that is supposed to mean. We were just doing our English homework.' Something that would never have happened here if Mum hadn't been out.

'This late?' She raises an eyebrow.

'Honest,' Bowie says. 'Shakespeare's *Richard III*. And we fell asleep.'

'Hardly surprising,' Mum says, and switches on lights, gestures towards the sofa.

Maybe a proper miracle will happen now; after all this I'm due one, I'm sure of it. Maybe he won't notice the photographs.

'That's you?' Bowie says, and goes straight up to the last on the wall. It's me and Mum almost a year ago, on my fifteenth birthday.

Don't, my eyes are saying to Mum, pleading, but she either doesn't notice or ignores me.

'You need to start at the beginning,' Mum says, and takes his arm and draws him to the other end of the room.

Starting at the beginning is a framed ultrasound – from before I was *born*. No privacy even in the womb.

'Now, this is a very special photograph,' Mum says. 'See, here, this is Liv.' She traces me as a foetus. 'And there, the smaller shadow next to her? That is Molly, her sister.'

'Twins?' Bowie turns to me. 'There aren't two of you?'

'It would explain her moods, wouldn't it?' Mum laughs. 'Sweet Liv, evil Liv.'

I glare.

'No. Sadly Molly died.'

Thankfully she spares him the details and he doesn't ask. But he will eventually. Won't he? He'll want to know, and then what? It's not like I can tell him anything like the truth about Molly.

Mum goes on to the photo of me seconds after birth: a great look.

Then follows one of Mum and me on each of my birthdays. For the first four years Dad was in them too, but when they split she had the photos enlarged and reframed with him neatly excised off the side. I see Dad so seldom now, leaving the photos as they were might have been useful for recognition purposes.

By the time Mum has Bowie back across the room to look again at the photo from my fifteenth, he comes up with the compliment she's been hoping for. She'd gone to lengths on that photo session, now that I was older. We're nearly the same height, though I'm a bit like a weed standing next to Marilyn Monroe. Eyes similar dark brown, both with long dark hair – hers straightened to look more like mine for the shoot – jeans and

8

white T-shirts that show off the tan we'd got on a beach in Spain at the end of the summer.

'No way do you look like her mum. You look like her sister,' he says. 'You could be twins: Lexi and Liv.'

He's made her night.

He finally leaves after many promises extracted to visit whenever he likes, with no necessity to use the window. Not sure, but I think Bowie just got granted a parental pass to my bedroom at any hour of the day or night.

Huh.

It starts as soon as the door shuts behind him.

'Liv, he's adorable.'

'Why don't you go out with him, then?'

'Liv!'

'What?'

She sighs. 'I'm just trying to help. He's a sweetie but he'll get away if blah blah blah blah . . .'

I tune out of Mum's guide to pleasing men. She should know, I guess. I eventually escape back upstairs.

My phone beeps as I shut my door. A text from Bowie: your mum is amazing, what were u worried about? xxx

Three kisses: he hasn't signed off a text like that before. My stomach lurches as I remember Bowie in moonlight: he held out his hands by the window. He kissed me. Did it really happen? It's confusing, he's my friend, I don't think of him like that – but then, all at once in that moment, I did.

But now Amazing Mum is all over it.

I put my phone on silent and chuck it on my desk. I throw

9

the window open wide, lean out into the night. The cool breeze is tangy from the sea; Brighton beach is close enough to hear the comforting murmur of the waves in the background, but far enough away that in daylight I have to stand on tiptoe in exactly the right place to see a stretch of blue.

Whatever I do, wherever I go, my friends . . . everything. If it's not her, then it's Mum. Wanting to be there. Crawling into my skin, living my life.

All I want – all I have *ever* wanted – is space. To be able to breathe.

Goosebumps creep up my arms, my back, like an army of little spiders. Mid October, a clear night; it's not that cold. I don't turn.

Mum's right: he's adorable.

'Go away.' I shut the window and get into bed. I should have known Molly had been lurking when Bowie was here, even though she promised not to. Not even that moment is mine, alone. Nothing ever could be, could it?

Sorry. I tried to stay away; I couldn't help it. That kiss was . . . yummy.

I touch my lips with my tongue; they tingle with the memory. I shake my head. 'He's not coming back. I'll see to it.'

Liv, come on. I hardly get to see anyone.

'I thought you didn't like it when I had friends over.'

Sometimes I don't. But Bowie is different.

'Bowie is my friend. Not yours.'

That's not fair!

'Life's not fair.'

Death isn't, either.

I don't reply. What is there to say to the ghost of your sister when you're the one who killed her?

Nothing.

Molly stretches alongside me, cradles her arms around me until the cold seeps into my bones.

It wasn't your fault. I don't blame you.

3

Echo

When the late train finally pulls into Brighton I hang back, last off the train. I watch the other passengers shuffle, stumble or power walk as they make their way to the gates, put their tickets in to exit. One girl has to empty out her whole bag to find hers. I stand in shadows by the wall, waiting for the last one to be gone, the guards to turn away. Now that I'm here I might as well not get caught.

I cross to the ticket barriers and, hands on the sides, vault up and over. Prepared to run if any of them notice, but they're tired this late, not really paying attention. Easy.

Now what?

For a moment I consider going to Mum's friend, Kashina. She wasn't just a friend; she was kind of like my adopted granny, as unlikely as that'd seem to most. She'd take me in, wouldn't she? If she's not too far into a bottle to hear the door. I dismiss it; maybe tomorrow. It's too late tonight to bother anyone, even Kashina.

I walk away from the station, aimless. Watchful. Avoiding people out on the party trail, other solitary figures like me who lean in the shadows.

I should find somewhere to get some sleep, but I don't sleep well, not any more. Not since it happened last year. Anyway, nowhere feels safe on my own: what might happen to me if I close my eyes on a bench?

There is a deep ache inside me for so many things that are missing. A longing – for warmth, light, someone who knows me that I can talk to – takes over so much that my feet are almost too heavy to go on.

Get a grip, Echo. I shake it off, keep walking.

There are fewer people out now; it's getting later. Without meaning to go there my feet take me to our house.

Gran and Grandad sold it and pocketed the money, I guess – at least I never saw any of it. I wonder who lives here now?

The lights are out. I know the way into the back garden from the lane behind – there are loose boards in the fence, assuming they haven't been fixed. Drawn there, I find the place. They're still loose.

I slip through the fence to the back garden.

It's an overgrown mess: whoever bought the house hasn't got green fingers like Mum did. She'd hate to see it like this.

But her summerhouse is still here.

I try the door; it isn't locked. Slip inside.

Instead of gardening supplies and a bench, there's a dusty reclining chair. A bunch of cushions are stacked up in a mess in the corner, the sort that go on outdoor furniture. I lower myself on to the chair, pull the cushions in around me.

I feel safer here.

After a while I close my eyes. I wish for sleep – for the blank, nothingness it can bring – but the night goes slowly by.

4

Liv

'Bad night, sweetie?'

Mum hands me a cup of tea when I finally make it downstairs. I shrug.

'Staying up late dreaming of Bowie, I bet.'

'No!'

I turn to go back up the stairs.

'Liv, wait. Eat something.'

I pause. 'I'm not hungry.'

'You're disappearing. Can't I make you something?'

'I'll do it myself. All right?'

'Fine.' She sighs and I turn back, clatter about the kitchen. Baked beans: breakfast of champions. I heat them on the stove while the bread toasts. It pops up and I tear a piece in half, dip it in the pot of beans.

'You could use a plate, Little Miss Sunshine.'

I glare and she glares back. I relent.

'All right, fine.' I stop dipping toast into the pot and take the plate she holds out. Put the toast on it and dump the beans on top. 'See, look what you've done: now I need cutlery, too.' She hands me a knife and fork and I sit at the table.

'Used to be you wouldn't eat toast unless I cut the crusts off.'

'Used to be I wore nappies, but isn't it good to move on?'

14

'Good point. But perhaps now you'd like to tell me what you are so angry about, this time?'

'I just wish you wouldn't show people that photo of the ultrasound, of me and Molly. Can't you put it away in a drawer?'

Mum sits next to me, slips an arm across my shoulders. Pushes a stray bit of hair off my face.

'It might be hard to understand why I still miss her so much, when I never even got to know her. But Molly will always be a part of me. That is the only photo I have of the two of you together; it belongs on that wall, with all the others.'

I don't answer. Molly has always been a part of me, too. She's been with me, in my shadow, every day of my life.

Imaginary friend, they began to say, when I was old enough to talk and got caught having conversations with someone who wasn't there. When I finally told Mum, years ago, that my 'imaginary' friend was really Molly, she cried, and I ended up with the first in a string of psychologists. Now I just keep Molly to myself. It's easier that way.

Easier for who? Molly sits on the counter, swinging her feet. She reaches out and puts her hand on Mum's cheek. *Tell her I miss her, too.*

Mum shivers, pulls her arms around herself. I say nothing and Molly glares, then disappears into the mirror hanging over the table.

With any luck she'll sulk for a few days and give me some peace.

'Do you have any plans for today?' Mum asks.

I shrug.

'I'm going to deliver a car to London this afternoon, get the train back. Want to come? We could squeeze in some shopping.'

I waver. Mum sells high-end sports cars; now and then she delivers them to buyers too busy or important to collect. But all that time trapped with Mum in traffic and then back on the train: more third degree about Bowie, or – worse – her telling me about her date last night.

'No. Homework calls.'

'Homework, or Bowie?' she teases.

'Homework!'

'I'm so pleased to see you've made a new friend.'

'By friend you mean boyfriend.'

'Whatever. You spend too much time alone.'

Of course she doesn't know I am almost never alone, or how I crave solitude. No one watching, reading my thoughts.

'Well, just in case you two get back to Shakespeare . . . you don't have to worry about me interrupting until late. I've got a date tonight.'

'How unusual. Which one is it?'

'Sarcasm, Liv? Tsk tsk. Same one as last night, and last weekend, and the weekend before that.'

'The fireman? Is it Todd or Clod or . . .'

She smiles. 'He's the policeman, actually. The fireman was Jamie. This one is Rod, cheeky thing. And he is hot. You should see his . . .'

I stuff hands over my ears. 'Not listening. La la la . . .'

She pulls one hand away.

'. . . you should see his dog, Merry. Cocker spaniel. She had puppies six weeks ago and they are so sweet.'

16

'Oh. Can we have one?'

'Maybe.'

'Really?' I'm staring back at her, looking for confirmation that she actually means it this time. I've wanted a dog as long as I can remember.

'You'd have to actually meet him, to get a puppy.'

'Bribery. Have you admitted to my existence yet?'

'Of course!'

'Must be serious, then. Does he think I'm three, or fifteen?'

'We haven't discussed your exact age.'

'Ha. How about your age?'

'That hasn't come up.'

Mum is a pretty good thirty-four. She doesn't look it; she often passes for younger. Admitting to a teenage daughter is tricky for her sometimes.

'How old is he?'

She shrugs. 'Aren't I the one who is supposed to be asking you the questions? How old is Bowie?'

'Sixteen – so what? How old is Rod?'

She mumbles something, walking out of the kitchen. I follow her.

'Wait. Did you say twenty-five?'

'Maybe.'

'Huh. I could go out with him. It's about ten years, either way.'

'No, you could not! Stick to sixteen a bit longer. But there is something . . .'

'What?'

'He knows you live here with me, but he sort of assumed

17

you are my sister, and I didn't set him straight.'

I groan. 'Are you serious?'

She doesn't answer and that says it all.

Molly won't like it. I glance uneasily at the mirror on the wall as I climb the stairs to my room. She often hides in mirrors. The surface stays flat, my face stares back. That doesn't mean anything, though. Sometimes I think I'm looking at myself and combing my hair or whatever, and it's Molly: copying my actions back at me, then suddenly jumping out and scaring the life out of me.

Bit by bit.

The calls to my mobile start soon after Mum leaves. I switch it off. Even on silent the vibrating was annoying, with Bowie's name on the screen, insisting I respond and me not knowing what to do, at all.

Now the land line is ringing.

I walk into the kitchen and stare at the phone; is it him? With all the reasons not to answer, my hand still itches to pick up.

RRRing! RRRing!

Why don't you answer? Molly says.

RRRing! RRRing!

I ignore it, and Molly. The machine clicks on.

'Hello, Liv? It's Bowie. Call me. Bye.' It clicks off.

Molly scowls. *Why didn't you pick up?*

'Why do you care?'

She doesn't say anything, just sits on the counter looking at her shoes.

I know that look. It's a lot like the one Mum wore when she

18

didn't want to admit how old Hot Rod was, or that he thought I was her sister.

'What have you done, Molly?'

Nothing.

'Tell me!'

She doesn't answer and I think back to last night. Bowie is my friend, that's all as far as I've ever been concerned. I met him four years ago – first year of secondary – when the seating plan in science had us being lab partners. I didn't talk to people much then – I still don't – and got labelled Loony Liv soon enough in the new school, much like the old one. But Bowie was friendly, persistent and hard to ignore. And then he worked out I was a maths whiz but useless at English; we started swapping homework help for the two subjects. Over time we started talking more and more, especially this last summer – and meeting up now and then for fish and chips on the beach. And then he started bugging me to meet up at his house, or mine, until finally I'd said yes, for him to come here – picking my time so Mum was out and Molly owed me a favour. She'd said it was OK and that she'd leave us alone.

And then last night he sat on the window and wanted a kiss, and for some reason, I went along with it. He's my friend, someone I can talk to – and I don't want to mess that up. The kiss was nice but that isn't the point. It wasn't like me to do that.

It wasn't ME. I gasp as it hits me; my hands curl into fists.

'You kissed him, didn't you!'

Don't look so angry.

'You promised. You promised you wouldn't come in any more without asking first.'

I thought you knew. Usually you can tell when I take over, and you didn't tell me to go.

I'm too angry to talk, too angry to do anything. I dash down the hall, pull my trainers on.

Don't leave like this, don't. Liv, wait. Talk to me. I'm sorry!

But the door is open, slammed behind and then I'm running. The houses blur past, the end of our road and then Brighton Lanes. Dodging shoppers, racks of clothes and café tables on the pavement, and still I run, not stopping, all the way to the promenade and the beach.

She's right. I can usually tell if she slips inside, comes along for the ride. There is a chill, a disorientation, almost nausea. I didn't pick up on it last night and that must have been Bowie. The whole kiss thing was so distracting, I didn't even notice it was really Molly's idea to go along with it.

Bowie is calling me, but he really wants the girl who kissed him. My sister. Slightly complicated by the fact that she is *dead*. That would freak him right out, wouldn't it? It freaks me out, and I'm the one who has to live with it.

My indecision is gone. This isn't just a question of Bowie staying a friend or maybe becoming something more – he can't be anything to me now. I'm losing my friend – my only real friend, if I'm honest with myself – and it's Molly's fault. There's no way he can come over again. God knows what she'd have me doing with him next.

I run the length of the promenade to Brighton Marina, and back again. Several times. If I go fast, very fast, Molly can't follow and I'm free.

I don't stop. Shadows start to lengthen. Sweat soaks through my trackies and T-shirt, my legs are giving out, my head pounding in time with my feet. My stomach heaves all at once and I vomit in a rubbish bin.

I'm bent double, clutching my stomach and trying to slow my breathing when there are footsteps behind. I turn at the sound of laughter: two girls from school.

'Aw, Liv dear,' one of them says, mock concern on her face. 'You really should try to keep your eating disorder out of the public eye.'

It is well and truly dark by the time I pull myself together enough to walk home. Mum's car is back in the drive and another parked out front, but she said they were going out?

I open the door quietly and start up the stairs, but obviously I wasn't quiet enough: Mum appears from the kitchen.

'Where've you been?'

'Running.'

'I can see that. Take your phone the next time. And you could turn out the lights before you go, maybe even lock the door.'

'Didn't think I'd be gone for so long.'

'Well next time, think. I've been worried.'

'Sorry,' I say, and I am, but also annoyed. Two years ago the older sister of one of my classmates disappeared. Maybe she ran away, maybe she didn't – no one knows. But ever since, Mum gets nervous if she doesn't know where I am. And even though I understand that, what does she want me to do: hide away behind locked doors for the rest of my life?

She wrinkles her nose. 'You need a shower. Rod is here so

make it a quick one, then come down so I can introduce you. We're making pizza.'

Fine. Wonderful. Perfect end to the day.

The heat of the shower works some magic on my sore muscles, and my empty stomach tells me that maybe some dinner would be a good thing. But Rod, here? I groan. And did she say they were making pizza? Maybe she ordered one, put it in the oven to stay warm and then hid the box.

Steam fogs up the shower door. Suddenly eyes look back at mine and, startled, I jump back, almost slip over.

Rod is gorgeous.

'Molly! Could you say hello or something before you join me in the shower?'

Sorry. He is gorgeous, though: seriously tall, dark and handsome. Sort of a more muscly Timothée Chalamet.

'First Bowie, now Rod. Are you having some sort of hormonal thing? I'm supposed to be the teenager.'

I am too! But at least you're speaking to me again.

'Huh. Like I have a choice.'

Molly bites her lip. *I could leave you alone, but think how much you'd miss me.*

5

Echo

'What, you again?' Kashina says – the same thing she always said when I'd visit her wanting biscuits when I was six. She's standing in the doorway. Her hair – what I can see of it with the colourful scarf wrapped around it – is whiter, lines are etched deeper in dark skin around unfathomable eyes, one alert, the other cloudy and scarred.

'Love you too,' I say.

She sighs, stands aside so I can go through the door.

'Is it OK if I stay for a few days?'

'Would it matter if I said no?' She shakes her head. 'Sorry, boy. Sofa is yours without asking, you know that.'

I bend to hug her, follow her in to the kitchen.

'You hungry? Want some toast?' she says.

I shake my head.

She makes hers and picks up a mug of tea already on the worktop. 'Come on.'

We go back to the front room. She fishes a bottle of whisky out from behind some books and adds a good glug to her tea.

'Early, isn't it?'

'Don't be cheeky, boy. My job keeps me more sober than I care to be.'

'Too many visitors lately?' Visitors are what Kashina and my mum used to call spirits – ghosts, the dead. They worked together;

23

both were mediums and psychics, and meant to be good at it, too, though Mum told me most of the predicting the future kind of stuff was made up.

Kashina shrugs. 'Now and then. So why are you here, Echo?'

'I couldn't stay away. Not when,' I swallow, 'you know. It's coming up – the anniversary. I was hoping my memory might come back.'

'I know, boy. But you can't change what happened, so what use is being here?' Her voice is gentle. 'Accept what happened and move on.'

'I can't.'

Her face is sad. 'I know.' Her hand grips mine.

'I thought time going by would make it easier. But it hasn't. If anything, it's worse. Will you help me?'

'Depends what kind of help you mean.'

'If I can't remember what happened the night she died, the only person who really knows is Mum. I need to ask her.'

'Even if I thought that contacting her beyond was a good idea for you, which I don't, you know I can't. I'm too close to her. It's dangerous: she could cross over and be trapped between worlds for ever.'

'What's the point of having an in with a medium if they can't give you a free séance now and then?'

'Don't be cheeky,' she says again. 'It's just not possible.' I've known Kashina since before I could talk; I know there is no point in arguing with her when she's made up her mind about something.

'There is something else you should do,' she says. 'It might help.'

24

'What's that?'

'Go to the cemetery – to your mother's grave. Pay your respects.'

I shake my head, a sick feeling inside. 'I hate going there.'

'I know. But maybe that is exactly why you should go: face what has happened, so you can let it go.'

'I know Mum is dead. Going there won't make any difference.'

'Do it. For me, if for no other reason.' She doesn't say anything else. For now. But I know she won't leave it alone, that sooner or later I'll have to go.

I have no choice.

6

Liv

Soon after my run and shower I am dried, dressed, and staring at the kitchen door.

Go on. What are you waiting for?

I stick my tongue out at Molly and push it open.

Mum is sitting at the breakfast bar, glass of red wine in hand, while Mr Tall Dark and Handsome spins pizza dough in the air. Of course: now it makes sense. *They* aren't making pizza, he is. He can cook?

Mum smiles, cheeks flushed. 'There you are at last. Rod, this is my daughter, Livia.' Slight emphasis on daughter; she has obviously told him the truth. Relief unknots my stomach. I'm not up to playing the sister act tonight.

He turns, smiles: dark hair, warm brown eyes. OK, so Molly wasn't exaggerating about the Timothée Chalamet thing. He is pretty all right.

'It's Liv, actually,' I say.

'Pleased to meet you, Liv.' He holds up his hands. 'I won't shake your hand just now – I'm covered in dough.'

Mum gestures and I sit next to her while Rod makes sauce and chops peppers and mushrooms, knife flying across the chopping board in true chef-like fashion. They talk and I pretend to listen, trying not to laugh as Molly starts dancing circles around Rod while he works in our own version of Happy Families.

Mum gives me half a glass of wine before the pizza is ready. After just a few sips in my empty stomach, warmth starts sliding through my veins, and I can feel from the heat of my cheeks that I'm going pink. Even Rod seems less objectionable than the last one she brought home, and when the pizza is done, it's scrummy. I wonder: what else can he cook? Will he be around long enough for me to find out? Then the doorbell rings.

'Who could that be?' Mum puts down her wine glass, a small frown between her eyes. Probably worried it is one of her previous.

'I'll go,' I say and jump up, already full enough of pizza to not eat for a week. I dash to the front door and yank it open.

Bowie?

'Hi,' he says, and smiles. His eyes do that boy thing I've never noticed him doing to me before – travelling up and down all of me – and I flush even more. 'You look awesome.'

'Uh, thanks.' Still thinking when dressing that I would be playing the role of sister not daughter, I'd dressed older: Molly had told me what to wear and I'd gone along with the short dress she'd picked. One Mum bought that I wouldn't normally choose. I even put on make-up, eyeliner and all – not a way Bowie has ever seen me at school or on the beach.

Mum appears at my shoulder and tugs my arm so I'm not blocking the door. 'Hello, Bowie. Hasn't Liv invited you in? Come on.'

She turns back towards the kitchen.

Bowie hesitates. 'Is it OK?' he says, close, in my ear. His warm breath tickles down my neck and I shiver.

'Of course.' Caught off guard like this, what else can I say? And we start to follow her down the hall.

'It's just . . .'

'What?'

'I've been trying to call you,' he says, lowering his voice.

My mind races, trying to work out what to say. 'Oh. Sorry. I . . .'

Mum is holding the door for us.

'This little idiot,' she says, and kisses me on the cheek, 'went out today without her phone. I was trying to call her for hours too. What if there was an emergency?'

'Sorry,' I say to both of them. Again.

Mum introduces him to Rod, and soon Bowie is devouring the rest of the pizza. So much for my plan of having it for breakfast. Mum and Rod start talking about going out next weekend, and I zone out.

Molly sits cross-legged on the table leaning into Rod and eyeing Bowie at the same time. *This night just gets better and better*, she says. I cross my eyes at her and she sticks out her tongue, then snuggles closer to Rod.

'What do you think?' Mum says. I look up. All faces are turned towards mine. 'Well, Liv?' she says, one eyebrow up.

'Uh . . .'

Say you think it is a great idea, Molly prompts, impish look on her face. It is always difficult to know when to listen to Molly and when not to.

'Sounds good?' I say tentatively, wondering what I am agreeing to this time.

'Then it is settled,' Mum says, and everyone smiles.

28

Soon Mum manoeuvres Bowie into taking me for a walk so she can be alone with Rod.

'What did I agree to?' I say once we clear the house.

Bowie laughs. 'You really have no idea, do you? Liv in the clouds, again.'

'None whatsoever,' I agree. Liv in the clouds: our English teacher called me that once from a poem we were reading, and it seemed to stick. I've learned to disconnect; to not react to what is around me. Molly jumping for attention all the time has made that a necessity.

'You just agreed to go out for a birthday dinner next weekend with your mum and Rod.'

'Oh. I guess that's not so bad.'

'And me,' he adds, and I feel myself smile. Even though I'm not going to see him, certainly not in a boy-girl kind of way; I decided that for definite. Didn't I? And maybe even not at all – isn't that what I thought earlier? But is it really necessary to cut him off completely? Maybe just not here, not alone. Anyhow, this is just one thing; one dinner, with Mum and Rod there too. Molly can't get up to much with both of them there.

'Though my birthday is actually tomorrow,' I say.

'I'll take you out for cake after school. Deal?'

Bowie's eyes are warm; looking into them makes my stomach do strange acrobatics.

'It's not such a big decision, is it?' he says, and suddenly, it isn't. Bowie is still my friend, isn't he?

'Can it be chocolate cake?'

'Sure.'

'Deal. But I need to stop somewhere first.'

His eyes look a question but I don't answer it for now. There is one visit I make every year on my birthday, no matter that we stopped doing it as a family thing when the latest in the string of counsellors the school insisted I have suggested to Mum that it wasn't healthy for me to always associate my birthday with the cemetery. With death. Now Molly tells me Mum always visits her grave on the morning of our birthday; I always do it after school, and neither of us mentions it to the other.

We walk through the Lanes down to the promenade. The wind is picking up, the tide nearly in, with growing white horses as the waves climb the beach.

I shiver. 'Cold?' Bowie asks and before I can answer slips his jacket over my shoulders.

It is warm and I pull it close around my body. It smells like him. Today that means vaguely of pizza.

'Let's sit,' he says and takes my hand, pulling me to a bench.

The moon is out again tonight, a few days off full. Clouds pulling in around us start swallowing the stars one by one.

He pulls at the hem of my skirt, just above my knee.

'This dress is, like, wow.'

Great vocab, but nice sentiment, Molly says, and sits on Bowie's lap, curling her arm around his neck. The moonlight, Bowie, and Molly.

I sigh. 'What am I doing here?'

Bowie raises an eyebrow. 'I've got a few ideas.'

I jump. Long habit of too much time alone with Molly: saying things out loud that should be kept quiet.

I pull at my skirt, too; trying to make it longer. 'Sorry. I should get home.'

'What's wrong, Liv? Tell me.'

I turn to face him.

Molly, still on his knee, frowns. *Don't you dare scare him away.*

I think at her: 'And who is the ghost here?'

Molly smiles. *But I'm not as scary as you are, just the same.*

'Come on, Liv. Tell me what's up.' Open, trusting Bowie. He doesn't deserve this.

'Nothing. I just want to get back before it starts to rain.'

'All right,' he says, but I can tell he knows there is something I'm not telling him. He takes my hand and we start to walk back uphill.

When we get to the house, Rod's car is still there and the light is on in Mum's bedroom.

Oh goody: Company tonight! Molly claps her hands. I hope Bowie won't put it together, and that Molly will go off to investigate. She does. Bowie and I are alone. I turn when we reach the door.

'Well, goodnight then. See you at school tomorrow,' I say.

'Bye.'

I open the door and start to step through it, quickly.

'Liv?' he says.

I stop, turn back to face him. Molly isn't here now, is she? I feel for her, inside. No Molly: we're alone. I look up, meet his eyes.

'Yes?'

'My jacket.'

'Oh. Of course.' I slip it off my shoulders, hand it to him. Close the door and go to the window, watch him disappear up the street just as light rain starts to fall. As if he can feel my eyes,

31

he turns at the corner, gives a friendly wave, then is gone.

Perhaps Bowie has worked out that I want us to go back to being just friends. But if that is how I want things, why do I feel so disappointed right now?

Molly appears at the bottom of the stairs. *I should think that is obvious. You clearly really like him and need my help.*

'No, I do not. And I don't need your help. I don't want your help. Do you understand?'

Molly laughs and skips up the stairs.

I follow more slowly behind, not sure whether to go to my room even though it is late. Mum's bedroom is only two doors down from mine, her study between us.

I open the door to my room; Molly is sprawled on the bed.

I wonder what they're doing now?

'You're sick,' I say, but she's already gone. I turn my radio up a little to be on the safe side; I'd been trying not to think about the same thing. There are some things I *so* don't want to overhear. Then I start to tackle my algebra homework. Anything to take my mind off what is or isn't going on in Mum's bedroom. And with Bowie, too.

I jump. Molly is back, sitting on my desk.

Wow.

'Don't tell me!'

You should see what he looks like without his clothes on.

'You're sick!' I say again.

I am not! You'd look if you could. And she mists into the mirror over my dressing table.

'I don't want to! Don't!' I say, but it's too late. One of Molly's tricks: she can melt into my mirror and out of another, and for a

32

moment I see everything out of the other mirror. This time, of course, it is the one in Mum's bedroom.

I close my eyes, but too late: Mum and Rod in bed flash across the mirror.

Even with my eyes clenched shut now, they are stuck there, in mirror reverse: an after image burned for ever into my mind.

YUCK.

7

Echo

Kashina is so bloody annoying.

I'm walking, fast – stomping really – up the road.

To the cemetery.

She seems to think if I see Mum's grave it'll give me some sort of closure or something.

I don't want to go there, but how can I say no when she's helping me with a place to stay? Somehow I found myself promising, and now I'm stuck, doing what she wants. As usual.

Kashina also seems to think there is something behind me not wanting to do this – she wouldn't say what or why she insisted I go. But she doesn't understand. There is just something about cemeteries; I hate them. It isn't visiting Mum's grave that is the problem; it's being around *any* graves.

Anyhow, it's just a bit of ground – a hole dug down – filled with a coffin. Bones inside of it. Dirt replaced above. Mum's not really there, not any more, so what does it matter? She won't care if I pay my respects, no matter what Kashina thinks.

The gates are ahead of me now and I slow down. There's a deep knot in my gut. I swallow, force myself to step through and walk up the path, counting my steps to avoid thinking about where I am, the headstones all around. What lies beneath them.

There are voices ahead. A couple and a little girl – they're holding her hands between them. The woman has flowers. I concentrate on them and not my surroundings.

They go to a grave and I follow at a distance. Their voices float on the breeze and I focus on them. It's the little girl's grandmother's grave – they're going to give flowers to Nanna, she says, her voice that high pitch of a child who only just knows how to talk. She doesn't get what this place really is, not yet.

They place the flowers – cut flowers – on a grave. They're dead, like what lies beneath them.

After they leave I find other voices, other people, to follow, focusing on them instead of where I am and what is under the earth. And so I wander through the cemetery, trying to get closer to Mum without going alone.

But no matter how hard I try to ignore what's all around me, it's too much. I can't. The darkness seeps inside of me more and more, and after a while my footsteps falter.

I lie down on a random grave. I wish something would happen to me to make everything stop.

Is that what being dead would be like?

8

Liv

'Happy birthday, Molly,' I say to her headstone and brace myself. She always does it on our birthday. The grand entrance. And sure enough, the grass growing in front of her marble slab shimmers, like mist, and she rises slowly out of the ground, hands crossed over her chest, eyes still and staring straight ahead. Then all at once she springs to her feet and laughs.

Right backatcha, chick. How does it feel to be sixteen?

I shrug. 'No different. It's no big deal.'

Molly sits on her headstone, swinging her feet.

It so is a big deal. This is THE year, you know.

'For what?' I say, though I'm pretty sure what she means, and that it involves Bowie. Understanding Bowie, who just this minute is waiting by the cemetery gates so I can do this alone.

For everything. And she winks.

I cross my arms. 'Don't for one minute think you're in charge. You're not.'

Molly stops swinging her feet. Tilts her head to one side. *Shut up*, she hisses.

I scowl. 'Stop telling me what to do all the time.'

Shut up! she says again, looking past my shoulder. I turn my head, uneasy now that someone has been watching, listening. Seeing me in conversation with a headstone.

But no one is there.

36

I frown. 'What's with you?' I say, starting to turn back to Molly, but then there is sound, movement, behind me.

'I should ask you the same question,' a voice says. Then a head appears over a memorial below Molly's. A dark-haired boy. He stares a moment then ducks down, out of sight.

I hesitate; then, curious, stand and walk around. He is stretched out not just on the ground but right on a grave, with his head by the headstone, his feet the other end. Arms crossed on his chest and staring ahead just like Molly was moments ago.

'What on earth are you doing?' I say.

'Imagining.'

'Imagining what?'

'What it's like to be dead. What on earth were you doing?'

'What do you mean?'

'I heard you, you know.' He sits up, faces me. 'Who's Molly?'

The colour drains from my face. I feel it go, as if my veins and arteries just opened and my blood poured out, all at once. Can he see her?

Molly stands by his feet, crosses her arms. *Don't be daft. Of course he can't. He heard you call me Molly.*

He stands up, walks over to me. He's tall, taller than Bowie. Maybe a year or two older. His long hair isn't just dark like mine, it's jet black, and his clothes are, too – black jeans, shirt, jacket also, and there is a black leather band around his neck. His cheekbones are high and stick out like he doesn't bother to eat enough, and his dark eyes are intense, curious, and outlined in black eyeliner. His face . . . it's interesting, different. The shape of his eyes, the cheekbones, the pale colour of his skin.

'Who is Molly? Or, should I say, who was she?' he asks.

37

I stare back at him. Molly stands next to him, then frowns. *Come on, leave this creep. Let's go meet Bowie.*

My eyes flick to Molly and then back to him.

He turns his head and looks exactly at Molly where she stands. She shudders and vanishes.

'Could you see?' I whisper.

His eyes are intent on mine once more. Serious. 'See what?'

I start to back away.

'Wait. See what?'

'I've got to go,' I say, and start down the path, each step faster.

'You believe, don't you?' he calls.

'Believe what?' I say, unable to stop myself from answering.

'In ghosts.'

I pause. Turn. 'That's stupid,' I say, but then can't stop myself from asking: 'Do you?'

'Of course,' he says, and there is no trace of mocking: he really means it. 'Why do you think I'm here, when it is the last place I want to be?'

I don't answer and hurry away, half afraid he'll follow, half disappointed when he doesn't. Even though there was definitely something about him that felt not quite right, at the same time the look in his eyes, his voice and what he said pulled at something inside me.

When I reach the exit Bowie is there, waiting, where I left him – looking safe, normal, as he always does. I breathe easier.

'Is something wrong?' he asks.

'No.'

'But you were almost running, looking upset?'

'It's nothing. Just some weirdo back there who hangs around cemeteries.'

Bowie glances back through the gates. 'Are you OK? Should we tell somebody?'

I shake my head. 'It was just some goth boy talking about ghosts. He didn't do anything.'

'But I'm guessing that with you visiting your sister's grave, that wasn't exactly what you needed.'

'Look, it's OK. Let's get out of here.'

Bowie slips his hand in mine as we walk. His fingers are reassuring, warm. Held tight there is a slight throb of blood pulsing through under the surface. It says he is real, alive. Here and now.

And, bonus: there's no sign of Molly coming back.

After huge slices of chocolate fudge cake at a beach café, we wander and then sit on a bench on the promenade away from the pier. The sugar rush makes me feel giddy. The sun is nearly gone. It's still, no wind, the sea almost flat. Seagulls dive bomb kids eating chips on the beach below us; a few runners pound past.

'Thanks for the cake.'

'You're welcome. I wasn't in a hurry to get home, anyhow.'

'Something wrong?'

He shrugs. 'Just the usual slamming doors and Tina-chaos. She's grounded again.'

Bowie has three sisters: two much younger and one older, Tina, who seems in trouble more than she's out of it. 'What is it for this time?'

'I think I've lost track. Anyhow she's arguing that now

she's eighteen they can't ground her. They're saying their house, their rules. She's threatening to take off. Just the usual. Anyhow, hope you're having a good birthday.'

'Thanks. But birthdays aren't a big deal for me.'

'Is that because of Molly? Because it is her birthday, too?'

'Strictly speaking, it isn't.'

His eyes look a question.

'Well, she wasn't born. She died before she had a chance.' And I can't believe what I just said. Danger, danger: I'm skirting too close to things I don't want to talk about.

I can see he is about to ask another question, and I don't want him to. *Kiss him* is in my mind and without any thought, I just do it: I reach up to catch his chin and turn his face, just a little. He leans down and his lips are there, pressing against mine. He tastes like chocolate.

Finally he pulls away. Smiles. 'You're confusing.'

'Tell me about it.'

His arm slips around my shoulders and I settle my head in the warm crook of his shoulder, and being here, his closeness, sends shivers up my spine.

'You're always so cold,' Bowie says, rubbing my hands between his. Goosebumps trail up and down my arms and back.

Cold . . . Molly?

I'm frozen in shock. How could she?

'Molly, get out!' I say, loud in my mind like a shout, and then I feel it. A slight pulling away, as if something under my skin is peeling, separating. A reluctant tug, and snap: she's out.

She sits on the other side of Bowie on the bench. *You liked that kiss, too. Don't lie.*

Did I? How could I really tell what I felt, what she felt? I back away from Bowie.

'I'm sorry,' I say.

'What for?'

'I'm just sorry.' And I get up, start walking away, fast. I can feel his eyes on my back but he says nothing, doesn't follow. He just lets me go.

9

Echo

I watched them leave: that girl and some blond boy she met by the gates. She made me forget why I was here, and when I remember I'm almost startled.

I'm here to visit Mum's grave. I promised Kashina.

Now it doesn't seem like as much of a big deal, at least, not like it did before.

I know the way.

Up the slope.

Down the path to the left.

It's near a tree: I remember the place from the funeral, though when I finally find it the tree is bigger than I thought.

There it is. Her name carved in stone: Rose Lee. I start to trace the letters of her name with my fingers, and the rest of it swims in my eyes.

'Hi Mum. It's me, Echo,' I say.

No answer.

See, Kashina, this was pointless. She's not here, not in any form I can hear or see. If she was, then she would answer.

Though if she is *anywhere* — if she stayed after she died — I know where she would be. The place. Where it happened. Where she died.

My hands form fists as I fight to keep myself together. Why can't I remember? I'm desperate for it, even if it isn't what I want to know. Even if it is the worst thing I can imagine: I have to know.

Kashina was wrong. Coming here hasn't done a thing. Nothing here will help trigger my memory.

If I can't make myself remember . . . there is another way. I'm the son of a psychic, after all; I was raised by her and Kashina. I know a few things. Even if Kashina won't help me, I know what to do to reach Mum.

But I don't think I can do it on my own – I don't think I can push myself far enough alone.

What about that girl? What I overheard wasn't just the usual, Hi Granny, here are your flowers. It was like she was trying to have an actual normal sort of conversation with Molly, whoever she was.

That is what I want – no, *need* – with Mum. If that girl wants the same thing with Molly, maybe we can help each other?

I walk back the way I came, to the grave where I saw her.

The headstone is marble, the carved lamb for a young child: Molly Jennifer Flynn. Date of birth – and date of death – the same. She would have been sixteen today.

So, Molly died at birth sixteen years ago. I'm thinking the girl I spoke to must be her sister; what other reason would a teenage girl have for visiting the grave of a baby from that many years ago?

She looked about sixteen too; if they were twins, that's even better.

The darkness that made me lie on a grave and wish to be in it before is gone. Something like hope is surging through me – together, we might actually be able to do this.

Now there is something else to focus on, something else I have to do.

Find her. Find that girl.

10

Liv

Goth boy is outside my school the next day.

Rinsing out beakers in our chemistry lab, I glance up through the window over the sink, and there he is. Across the road and leaning against the bus stop. He's hard to miss really, even at this distance. He's so different from everyone else I know that my eyes are drawn to him, and it's not just the whole dressed-in-black goth thing either. Even the way he stands, holds himself – casual but poised and watchful at the same time. I glance at the clock: twenty minutes or so before end of day.

The seconds tick slowly by.

The final bell goes at last. I check out the window: he's still there.

He could be waiting for anyone – a friend, a girlfriend. But even as I try to ignore my instinct, I can't dismiss the thought that he's here because he's trying to find me.

Side gate? Molly suggests.

I go through school the long way, avoiding anywhere Bowie is likely to be. I head out through the side gate and walk around behind the school instead of to the front.

I hurry home. Shut the door when I get there and lean against it.

How long can I avoid both of them? I don't know about goth boy, but I'll have to face Bowie in English tomorrow afternoon. I think about inventing a headache, staying home.

Phone on silent, I curl up in my room with a history assignment but can't concentrate. I keep sneaking looks at my phone.

Bowie doesn't call.

11

Echo

The sun is shining but I'm cold. There's the sense of a storm building, pressure increasing inside me. The internal doesn't match the external and I can't stay still.

I'm disappointed I didn't see her come out of her school yesterday. Maybe I missed her; maybe she wasn't there for some reason. Is she just a distraction? I don't know. She might not want to help me, it could be a waste of time, but I can't stop thinking about her.

I wander, aimless, around Brighton. Avoiding what must be done. I know I need to go there – where it happened – but somehow can't make myself walk any further than the marina.

People around me amble or march and I hang back, stay out of the way. Cars and buses rumble past in both directions. Maybe that is the answer: if I get on a bus, one that goes where I need to go, then it'll be like the train to Brighton. Once I'm on it I'll have no choice and the battle will be over.

There's no one else at the bus stop, the one on the side of the road heading from Brighton to Saltdean. After a while a bus comes but I hang back, don't flag it down, and no one is getting off at this stop; it goes by.

A woman with a baby in a pram comes to the stop, then an old man, and another bus comes. I watch them get on, the doors shut. The bus leaves without me.

Things come in threes and there's something about that number: the third bus. That's the one I'll get on.

Seconds and minutes tick slowly by. When I finally see the next bus coming in the distance, there isn't anybody else at this stop. Standing back in the shadows, I can't bring myself to flag it down. I'm frozen.

But it's slowing down anyhow, pulling in. It stops, the doors open and two old ladies slowly climb down the steps.

Go, Echo. Do it.

I slip in through the back door, waiting for someone to call out, ask me for a fare I haven't got. But no one notices me sneaking on the mostly empty bus.

I sit at the back. I did it! But I feel nauseous, my head is pounding as it pulls back on to the road, even worse when it drops gear to start up the hill – oh-so-slowly, dragging it out.

This is wrong. We were coming the other way.

I'm startled; my eyes open wider. We were? Do I remember this?

Yes. I'm sure of it! We came the other way. Am I starting to remember – will more come?

I close my eyes. We came over the top of the hill, fast and then faster. And then . . .

And then . . .

That's it. That's all. But it's something more than I had before.

When I open my eyes, we're almost there. I know the place from what came after – waking up on the side of the road. Getting up and seeing the wreckage below. My eyes are seeing green grass, sunshine, and remembering pain and

48

darkness – putting one on the other, a jigsaw of light and dark, life and death.

They've repaired the boundary. Of course they have; it's been almost a year. The tracks in the grass are gone; the chain fence is seamless, like nothing ever happened.

And then the bus continues on and the place is gone, lost behind us.

I stay on the bus when it turns around for the return trip, and then again; I stay on the bus for hours. Each time we go past the place I push my thoughts to that night, trying to recapture something else, some detail.

I fail.

I need help.

People get on and off: happy, miserable or anywhere in-between, in groups or alone. They all have somewhere to go.

I don't. At least not until school knocking-off time.

I think back to when I met that girl in the cemetery. Those eyes, the way she stood – the way being near her took me out of myself. I shake my head. Concentrate, Echo, on what she was wearing: her school uniform. Did I get it wrong?

No. I'm sure I didn't. That was her school; the girls all had the exact same skirt, top, blazer. Maybe she had a day off yesterday or was on a field trip. I'll try again today.

One last trip back on this road, going in the right direction – the way we did in our car that day. One last push to remember something else – anything. One last failure.

I get off in Brighton.

I have to find her.

12

Liv

I am late to English. On purpose.

'Lost in the clouds again, Liv?' our teacher says as I walk across the room to my seat. To the table I share with Bowie.

Bowie moves his books over slightly to make more room, as if he isn't sure he wants me to get too close. Not that I can blame him after I ran off Monday night and avoided him all day yesterday.

Part way in I lean across and write *sorry* on the margin of his notebook. He lightly touches my hand under the desk for a moment, but says nothing.

When the final bell goes, he gets up, gathers his things and leaves. Without saying a word.

I drag behind, not wanting to catch him up. He's made it clear he doesn't want to talk to me, hasn't he? And I can't blame him. He must think I've been playing him – kissing him one minute, running away the next.

The halls are nearly empty when I reach the front doors and I almost step out without thinking. I hang back, go to the library instead and look out the window.

And there he is again. Goth boy. Across from the front gates like he was yesterday. The library will close soon, it's past time to go, but I'm still staring out through the library window. Standing back in shadows in case he looks up. He stays put, watching as students file out. If he keeps this up the school will call the police or something.

This is stupid. With avoiding Bowie between classes and goth boy at the end of day, I'm looking over my shoulder every second.

He'll give up if he doesn't see you, Molly says. *Just two more days to half term and he'll have to give up.*

I shrug. Maybe. We could tell Rod I've got a stalker, let him sort it out. What is the point of having an in with the police if you can't give them a call when you need them?

Just keep away from him, Molly pleads.

I feel uneasy enough to listen to her, and again slip out the side gate and take the back way.

Molly is right; he'll give up soon. Won't he?

13

Echo

The flood of students released from her school slows to a trickle, then a last few stragglers, and then stops altogether.

I wait as the shadows lengthen, but I'm kidding myself. She's not going to come out this late, is she? Kicking at leaves on the ground I walk back down the road.

Where is she?

Either she's got the flu, skives off class regularly, or . . . she's avoiding me. Maybe she spotted me out the school gates, then waited until I was gone or left another way.

If she did see me, she must think I'm following her, that I'm some sort of stalker. Then how will I convince her to talk to me?

It hurts to think that she could be avoiding me when I can't stop thinking about her. We met so briefly, I'm not even sure if my memory matches reality.

I don't know her, not really, so why can't I leave this alone?

I'll have to find another way.

14

Liv

The next morning it's raining, grey and cold. Late, I rush up the hill to the school, hunched over, pulling my jacket hood down over my face, unable to see much more than my feet as I race along. The first bell rings up ahead, and I go faster.

Someone steps out in front of me. Too late to stop, I crash straight into them.

'Sorry!' I say and glance up, water dripping down my face. Then I gasp in shock. It's him: goth boy.

He holds an umbrella up over both of us. 'At last,' he says. 'Where've you been?'

I step back but school is the other way, and he is between me and it.

The final bell sounds.

'You might as well stay a minute, you're already late.'

I dodge around him and start walking fast towards the school gates.

'Wait. Please?' he says, and there is something in his voice that makes me pause, turn to face him. 'Meet me after school, at the end of the pier. I just want to talk to you, that's all. Will you meet me there?' There is something I can't name in his eyes, like nothing I've seen or felt before. I'm drawn so strongly to him, but at the same time I want – *need* – to get away.

'I don't know. I've got to go.' I turn, half run to the school gates.

He calls softly after me.

'I know about Molly.'

15

Echo

I'm there early – at the pier – and walk to the end while I wait.

Will she come?

I don't know. I hope so.

It really didn't go well this morning, not how I wanted, at all. I said the wrong things – didn't reassure her like I should have done. And she didn't react to me asking where she's been. Does that mean she *did* notice me waiting for her there the other days and deliberately avoided me?

I shake my head, not entirely sure why I'm so desperate to see her, talk to her again. Ask for her help.

Somehow, this girl – thinking about the way she stands, her voice – eases something inside of me. Stops me from thinking over and over again about the things I can't remember, and Mum, and how she died.

Fills a space that is otherwise only darkness.

16

Liv

Don't go.

'How can I not?'

He doesn't know anything about me. How could he? And even if he does, who cares?

I don't answer. Molly can't possibly understand how I feel. How I long for someone, anyone, to know about her. To understand. At the very least I want to find out what he thinks he knows.

Don't be stupid! Remember how creeped out you were this morning.

'All the more reason to meet him in a public place, yeah, and find out what he wants.' I turn and glare. 'No one is asking you to come along.'

Molly flips her hair and vanishes.

Two women walking the other way give me a funny look; I ignore them, breathing a sigh of relief at Molly's departure. I hadn't said anything they could hear: this conversation had been with thoughts, not out loud. But it is so hard to talk to Molly in public, even that way, without looking like I'm talking to myself.

The rain has stopped but the sky is grey and heavy, more on the way. The closer I get to the pier, the slower my steps. Maybe Molly is right.

She appears in front of me. *I'm always right.*

'Naff off!' I say out loud, forgetting. Three boys, twelve or so, walking past the other way laugh and give me the one-fingered salute: nice. I flush, annoyed with Molly, with myself.

When I get to the pier I can't see him, so walk along it towards the end. The sea is dark and angry in this light, choppy and churned up as it smacks against the pillars that support the pier. There aren't many people about: a few fishermen, some teenagers walking hand in hand. Joggers who don't care about the weather pound along the beach, or maybe they are avoiding ghosts of their own.

There he is. Leaning against the rail at the end of the pier, just like he said. Not facing this way, but staring out to sea.

I stop a couple of metres away, and he turns.

'You came,' he says, and his lips curve into a hesitant smile. I haven't seen him smile before; he looks different with it. A bit more shy and uncertain, not so intense.

I walk over to him and half smile back; he looks unsure what to say now I am here. Standing closer to him he is so tall that I tilt my head back a little.

Rain starts to spatter down, and he puts his umbrella up over both of us.

'Well? You wanted to talk,' I say.

'How about we start with names? I'm Echo. Echo Lee.'

'What sort of name is that? Sorry,' I add, hastily.

He shrugs. 'It is a different sort of name. My mum was a different sort of person and she picked it. And you are . . . ?' he prompts, but I stay silent. 'Molly Flynn was your sister, wasn't she? You know what it feels like to lose somebody.'

'How do you know? And how did you find me?'

'Not so mysterious. You were talking to someone named Molly in the cemetery, standing next to a grave with "Molly Flynn" on it. On her birthday, saying happy birthday. Born and died the same day sixteen years ago, according to the headstone. And I found your school because you were wearing your school uniform when we met. I just wandered around until I saw someone in the same uniform, then followed them to the gates.'

'You are . . . ?' he says again.

'Liv,' I say, finally. There doesn't seem much point in holding it back when he knows so much.

'You look about that age: were you and Molly twins?'

I nod.

'I thought so! Twins share links that can stretch beyond this life.'

He's just fishing for information, Molly says, back again. She stands well away from Echo, like she can't bear to get too close to him.

'What do you mean?' I say, careful to sound neutral, to not react. Trying not to look at Molly.

'I asked you the other day, but you lied.'

'You asked me what?'

'If you believe in ghosts.'

I look up at him, and there is this weird feeling, like something in his eyes is pulling me in to a deep, dark, desperate place.

I back away and start walking up the pier.

'Wait. Please, Liv,' he says. 'I need your help.'

'You need help of some sort. But why my help?'

He catches up and stands between me and the beach. 'I know the way to contact spirits that have moved on: to lift the veil

58

between the world of the living and the world of the dead. You want to see your sister again, to talk to her, don't you?'

'Why would I want to do that?' I say, and walk around him and away.

His words drift out after me. 'If you want to find out more, meet me here again. Tomorrow night. At ten.'

17

Echo

I watch Liv walk away.

There's something about her. I was right: this isn't just about getting her help to contact my mum and her sister, even though that was why I convinced myself to track her down.

It isn't how she looks, though she is attractive enough; very, really, slender, with long dark hair. Watching her move, too, sort of precisely and not wasting energy, but with a sense that if she took fright she could leap away and disappear, like a cat. The way her lips part slightly when she's listening. But even more, there is something about her eyes, the way she looked at me. Even though I frightened her a little — I know I did — there was still something there, and I want to see her look at me like that again.

It's been so long since I've felt this kind of pull towards a girl . . . it feels strange.

But that's not why I'm here, is it?

I wander around Brighton for hours in the rain. Walking ways I used to go with Mum, places she used to take me. Reliving moments I can remember, hoping they'll trigger the things that I can't.

Here, we had ice cream on my birthday.

There, I got my skateboard fixed.

This is the skateboard park where I wiped out, took the skin off my knees. One of the other mums said I should have had kneepads. Mum looked at her, and said there can be no joy without risk of pain.

She often said things like that, unsmiling: the kind of things that made people look nervous and back away.

Maybe that's where I get it from.

Kashina once said Mum didn't drink enough. That bad habits were necessary for their job; that without occasional moments of oblivion, they couldn't recover. She never says it in so many words, but I know Kashina thinks Mum did it on purpose – that she sought oblivion.

But she's wrong. And I'm going to prove it.

18

Liv

'You're soaked,' Mum chides when I get in. 'Don't even have the sense to come out of the rain.'

'It's just a little water,' I say, but start shivering. 'And why are you home from work so early?' As if I need to ask: a man must be involved.

'Rod's coming over. We've got a surprise for you.'

Haven't I had enough surprises for one day?

Rod's car pulls in out front while I am changing into dry clothes. What sort of surprise can I expect from Mum and her new boyfriend? Let's see: they're engaged. Possible: there is precedent, though this would be quick work even for her. Of course her engagements don't usually last beyond getting jewellery. Or—

I could think of a few surprises I'd like from Rod.

'Molly! Honestly. Have you got over your strop?'

No. Why you'd want to talk to that creep I can't begin to imagine.

'Echo. His name is Echo.'

Whatever. There is something seriously wrong with that boy. Promise me you'll keep away from him.

'Get a grip, Molly.'

'Liv?' Mum calls up the stairs.

The surprise is a chubby warm ball of golden fur named Amber, though Rod assures me her name can be changed if I want to keep her: six weeks old of squirming cocker spaniel puppy, the last of his dog's litter to need a home to go to in a few weeks' time when they are old enough. And she is the most beautiful thing I have ever seen.

'She's gorgeous!' I say, holding her up while she licks my face. 'Is she mine?'

'She could be your birthday present,' Mum says. 'But we thought we'd bring her over for a visit first so you can get to know each other and see what you think.'

'Looking after a puppy is a big responsibility,' Rod says, and starts going on about walks and feeding and vet visits, but I am away. Gone. In puppy bliss. I've wanted a dog for as long as I can remember; Mum always said no.

I look up at Mum now. 'Are you sure I can really have her?' I say, suddenly suspicious.

But Mum is in a different sort of bliss, with Rod's arm curled around her. She'd probably agree to anything. They start dinner while Amber and I get acquainted.

Molly sits with her arms crossed on the sofa.

'What?' I say.

She shrugs. *Why do you want a puppy?*

'Why do you need to ask? Look at her – she's adorable.' After chasing about the room non-stop, Amber suddenly flops on my knee, sound asleep. I sink in the sofa next to Molly and hold Amber up against my chest. 'Her fur is so soft. And her little heart is beating th-thump, th-thump, th-thump.'

Molly edges closer. *Can I come in? To see what it feels like?*

I hesitate. Well, at least she asked. Reluctant, I nod yes. It's easier if I relax, so I do, as much as I can, and close my eyes.

Molly settles herself around me like a cold blanket, then slips under my skin. I open my eyes again and she is me, I am her – together as one. *We used to be like this most of the time*, she whispers inside me, and she's right. Somewhere along the way I stopped liking it. I can prevent it from happening, if I'm paying enough attention when she tries: visualise boundaries that she can't easily cross.

Amber stirs.

My/Molly's hand reaches up to stroke her and she whimpers. Pulls away and jumps to the floor.

I don't think I like puppies, Molly says, and all at once she pulls out in a rush, so fast her leaving me is like a snap, an elastic recoil that smacks me in the face. She walks across to Amber and kneels down to look her right in the eye.

Amber backs up and barks.

'She can see you. She can!' I say, shocked.

Get rid of her! I don't want her! Molly is angry now and steps towards Amber, backing her towards the closed door. Amber piddles on the floor.

How disgusting.

'You scared her!' I dash across the room and scoop her up, tears smarting in my eyes. 'Leave her alone,' I say.

Rod opens the door. Looks around the room.

'Is everything all right?'

'Just fine,' I say, and bite my lip. 'But as lovely as she is, I don't think I want to have a pet.'

'Are you sure? I thought you loved her. And Lexi said you've always wanted a dog.'

Rod looks down and realises he is standing in puppy wee.

'I'm sure,' I say, and hand her to Rod.

Mum backs up my decision when she sees what Amber did on the carpet.

That night, I wrap myself up in my duvet, eyes clenched shut tight, barriers up as much as they can go.

Trying not to cry.

I'm sorry about the stupid puppy! She can hardly stay here if we don't get along, can she? Liv?

I finally open my eyes. Molly sits on my desk, looking as contrite as she can. 'I suppose not,' I say.

What has happened to us lately? It is like we don't know each other any more.

'I don't know.' It's true that we used to be inseparable and seemed to share the same brain even when we weren't sharing the same body. The last year or so, things have been changing.

Are you all right?

I shrug. 'I don't know. It's not just the puppy.'

Molly waits. She doesn't try to dip inside me to see what is up, so I answer.

'It's Bowie, too.'

You're the one who ran away from him.

'You're the one who kissed him – twice. But he's my friend! At least, he was.'

I'm sorry. Is he still coming for our birthday dinner?

'I don't know.'

Call him.

'I don't think I should.'

Call him.

Eventually, after thinking a while, I do. It's a bit late; his phone rings four times, then five. My finger is just sneaking towards the end call button when he answers.

'Hello?'

'Hi. It's Liv.'

There is a small pause.

'Hi.'

'Look, I just wanted to—'

'You don't have to keep apologising, Liv. It's all right,' he says, but his voice is distant. It is *so* not all right.

I pause, unsure what to say, then remember why I called. 'What about this weekend?'

'What about it?'

'My birthday dinner on Saturday. Mum invited you: are you still coming?'

'Do you want me to?'

'Yes.' And I realise as I say it, that I do; I really do.

'All right, I'll come.' But he sounds like he isn't sure it is a good idea.

Neither am I.

19

Echo

'What are you smiling at?' Kashina says. I was draped across her sofa, thinking about Liv, when she came in. It's gone 2 a.m. and her feet aren't steady. She's been at the pub.

I shake my head. 'None of your business,' I say, but then relent. 'If you must know, it's a girl.'

She crosses the room from the door, then uses her hands on the sides of the chair to lower herself carefully.

'A girl!' she says, looking both amazed and fascinated. 'Tell me about her. Where did you meet?'

'In the cemetery.'

'Now there's a surprise.' She raises an eyebrow and giggles at the same time.

'You sent me there. It's your fault.'

'Oh, yes. Why, so I did. Did you visit your mother's grave?'

My smile falls away. 'Yes. I said I would, didn't I?'

'And?'

'And what?'

Her look is impossible to read. Her giggles are gone; her face is sad again.

'Never mind.'

20

Liv

You're not seriously thinking of going to meet him, Molly says. *I mean, what is he – some kind of stalker? Staking out your school like that to find you? That is beyond weird.*

'Some might say it is romantic: a boy meets a girl and can't get her out of his mind, so much so that he does everything he can to find her.'

Huh. Maybe in a book or a movie – in real life it's just weird. And there's something about that boy that isn't right.

'That boy has a name: Echo. What is it you don't like about him? Tell me what it is, and maybe I'll listen.'

But she won't say any more.

Is this just Molly's usual jealousy? Apart from Bowie, she's usually like that with anyone who gets too close to me, being so disruptive that I've mostly given up trying to have friends. It's hard to talk in anything like a normal fashion if she's there and determined to be a pain.

Maybe she has a point about how Echo tracked me down. But there is *something* about him – I don't know what it is. I can't stop thinking about him. And I want to know if he really does know anything about Molly.

Though, if I'm honest, maybe it is exactly because she doesn't want me to meet him that I can't put it out of my mind.

Mum and Rod are at some party; she said they'd be late. Just before ten I find myself locking up the house and walking to the pier, Molly keeping close all the way.

When we get there, I'm a few minutes late and can't see Echo. Maybe he gave up waiting when I didn't show? Or maybe he walked down the pier again.

Let's go home, Molly pleads. *It's cold.*

It is, but as if she can tell. I walk the length of the pier, then back to the promenade.

See? He didn't even bother to turn up. Let's go home.

'Liv!'

I turn and there he is, leaning on a bench by the bus stop.

I wave, walk over to him.

'Are you ready?' Echo says.

'For what?'

He grins. 'Adventure. Perfect timing.' He gestures at an approaching bus.

Don't! Molly says.

'Where are we going?'

'You'll see,' Echo says. 'After you.'

I get on. I hold up my student pass for the driver, start to walk down the aisle and then realise Echo hasn't followed. Then catch movement further along. He's snuck in the back door and makes for an empty seat near the back.

I roll my eyes as I sit next to him. 'OK, so we're on a bus. Where are we going?'

'To a special place,' he says, and won't say any more.

We change buses, and the second one twists up and down back roads until I have no idea where we are. I start to get nervous. Nobody knows where I am, who I'm with.

Get a grip, I say to myself. You're on a bus, what could possibly happen?

'It's all right, Liv,' he says, as if he can read my mind. 'I just want to show you something, a place that is important to me. I promise not to murder you with an axe. Besides, I totally forgot to bring one along.'

And it sounds so ridiculous when he says it that I stop worrying.

The bus winds down narrow roads. 'This is where we get off,' Echo says, and I push the button. The bus comes to a stop on the road, but there isn't an actual stop I can see – it must be only on demand.

'Where are we?' I say as I get up, follow Echo down the aisle to the door.

'My mum used to bring me here,' he says – doesn't explain why.

We get off the bus. There are no streetlights and the lights of the bus are soon gone. My unease is coming back. What was I thinking – getting off a bus in the middle of nowhere with someone I barely know? My eyes begin to adjust to the thin light from the half-moon as I follow Echo past a few old houses, dark and shuttered. There are no lights in windows, no cars parked anywhere. We walk along a single-track, rutted lane, up a steep hill.

'This way,' he says and gestures at an old church. It's not just old, it's ancient. It looks spooky, crumbling graves all around, half tilted over or cracked. My eyes open wide and then wider but somehow it seems even darker than what surrounds it, as if this place rejects even moonlight.

We go through a gate that is open, hanging crookedly from

its hinges, and then down an overgrown path. The path winds around the church to the back.

'Watch your step,' he says.

I follow him in the moonlight, goosebumps prickling the back of my neck, my arms, but they have nothing to do with Molly this time. She seems to have vanished; either she hasn't come or is keeping well back and quiet. How I feel isn't just because it is cold – it's this place. There isn't a sound except for our feet on the path, our breathing. Not a bird, nothing. Then I realise the silence is even deeper because I can't hear the background throb of the sea that is always there in Brighton, not even as a distant murmur. We are further inland than I realised.

Echo walks through old graves along the thread of a path, and I follow close behind.

Boo! Molly jumps out from behind a headstone. I just manage to stop myself from crying out in fright.

'How could you!' I say to her in my mind, but smile: the tension is broken.

See: just what you needed. Even though I still think it was stupid to come here with that weirdo.

I ignore her. Echo has stopped now against a crumbling wall that lines the back of the graveyard. He pulls himself up to sit on it; it is a bit high for me and he holds out his hands, helps me scramble up next to him.

'So, are you going to tell me why we are here?'

'Two reasons. The first is that it is meant to be haunted. My mum told me that a girl who lived here went missing; everyone thinks she was murdered, but her body was never found. She lived in the first house we passed when we got off the bus. Her family

71

moved away and it was sold, but the people who bought it soon left – they were scared. Said there were noises at night – banging sounds, like fists pounding against a door, crying and wailing. The neighbours soon followed. Both are boarded up – no one will live there.' As he speaks his voice is different, breathless, as if he is running instead of sitting still in the dark.

'Are you all right?' I say.

'Yes. Well, sort of. It's just that this place scares me.'

'It does?' I say, surprised. 'I figured since, you know, you said you want to pull spirits from beyond, you should be pretty comfortable in a haunted graveyard at night.'

'It's not that. Well, not only that.'

'What is it, then?'

'It's the second reason we're here.' He curves an arm around my waist. Something leaps and flutters inside of me at his closeness, the dark, even as fear of what he might say next, what he might do, is growing inside me; the butterflies and the fear combine like a drug that rushes hot through my veins. 'It's OK, Liv,' he says. 'I'm just keeping you safe.'

'From what?'

'Look the other way,' he says, and I turn away from the graveyard, and gasp.

The crumbling wall where we sit is at the top of a cliff. In the watery moonlight it's hard to tell how far down the drop goes, but it doesn't look good. I start to lean back further to peer over the edge but Echo pulls me away from it.

His hands are cold and shaking.

'I'm afraid of heights,' he says. 'Not just afraid: it's all I can do to even stay here.'

72

'Why come, then?'

'Being scared is the point. It's the way. What are you scared of?'

'You,' I say, the word out before I can call it back.

His eyes crinkle at the corners a little as he smiles and some of my fear eases. 'Then why did you come here with me?'

I tilt my head to one side. 'I don't know,' I finally say, honestly.

'I do. It's the same reason I can't stay away from places like this. You couldn't stop yourself, could you?'

'No,' I say, and my voice doesn't sound like my own. It's like I've caught his breathlessness. I can feel his fear and mine combining together, my blood throbbing fast as my heart pumps it through my body. I look at his eyes and know I've never felt anything like this before, like I'm tumbling, falling, over this cliff and inside of him, both at the same time. It's wild.

His hand touches the side of my face and I lean into his touch, almost vibrate with it.

'Apart from me, then,' he says. 'What are you scared of?'

'Lots of things. Almost everything, really,' I say.

'Like what?' he asks. And there is something about his closeness and where we are that makes me answer. With the truth.

'Terrorism, global warming, economic collapse, pandemics; being alone; not being alone; earthquakes, tsunamis, nuclear accidents; war; falling down stairs and hitting my head; getting blood poisoning from a splinter; Mum marrying somebody I don't like; getting cancer; Mum getting cancer. You name it.'

He nods. 'But not ghosts.'

'No.'

'Still, that is a lot of stuff to be scared of.' He half smiles again

73

and leans as far away from the drop behind us as he can and still be sitting on the wall, pulling me away from the edge a little with him. 'But that isn't what I meant.'

'What, then?'

'What is the thing that terrifies you, that makes you shake and scream and panic until your guts turn to liquid. Takes over until you are not even yourself any more – all you are, is fear.'

His face is white in the dim light of the moon – paler than white. It almost glows in the dark, black eyes burning with some fire that I can feel and almost name; one I want to run from and have consume me at the same time, and I don't know which impulse is stronger.

There is only one answer. My darkest nightmare.

Don't tell him, Molly hisses, next to him now where before all was empty space.

I flinch and Echo tightens his grip around me, as if afraid I'll fall or jump.

'Well?' he says.

'I'm claustrophobic,' I whisper. Molly scowls and vanishes. 'I'm scared of being trapped in closed-in spaces. Like I can't go in lifts or I totally freak out; I can't even be in a car without opening the window. It might be because I climbed into our washing machine once when I was little and somehow locked myself in: I screamed the place down until Mum found me.' Though I'm sure there is another reason for my fear, an even earlier, more fundamental source of the panic I feel when things close in around me. But I shy away from thinking about it, let alone saying it out loud.

74

'Why sit here if it scares you?' I say. I'm not afraid of heights, but his fear is so infectious I can almost feel it too. If this is his version of being shut in a lift, how can he stop himself from dropping down and getting away from it?

'Remember when I told you that I know how to open a way between the living and the dead?'

I nod.

'It's fear. Not just fear, really: complete terror. That is the moment the veil between the worlds of the living and the dead lifts, and you can talk to the dead.'

He says the words so seriously, with such belief. I look at the graves around us, as if the fear we share should show us the ghost he says is here. For a moment I can almost imagine I see something, some form, shimmering in the dark. I blink and all I see is Molly sitting on a gravestone below us.

'Well, you're scared sitting here,' I say. 'Are any of the dead saying anything, just now?'

Molly waves. *Hi Echo!*

He glances around the graveyard. Do his eyes pause on Molly? A slight frown appears between his eyes, then he shakes his head.

'No. But I'm not scared enough, not on my own. I need more fear,' he says. 'I need your fear.' His eyes are locked on to mine, and like yesterday on the pier, there is this feeling, a pulling, like his eyes can drag me out of my body, and I can't move, can't breathe, can't anything.

'Why me?' I whisper.

'Two reasons. You believe in ghosts – don't bother denying it. And you lost a twin. Twins are so close, it should make it easier

75

to lift the veil and open the door. And once it is open . . .' His voice trails away.

'What then?'

He stares back. Doesn't answer.

'You must want to contact somebody,' I say. 'Who is it?'

His head turns away. 'My mum,' he says, so quietly I barely hear, yet those two words and how he says them carry such sadness and pain that my hand reaches out to his, holds it. His tightens on mine in return.

'I'm so sorry,' I say, shocked, and not sure what else to say.

'Don't be. You didn't have anything to do with it,' he says, his eyes back on mine now. 'It was almost a year ago – a car accident.' There is anger there too – in his eyes. Because she was taken from him, or some other reason?

'Why do you want to reach her?'

'Let's just say there's something I need to ask her.' He jumps down off the wall. 'Come on. Let's go.'

He doesn't say much on the late bus back to Brighton. When we get off, he asks if he can walk me home.

'Let's say goodbye here,' I say.

'Think about what I told you. Let me know what you want to do.'

'Sure. Of course I will,' I say, but now that we're back in normal Brighton, with the comforting sound of the sea, people wandering about the promenade with streetlights showing the way, we're so far away from that insane moment in a dark graveyard that *no way* is what I'm thinking. Try to scare each other until we're completely terrified? I don't think so.

'I haven't got a mobile, but I'm staying with a friend of my mum's. I'll give you her number.'

Thinking it best to play along, I take out my phone. Enter the numbers as he says each digit, marvelling as I do that he hasn't got a mobile – he didn't say he lost it or it's broken or something; he said he doesn't have one.

'Got it,' I say, and stuff my phone back in my bag.

'Call me. We can do this together. Are you sure you don't want me to walk you home?'

'No, I'm fine.'

There's amusement on his face, like he's worked out that I don't want him to know where I live. He says goodbye, walks off in the night. Dressed in black as he is, he's soon lost from sight.

I walk home, fast, checking behind me now and then to make sure he isn't following.

When I get there I unlock the door, and quickly lock it behind me. I lean against it, breathing deep, then switch on the light.

Mum isn't home yet, and I'm relieved. She'd see something has happened, would want to know what it was – and even though she's not a traditional sort of mum, it would be hard to explain without freaking her out completely.

I head up the stairs to my room. Molly sits cross-legged on the desk.

I hope that after all that major weirdness tonight you've got him out of your system.

'Why? Why do you care so much? Lately you're always after me to see people and go places so you can come along. And Echo is certainly interesting. He's actually pretty gorgeous, in a goth boy sort of way. I'm sure he turned heads when he was watching for me at school.'

True, she admits.

'Tell me,' I say again.

There's something about him that I don't like, she says, the same thing she said earlier. She hesitates. *But it isn't him, exactly, either.*

'You're not making sense. What do you mean?'

But Molly doesn't feel like explaining. *Just delete his number. Please!* She disappears into the mirror on my dressing table.

I look at his name, the number he gave me, on my phone. Maybe deleting it – even though it was Molly's idea – would be sensible. If I'm not going to call, why keep it? But somehow I can't bring myself to do it.

Anyhow, just because I have his number doesn't mean I have to call him, does it? It's just there. Waiting. Just in case. I don't have to decide this instant.

I flop down on my bed, though doubt there is any way I am going to get to sleep anytime soon. My heart is still racing.

I had been scared. Afraid of Echo, where we were, what he might do. But that isn't what is keeping me awake.

I can't stop thinking about him. His eyes, the pain inside them. How he made me feel when he sat close, his arm around me, the touch of his hand.

Being with him made me feel more alive than I ever have before.

21

Echo

I don't follow Liv to see where she lives. I want to and I do think about it, but what if she spots me? I can't risk giving her more reason not to trust me than I have already.

Restless, I walk the other way – to the end of the dark pier – and make myself lean over the railing. Over the swirling, dark water below.

The familiar rush of fear grips me, but for a change I don't pull away; I want to lean further and further out. It's Liv that makes me feel this way – like I can do anything.

I almost kissed her. In the dark, on the wall. Her fear and mine mixed together like a drug, one that made me want to wrap myself around her, hold her close.

But instead I pulled her away from the edge. I kept her safe.

I stare at the water below. If I plunged into it right now, would it be so cold that it would take my breath away, stop me from breathing like my mum stopped breathing almost a year ago?

The sea I love and hate. Each molecule of water could be one that filled her lungs when she drowned. Each drop of rain that falls from the sky could be too; evaporated to the clouds to fall down to the depths again.

I have to remember why I'm here, what I need to do. Not be distracted by this battle between kissing Liv and keeping her safe. After all, everything we need to do is the opposite of safe.

If she calls.

What if she doesn't call?

She will; she has to.

But what if she doesn't?

22

Liv

'Here. Try this.'

Mum thrusts a white dress through the changing room door and I sigh. First Saturday of term break and we've been trying on clothes since the shops opened, even though she'd had trouble dragging me out of bed. She might have come home later than me but I was still awake when she got in.

I like this one, Molly says when I slip it over my head, and she stands in front of me in the exact same dress so I can see it: no mirror needed. She mimics my actions as if she is my reflection, looking back at me with my face.

When Molly died she wasn't even born yet, but she has always looked exactly like me. When I was two or three, about the time I first remember seeing her as being separate from myself, she was a toddler in a horrible matching pink dress. At eight it was school uniforms and pigtails; now, at sixteen, it's jeans and T-shirts when not in school uniform. And now, this floaty white dress.

'Why do you always look like me?' I ask her.

Who else should I look like? We're twins, remember?

Mum bangs on the door. 'Come out. I want to see,' she says.

Did you ever think maybe I don't look like you? Maybe, you look like me.

I step out of the changing room. A cluster of doors face a three-way mirror, and there are mirrors on the wall behind reflecting me back and forth, in endless, multiplied images. This all seems unreal, strange, like I'm not really here. Part of me is still sitting on a crumbling, graveyard wall, with the shiver of a dark cliff below it. My eyes are heavy, and my handbag seems to sag on the floor as if my mobile weighs it down, laden with Echo's phone number.

'Well, what do you think?' Mum demands.

I try to focus on the here and now; the mirrors. The dress is OK, but who wears white in October? That's when I notice: Mum is in the exact same dress, but in black.

She smiles. 'This will be perfect for our session.' This year's birthday photo shoot for our own wall of horrors is scheduled in a few days.

'Not in the same colour this time?' I say, surprised. Usually she has us in identical kit as much as possible.

'See: I'll wear the black dress, white belt, white shoes; and you, the white dress, black belt, black shoes. I've been to see Charley – he's going to do something arty in black and white.' Charley is her favourite photographer.

She's all excited, but I most definitely am not.

'I really hate this dress,' I say.

'How can you say that! It fits perfectly, and . . .'

'It's white! It's like a wedding dress, or a summer dress. It's stupid in October.'

Tell her you want the black one.

I grin: perfect. 'Tell you what, I'll do it however you and Charley like, in endless uncomfortable poses, if I can have the black dress and you the white one.'

'What?' Mum says, mouth hanging open. 'But you're the

82

sweet young thing. You should wear the white dress.'

I raise an eyebrow. 'Does that mean you're the old wicked witch and must wear black?'

By the horrified look on her face I know I've won.

'You're not so sweet at all, are you? Fine. I'll wear the white one,' she says.

The sales attendant finds our sizes in opposite colours. We put them on and pose together, black and white, white and black, reflecting in endless sequence to infinity. But there is just one Molly – she may be able to disappear in mirrors but has no reflection.

Much better. Say: thank you Molly, that was a brilliant idea.

'Thank you!' I say.

Mum smiles and kisses my cheek. 'You're very welcome.'

Which dress shall I wear for the photos next week? Molly twirls around my room as I hang up my new things and look for something to wear tonight: my birthday dinner with Mum, Rod and Bowie.

I shrug. 'You know what you'll wear: same as me.'

Maybe I won't!

'Sure. Maybe you won't.' She scowls and this isn't how I want to start the evening. 'Look, Molly, I need your help with something.'

What?

'Tonight, when we're at dinner, can you not jump out at me, or say stuff, when I'm trying to talk to everyone?'

She crosses her arms. *Why should you have all the fun?*

'It's just it is really hard to look anything like normal if I talk

83

to you in front of other people! You don't want me to scare
Bowie away, or Rod either, do you? Please.'

She stares back at me a while, then smiles.

You'd have to owe me a favour.

'What kind of favour?'

I don't know yet. But I'll think of something.

23

Echo

At first I think I've imagined her, that I've spent so much of today thinking about Liv and willing Kashina's phone to ring that my mind is playing tricks on me. But I blink a few times and Liv is still there – across the road, walking.

She's in a dress. I haven't seen her in a dress before, just jeans, school uniform. She looks somehow more poised, older, and she's stunning. Her dress is a dark aquamarine, not too tight but skimming her body in the right places. Her hair is swept back, and when she moves her head it sways softly side to side. I almost step forward to cross the road, ready to call her name and have her turn towards me, but then I see she's not alone.

There is a woman who must be her mother; her hair is long and dark, too, curly where Liv's is straight, but apart from that there's so much likeness between them. She's holding hands with a man younger than her. And then there is a boy about Liv's age walking next to her.

Liv says something to him; there is a lurch in my stomach when I see the way he looks at her. He's blond, moves easily, like an athlete. Somehow you can just tell by looking at him that he's popular, good-natured, likeable; his face looks like it is made for smiling. He's everything that I'm not.

I step back, away from the curb, meaning to lose myself on the busy pavement, but can't stop myself from following. I keep back, let them pull ahead on the other side of the road.

Now blond boy is saying something; Liv is laughing. I haven't heard her laugh before and I'm not close enough to hear it now, but I want to.

They're not holding hands; he's not standing close to her as they walk, not even as close as I was to her last night. Despite the way he looked at her before, I'm unsure: is he a friend or a boyfriend? She wouldn't have met me like that at night if she had a boyfriend, would she? I don't know.

Though maybe that's why she hasn't called.

Please call me, Liv.

The four of them go into a restaurant and I stay in shadows across the road, watching. I lose sight of them for a moment, then see first Liv's mother and then the rest of them being led to a table in the window on one side of the door.

They sit down. Liv is in profile to me, blond boy's back to the window; her mum opposite Liv and the other one on Liv's other side.

They're talking, opening menus, and I'm standing in the dark. Watching. The evening moves slowly by while they talk some more, smile and laugh and eat, and still I watch, feeling creepy to be doing it but somehow unable to make myself walk away.

A cake is brought out, with candles. It was Liv's birthday the day I met her, wasn't it? This must be her birthday celebration.

I wish I could be closer, be there with her. Without thinking it through I'm crossing the road, but before I get to the door of the restaurant I come to my senses. What would she think if I just barged in on their dinner? Get a grip, Echo.

Instead I turn and walk away.

86

24

Liv/Molly

Despite Molly's promises, I was nervous tonight, and it's not even just because of anything she might say or do. First there was Bowie and how weird things have been between us since I dashed off after we kissed. Then there was Mum and how she might go on about Bowie and me being a lovely little couple or something else equally cringeworthy, and also how touchy-feely she and Rod might be with each other in public.

But all that worry was for nothing. We've had a nice dinner in my favourite restaurant. Molly stayed sitting on the window ledge next to us swinging her feet, alternatively mooning over Rod, then Bowie, then Rod, but she did so quietly. Mum hasn't been too embarrassing, and Rod guided the conversation around on relatively safe topics, like the chances of the Seagulls being relegated this year, local knife crime and Amber, the world's cutest puppy, whom he has decided to keep.

But best of all is Bowie. From the beginning tonight he has been just himself: my friend like he always was, as if the last week never happened.

In fact everything was completely fine until I was trying to decide what to wish for when I blew out the candles, and glanced at Molly to see if she had any ideas. Then – just for a split second – I thought I could see Echo's reflection in the glass of the window.

Startled, I turned my head to look for him outside, but he wasn't there.

Echo had been wandering through my thoughts all day and just had to do so again then. I turned back to the cake and blew out the candles, but, concentration gone, forgot to make a proper wish. And I got them all out, too. What a waste.

'Here you go,' Mum says, and passes me a small gift bag. 'I hope you like it.'

I shake it. There's a faint slithery noise – jewellery?

'Go on,' she says, and I reach in, take out a small box. Open it. Inside is a chunky silver charm bracelet with letter charms that spell out Livia, and one of the number sixteen.

'Thank you!' I say, and take it out to put it on, struggling with the clasp.

'Let me,' Bowie says, and I hold out my hand. His fingers lightly touch my wrist as he fiddles with the catch and I watch him. He fastens it and looks up, and for a moment our eyes meet and his seem to be saying something, but I don't know what.

'Do you like it?' Mum says and I glance at her, the moment gone.

'I do!' I spin it around my wrist to line my name up at the front, and I actually really do like it. Maybe it's a bit naff to have a name badge on your jewellery, but it's pretty.

Not much later we're walking home, back to ours. The evening would have been perfect if it hadn't been for stray thoughts of Echo intruding now and then. Where did he get his ideas? What do they have to do with me?

And not so much 'should I call him?', because I know I shouldn't, but 'will I?'

'Beautiful night, isn't it?' Mum says, looking up as we near our house. The sky is clear and the stars are twinkling. She looks pointedly at Bowie and me. 'Nice night for a walk.' Nice night to be alone with Rod is what she really means.

'Why not?' Bowie says.

I can think of a few reasons. But what I say instead is, 'Wait a minute, I'll go change.'

Upstairs in my room I kick off my heels and do a quick change from dress to jeans. Is this a bad idea?

No, it is the very best idea. Molly is grinning like a maniac.

'Don't get carried away. We're just going for a walk.'

Haven't I been good tonight? Done exactly as you asked?

'You have,' I admit, uneasy as to where this is going.

It's time for my favour.

'What? But it's still tonight. You're still being good, like you promised.'

No way. The deal was for over dinner. Dinner is well and truly finished. Your pasta looked yummy, by the way.

'It was. What do you want?'

Let me in. Not just hitching. Let me be in charge for a little while.

I'm trapped. How can I say no after how well the evening has gone? But we have a quick debate, and setting of rules. No hitting on Bowie allowed: things are finally normal between us. She adds an addendum that if he starts anything, she is allowed to kiss back; I add that she can't let it go any further than a kiss. She argues, then agrees.

Mum bangs on my door. 'Come on, Sunshine, Bowie is waiting.'

'Just a minute!' I say. Then in a lower voice: 'Molly, are you sure you wouldn't rather stay here with Mum and Rod? It might be more entertaining than coming with us.'

No way.

As hard as it is to do when I'm feeling uneasy and unsure about the whole idea, I make myself relax. Molly drapes herself around me and then slips in, like a very sharp knife, so sharp you don't feel the pain but wonder at the damage.

What a horrible thing to think, she says and I start to apologise, but then Molly's thoughts shimmer together with mine. We are one, and I curl up, small, inside. Molly is in charge.

Molly goes downstairs, kisses Mum goodnight and walks out the door with Bowie.

25

Echo

Kashina is home, sitting lotus style on the sofa with Abba on loud and a half empty bottle of whisky next to her. Her eyes are closed and I almost back out again, but where have I got to go?

'Hey,' I shout.

Her eyes open part way. 'What, you again?' she says, or at least I think she does – I can't hear her so that is guesswork.

'The one and only,' I say, and slump down on the chair opposite her, wondering how long she'll be camped out on my bed, the sofa. Not that I'll be able to sleep, so what does it really matter? If I close my eyes all I see is Liv, laughing with that blond boy next to her. I wonder what they're doing now.

Kashina stirs, stretches; her lips move again but reading them fails me this time. I shrug, point at the stereo, and she finds the remote for it under a cushion and 'Dancing Queen' goes down a few notches.

'How can you stand it so loud?' I say. 'Especially that.'

'You don't like it? You choose the next song.'

'I know you won't have anything decent.'

'We can listen to anything you want – it's streaming!' She has a drink of whisky, holds the bottle out.

'No, thanks.'

The final strains of the song are fading. She waggles her phone in her hand. 'Quick now, what will it be?'

'Anything at all?' I say, and she nods. 'OK. "Disintegration" by The Cure.'

A moment later it is blaring out of her speakers and I close my eyes to listen. Music comes through me more with my eyes closed. I can't remember the last time I heard this song.

'You need to lighten up,' she says when it is over. 'Pick something fun.'

'It's your turn,' I say.

There's a pause, then she's bellowing out 'YMCA'. I'm actually laughing when she gets up and starts doing the classic arm movements to spell out the letters – a white-haired, half-drunk psychic in some sort of kimono dancing to the Village People.

But she stops on the next chorus, somewhere between changing from M to C.

'Ouch! I think I strained something,' she says, rubbing her right shoulder with her other hand. 'Let's take a break.' She's puffing a bit and lowers herself back on the sofa; she aims the remote to turn it down further. 'So, what have you been up to today?'

My mind turns back to spying on Liv and now my laughter is gone. 'Nothing I care to admit to. You?'

'It's Saturday, so much the same.' Her eyes crinkle at the corners.

'The usual shtick down by the pier?'

'Yes.'

She and Mum used to do this together: fortune telling, but not for real. Kashina always said if you tell people what they want to hear, they pay more.

My smile fades further, remembering. 'Mum used to argue

with you, didn't she? She said that if she could see something real about someone, she should tell it no matter what it was.'

'She always took things too seriously,' Kashina says. Sadness in her eyes, she starts to twist off the lid of the bottle in her hand again. I get up, sit next to her. Put my hand over hers.

'Maybe you don't take them seriously enough. That stuff is going to kill you.'

'There are worse ways to die. I've seen – felt, lived through – most of them over and again.'

'Can't you just say no? Walk away. Don't listen.'

'It's not a choice, Echo. It's what I am, though it can be a heavy burden. One that your mother carried as well.'

Again, she doesn't say it directly but I know what she means: that it was too heavy, that Mum couldn't go on.

'It was an open verdict,' I say. 'If people who didn't even know Mum couldn't believe she meant to take her own life, how can you?'

'Open just means they couldn't prove it.'

'Look. I know that Mum kept stuff inside, and maybe I didn't know or understand how difficult things were for her. I can even accept, for the sake of argument, that she could have been driven to that point without me being aware of it. But she would *never* have tried to take me with her. I'll never believe that.'

'If she was in her right mind, I've no doubt you are right.' She squeezes my hand and heads up to bed soon after.

I can't stop thinking about what she said, what she didn't say.

I hate that Kashina is making me doubt myself, doubt the things I know to be true: Mum loved me. She'd never, ever have done anything to hurt me.

I have to remember why I'm here. I've been distracted by Liv, by how I feel about her. But I need to focus on what is important: getting Liv to help me reach Mum.

26

Molly/Liv

'Look, here. This knob? You can focus with this if you need to.'

Bowie is demonstrating the workings of his telescope. We are on the roof terrace at his house; no one is home except for his grounded sister, Tina, who waved from the sofa as we went through but didn't even look up from some horror flick.

I lean over and look through the eyepiece, then make a slight adjustment to the focus. The stars! So many, so bright. So different to how they look normally, in half-light and shadows.

'It's beautiful.' I almost breathe rather than say the words.

Bowie shows me different stars, constellations. He's standing so close to me that every bit of me tingles, almost vibrates, with awareness, as if my skin can feel his across this small space between us.

Finally I look up from the eyepiece, and into Bowie's eyes. A shiver goes through me from deep inside. This feeling: it must be the moment. I wasn't supposed to kiss him, though why that is has gone, slipped into some shadow of a memory, and it is all I can do to stay still, to wait for him to bridge the gap.

His eyes are blue: not a wishy-washy pale colour, but a deep blue, like the sea under midday sun. His lashes are long and curly, a streaky dark blond like his hair. My hand aches to brush his hair away from his eyes, but something stops it.

'Look, Liv. There is something I want to talk to you about,'

Bowie says. He steps back, away from me, and leans against the railing.

Liv. That sounds wrong. But that's my name, isn't it?

I smile up at him, look at his lips, then back to his eyes.

'That kiss last week was a mistake, wasn't it?' he says. 'We're friends, good friends. I don't want to risk losing your friendship. I want things to stay the way they are, like they've been tonight.'

I blink, stunned, unable to react, to speak. It hurts, like a knife slipping in without resistance.

Sssssh, Molly, it's all right. Someone cradles me, soothes me, inside. I slip away and the colours fade, dim down. Everything goes back to half-light and shadows.

I blink. Molly was so in control that for a while I didn't know where I was or if I could even come back again without her help. If the shock she felt with what Bowie said hadn't made her want to retreat, would she have done so?

'Are you all right?' Bowie says, concern in his eyes – did we zone out while I was coming back?

'Yes.' I smile, relieved both at what he said and to be back in myself, where I belong. 'I'm fine, everything is fine. And you're right. I want us to stay friends too.'

He looks uncertain, then smiles too.

Later in my room, Molly is sitting on the desk as usual. Though not talking: unusual.

'Well, how was it?' I say. 'Being in control.'

Weird. It was definitely weird. I felt all . . . confused. Like I didn't know what to do, or what to say.

'Welcome to my life.'

Look, Molly says and holds up her wrist. She is wearing a charm bracelet like mine, the one Mum gave me earlier. She twirls it round. Instead of L – I – V – I – A, it has M – O – L – L – Y hanging on it. But she has always had exactly the same things on as me, as far back as I can remember.

'That is different,' I say, feeling somehow disturbed, like she is changing and leaving me behind.

Molly slips into bed next to me. *Don't worry, I'm not going anywhere. We made a good team tonight, didn't we?*

'I guess. But why are you here, really? When you died, why did you stay?'

Molly shrugs. *I've told you this before: to look after you. To look after Mum. I couldn't leave you alone.*

'If that was how it worked, if dead people could just decide to stay if they want to with people who love them, no one would ever leave. You wouldn't be able to move for the crowds of ghosts.'

You needed me and I couldn't bear to leave you alone. You still need me, don't you?

And there is no point in denying what she can see and feel inside me. As much trouble as she causes sometimes, Molly is part of me, and I am part of her. I couldn't get rid of her any more than I could get rid of myself.

As far as I know, no one else has someone like Molly with them. And this is what Echo wants, isn't it? He doesn't know Molly is already here; he thinks we can scare ourselves enough to move her into our world. So if he wants what I have, who am I to judge?

Molly has been there from the beginning – my beginning.

I don't remember being born, but Molly was there — and aware — when I took my first breath of air in the world.

And then you cried — more like screamed the place down!

'But you didn't. What was it like — dying?' A question I've asked many times before; one she has answered in different ways at different times.

Being slowly crushed, suffocated. Starved. It didn't hurt like you'd think it would. I remember a vague sense of panic, of trying to move and get away.

'From me.'

But there was nowhere to go.

We were special twins. Not just identical, but even more: we were momos. Momo is easier to say than what it stands for: monoamniotic and monochorionic — we shared the same amniotic sac, the same placenta. So from days after conception — when our fertilised egg split and we became two identical beings — we were in competition: for food, for space. Whether I was bigger because I was winning the battle, or I was bigger anyhow and that was why I was winning, she doesn't know. But I was the bully who wouldn't share and slowly crushed her cord until oxygen and food went from a stream to a trickle to nothing at all, and just before she should have been born, she died.

Why are you thinking of all of this now?

'I don't know. With us being together and then apart tonight, I'm trying to make sense of who we are, I guess. But all I know about what happened is what you say. I don't remember any of it.'

It wasn't your fault. I don't blame you.

This is Molly's litany: something she says now and then when

I need to hear it. Two short lines meant to comfort, but I'm not sure I believe either of them.

It's all right. Go to sleep, Molly says. As I eventually drift away, she whispers and murmurs, words too faint to hear.

Something about dreams?

Another place . . . another time: an end and a beginning.

Pulling away from myself I feel relief, separation. I stay to watch. Mum looks different from the outside; so does she, the one I shadowed for so long, the one who surrounded, held and then finally crushed me.

Mum lies on her back, knees up, screaming and yelling at Dad, and her hair and face are a mess. Nurses and doctors come and go, then a few stay and Mum screams and screams.

Always first to stake a claim, to food, to space – to life – the other one pushes her way out first. She sucks in air and hollers. Dad holds up a little camera and takes her first photo, if you don't count the ultrasound.

Everyone smiles.

Then it's my turn, but there's panic in the room now. They know something is wrong.

When I come out a moment later, I am small and still and silent – blue, not red like my sister – and there is a flurry of determined activity by the medical staff on what is left of me.

Too late.

Dad puts down the camera. A nurse tries to press the other one to Mum, all squirming, furious life, wailing, as if she were the one who died. But all Mum does is cry, and clutch what I was, tight against her.

My sister is forgotten, alone, screaming and ignored. I settle around her and think soothing thoughts. She stops crying and looks into my eyes.

She needs me, doesn't she?

So I stay.

27

Echo

What happened must be buried somewhere in my mind. Maybe it's like when you've lost your keys and can't find them for looking, but when you forget about them and go do something else – or even, nothing at all – suddenly, there they are: in your pocket or under a book or hanging from the lock in the front door, there all along. If memory works the same way, maybe I've been trying too hard.

It's quiet. Even in this busy part of Brighton, there is an hour or two when the parties have stopped and the early birds haven't started tweeting. Quiet, that is, unless you count Kashina snoring upstairs, the waves washing up the beach far down the road and the suddenly loud tick, tick of the clock on the mantle.

I'm stretched out on the sofa. I close my eyes, willing myself to relax, but relaxing doesn't work quite like that, does it?

Tick, tick . . .

I can't stop my thoughts, make myself go blank. Think of something else instead?

Kashina, her awful music tonight; her even worse dancing. Y – M – C – A

Tick, tick . . .

Sometimes I made Mum and Kashina listen to some of my music; Mum didn't mind but Kashina hated it – said it was too dark. Nice of her to play some tonight, though.

Music is noise; I remember Mum saying that once. It distracts. But Kashina said it drowns out things she doesn't want to hear. She meant visitors – the dead. They used to say things like that to each other in vague-speak, as if I wouldn't understand.

Tick, tick . . .

Mum wanted to listen, Kashina to drown out. They'd argue, not in a way that mattered – it was like how I could argue with Mum. Kashina really was like her mum – my gran – wasn't she?

Though their disagreements had seemed more serious, more heated, not long before Mum died.

Tick . . .

I creep closer to the kitchen door. Their voices were raised and now that they aren't any more, I'm worried.

'. . . not listening to me.' Kashina.

'I listen better than most. You know that.' Mum.

'That's not what I mean.'

'I know.'

'I'm worried about you.'

'I know that, too.'

'What about Echo? If you won't think of yourself, then think of him. What if . . .'

Her voice drops lower, I can't hear. I shift closer to the door, put my ear against it,

'. . . can't walk away. She needs my help.' Mum.

'You can't go there again and again – it could overwhelm you, your mind. Break you. You're not strong enough.'

Not strong enough . . .

★

102

Tick.

I open my eyes wide. I'd forgotten about that day, listening in. It sounded like stuff Kashina said to Mum a lot of the time, really, though more serious than the usual version.

Mum said she couldn't walk away, that she needed to help someone – who was it?

But now I'm thinking of the words Kashina used this time: overwhelm your mind; break you; not strong enough . . . Did something break my mother, lead her to a place so dark that she took her own life?

And nearly mine, too.

No.

No! I won't believe it.

I can't.

Tick, tick . . .

28

Liv

Waking up the next morning is a gradual thing, with part of me still drifting in Molly's memory – my dream – or whatever it was. I don't want to wake up and have to think about it.

When I finally do open my eyes, I'm alone. Did Molly know I needed some time to myself right now, or is she off spying on Mum and Rod?

I don't understand how Molly and I fit together any more. Things used to be simpler – well, as simple as they can be when you spend most of your time with someone that no one else can see or hear. But it used to be that I only needed Molly, no one else. Well, Mum too, of course, but in a different way. Now things are changing; I'm changing. That's it, isn't it? I don't want to be part of a committee any more. I want to do what I want – what I need. I want things that are only for me.

I'm selfish.

Yes, you are. Molly is back, sitting cross-legged on my desk. How long has she been eavesdropping on my thoughts?

Long enough. Are you getting up? It's breakfast time. Rod is making pancakes, and he's wearing one of Mum's dressing gowns. And it's too small. She grins.

I pull a pillow over my head and make a gagging noise. My phone vibrates on my bedside table.

Who is it?

I sit up, pick up my phone. There's a text, from Bowie: last night was fun, glad I came. Are you sure you're all right?

Molly cranes to look over my shoulder. *Who is it*? she says again.

'Don't be so nosy.' I sigh, shake my head. 'Bowie. It was Bowie, all right?'

Does he want to see us? Her eyes widen when she realises what she said. *I mean, you.*

'I know what you meant, and we've decided to stay just friends, remember?' And now I'm also remembering Molly's pain last night – I felt her feelings as my own when she was running things. 'I'm sorry, Molly.'

Are you? Are you really? You should be.

I'm about to apologise again, but then I'm annoyed at feeling that way. Before I can say anything else, there's a knock at the door.

'Are you awake, Liv?' Mum says. 'Do you want some pancakes?'

Forewarned about the dressing gown I stay silent; Molly looks through the door. *She's got a tray.*

'Yes, please!' I call out.

The door opens. Mum has a tray with pancakes, strawberries, juice and tea.

'Wow!' I say. 'Thank you.'

She quickly sets it down on my desk, leaves and shuts my door again.

Message received, loud and clear: stay in your room.

So Mum doesn't want you around? Now you know how it feels.

Molly flips her hair and vanishes through the door.

I get up and pick at breakfast; it's yum, but I'm feeling . . . I don't know. Out of sorts. Abandoned. Wondering what is going on downstairs and not wanting to know at the same time.

Later I shower, get dressed. Still no sign of Molly. Is it safe to go down yet?

While I hesitate at the door, my phone vibrates: it's Bowie again. I think you need to talk to your mum.

A sinking feeling joins the rest. Why? What's going on?

She called mine, asked us all for dinner. Then Mum was on my case, asking why I haven't told them I've got a *girlfriend*. What have you been telling her?

I stare at the words on my screen, unable to take them in. She did *what*? Without asking me, first? I lean against the door, thunk my head against it – several times, hard. And does Bowie really think I've been telling her we're together or something?

This can't be happening.

I text back: NOTHING, I've said nothing. It's all Mum. Sorry, I'm on it.

No longer caring what I might walk in on, I march downstairs – but it's safe. Mum is on her own, at the breakfast bar with the newspapers and tea. No sign of Rod, though through the window I can see his car is still here. She's on her own, except for Molly, who is cross-legged on the counter with that look on her face – a cross between innocent and wicked.

'You knew, and you didn't tell me?' I think at her.

Knew what?

'Mum! How could you!'

'What is it this time?'

106

'Did you actually call Bowie's parents and invite them for dinner?'

'Don't worry, Rod said he'd cook. They're coming next Saturday.'

'I'm not worried about the menu! You told Bowie's mum that I'm like, his girlfriend or something?'

'So? Shouldn't she know?' She shrugs.

'You don't get it, do you? Even if I was – which I'm *not* – it's just . . . it's so . . . embarrassing! Parents don't call other parents and tell them stuff like that!'

'I really don't understand what the problem is.'

My mouth is hanging open, words actually failing me now. 'Cancel it,' I finally manage to say.

'I can't do that – it'd be rude. Honestly, Liv. What's got into you?' She shakes her head. Molly is watching us, back and forth like a tennis match, laughing, almost hysterically.

'Just keep the hell out of my life, both of you!' I shout, just as the door opens and Rod steps through.

I stomp out of the kitchen to the front room, slam the door. I hear Mum apologising, then she comes through to me.

'Liv! That was beyond belief. How could you speak to Rod like that?'

I didn't. But how can I tell her that wasn't directed at the two of them, but at her and Molly?

I can't.

I've had enough of everything, this whole ridiculous situation. Out. I'm getting out of here.

I head for the front door.

'Liv, you come back here, right now, and apologise!'

But I'm opening the door, slamming it behind me, running up the road. As each foot hits the pavement it is like it jars the anger and the completely, total, cringeworthy mortification through my entire body.

Oh my God – I just – can't believe – she did that – called Bowie's Mum –

And Molly – didn't say – didn't warn me –

Then Rod – he thought – I meant him –

Is it possible to actually die of embarrassment?

A bit later I find myself on a bench opposite the beach. My phone is in my hand. I ignore the missed calls from Mum; I'm not listening to her, or to Molly, or anybody else any more.

I need something that is just for me.

Contacts . . .

Echo . . .

I hesitate, then hit the call button.

29

Echo

'Echo? Echo!' Kashina calls, excitement all through her voice.

I go through to the kitchen. 'What is it?'

Her eyes are wide, she points at the phone, shakes her head like she doesn't know what to say, and then pushes a button on it.

Beep. 'Hi, this is Liv, calling Echo. I'm down by the beach near the pier if you want to talk. Bye.' Beep.

'When did she call?'

'Must have been when I was in the shower. I just noticed it now. That was the girl you met at the cemetery?' She can't believe it – she's shaking her head as if to make sense of it, but is it so impossible to imagine that a girl would call me?

Will she still be there? I'm running for the door.

'Echo?'

'Later, gotta go.'

I run all the way. When I get to the promenade I scan up and down, the benches, the beach. I can't see her – has she left? It's a sunny Sunday afternoon, crowds of people everywhere; I might have missed her. I start checking faces more methodically, but no luck. Hope is starting to fade. Should I keep looking or go back to Kashina's in case she calls again?

'Echo?' a voice – behind me. I spin round, and there she is. I feel a smile take over my face.

She's smiling back. A bit hesitantly, maybe, but still, it's a smile. One that is only for me.

30

Liv

'I couldn't see you. I thought you'd given up, left,' Echo says.

'I didn't have anywhere else I wanted to be just now,' I say, then mentally give myself a slap. Way to sound desperate, Liv.

'You're going to help me, aren't you? That's why you called; that's why you're still here,' he says.

We're standing in the middle of a crowded pavement, people all around, but the way he looks at me – like I'm the only girl in the world – makes me want to agree to anything he says.

But there is still some caution inside that has me shaking my head. 'Wait a minute, not so fast. I need you to explain things a bit more, about what you are trying to do, and why.'

A silent pause follows. 'That's fair,' he finally says. 'Come on, let's find somewhere a bit quieter we can talk.'

We walk along the promenade. It's a beautiful day, something I'm only really noticing now, and as it's term break there are people everywhere. The sun is shining, kids are eating ice cream and everyone is just generally enjoying the seaside, on this, a rare autumn day that is more like July than October.

We wander past the endless line of touristy shops, art good and bad on easels, rock, ice cream and fish and chips. We walk down from the promenade to the pebble beach, and down to the edge of the sea. The tide is going out.

He stoops to pick up a pebble. 'I wonder how long this

111

has been here, on this beach, its edges rounded by the sea and the tide?'

I take it from his hand and throw it as far as I can into the water. 'There. A change of scene.'

He laughs; he has a nice laugh, not too loud but somehow just right for him. I'm guessing it's something he doesn't do often.

'So, you want the full story,' he says, and walks back from the water to where it is dry and sits down. I sit next to him. He's gazing off in the distance as if there is something only he can see, then lies back, knees up, facing the sky. He turns on his side, leans up on one elbow, and takes off his sunglasses. His dark eyes flicker with something, some pain, and I settle next to him, half lying down also, facing him, and wait.

'I told you my mum died in an accident. What I didn't tell you is that she drove her car off a cliff.'

My eyes widen. I don't know what I expected to hear, but it wasn't that.

'I'm so sorry,' I say, one hand reaching to his but he turns away and my hand falls back. He puts his glasses back on, lies on his back again and looks up at the sky.

'Stop apologising like you had something to do with it.'

'I'm so—' I start to say, then stop, trying and failing to imagine what he must have gone through, and instantly feeling bad about running out this morning and not returning Mum's calls.

'Why do you want to contact her?'

'There's something I have to ask her. Something important.'

'But why do you think fear is the way? How do you know this?'

He sits up, stands, and holds out a hand to help me up.

'Come on. There's a place I want to show you. It's just a short bus ride away.'

We walk back up the beach and promenade, through cafés and shops towards the bus stop.

There is a bottleneck of people to get around and then Echo stops like he's startled, starts to reverse as people part. Before us is an old woman crouched on a blanket, a nearly empty hat next to her with some loose coins. A sign that says 'Fortunes: pay Kashina what they are worth.' She looks vaguely familiar: part of the colourful human landscape of Brighton that I've seen before, but never this close.

'Liv?' she says, and holds out a hand.

31

Echo

Great timing.

'How do you know my name?' Liv says.

'I know many things about you. Come, and I'll tell your fortune.'

Liv glances back at me, eyes wide.

'We're kind of in a hurry just now,' I say, hoping Kashina will just let us go, though knowing her, it's unlikely. What is she up to?

'Sit,' she says. 'Both of you.'

'Could be fun?' Liv sits down on the edge of the blanket. I sigh and sit next to her.

Kashina fixes her brown eye on Liv; her other eye is turned inward and is a cloudy grey.

'Your left hand,' she demands and Liv holds it out. Kashina grips it in hers, stares intently at it, mumbles to herself. Liv looks at me; I shrug. Kashina suddenly grasps Liv's hand tight and sits bolt upright. Her eyes have changed. The brown eye looks away, off to the side, and her blind eye seems to stare straight at Liv. Even though I've seen this before, it's still freaky.

'You are at a crossroads.' Her voice is different: deeper, clearer. 'A crossroads between what is safe and what is not. The choices you make now will change you for ever. Take care or you may lose everything.' Then her clouded eye wanders across, seems to focus behind us.

'There is another? One from the other side who always stays close to you.'

Liv twists to look behind, and then back at Kashina. Her face has gone pale. 'What do you mean? What do you see?'

With her free hand Kashina taps on her hat until it jingles. Liv reaches into her pocket, puts some coins in.

'Who is it you see?' Liv says.

Kashina's other eye – the brown one – wanders back to focus on Liv. 'Why should I tell you what you already know?'

32

Liv

I get up fast, almost run to the bus stop until I make myself slow down. Was Molly there? Did that so-called fortune teller actually see her? I didn't see Molly when I turned around, but she could have been and gone – especially if Kashina freaked her out.

'Are you all right?' Echo says once he catches me up.

'Of course. Such nonsense, don't you think?' Is it?

He shrugs. 'Sometimes yes, sometimes no.'

'What is that supposed to mean?'

'There's something I should tell you. Kashina knew your name from the message you left on her answer machine.'

'What?' I shake my head, trying to knock sense into it. 'Do you mean she is the friend of your mum that you are staying with?'

'Yep. She must have spotted us together and worked out you were Liv. Sorry if she scared you with what she said. She's really good at reading little things with people and coming up with stuff that freaks them out.'

'Do you mean what she says is all made up?' I feel disquieted, maybe disappointed too.

'Most of the time. Not always. That's why I said, sometimes yes, sometimes no.'

I say nothing, trying to take in what he means. But now the bus is here, and we're getting on. It lumbers past the marina, along the coast and towards Rottingdean. It's not long before Echo says to ring the bell.

I push the button; the bus stops. We get out and cross the road. He stares over the chain fence at the side of the road, at the cliff, the paved Undercliff Walk below and the sea just beyond.

And I start to wonder what he then confirms.

'It was here – my mum's accident. Her car drove off the cliff just here. At speed. She crashed through the fence and her car went over and crashed on the pavement below, rolled to the rocks and sea just beyond. The car was a wreck. She died.'

I stare at Echo. The way he told me . . . he stated the facts calmly, remotely. As if he was reading the news.

'I'm so sorr—' Then I catch myself and bite off the apology.

'It was at night, but the road was dry and visibility good. Traffic was light and nobody saw it happen. There was no reason for her car to go off the road here. Some thought she did it on purpose, but she didn't leave a note or anything. There was an inquest into her death but it gave an open verdict – there was insufficient evidence for them to decide if it was an accident or suicide.'

Unable to begin to know what to say, I stare below. The rocks are jagged; the cliff isn't that high, but high enough. How could anyone point their car for the sea and accelerate . . . into nothing?

I slip my hand into his. He grips it tight for a moment then lets go. Crosses his arms and stares at the sea.

'But I'm sure she didn't do it on purpose. She wouldn't have left me like that. She was a clairvoyant, a psychic, and worked with Kashina. They had an actual storefront then, for fortunes

117

and horoscopes. Séances too. And Mum was for real. Kashina is too, but she plays games with it sometimes, makes things up, either that people want to hear or just to play with them. Mum didn't. She took it all seriously. It's from her that I understand how to reach the dead, using fear. It's what she used to do.'

He reaches into his pocket, takes out an old, creased photograph. A young woman with jet black hair. Pretty, slight. There's something about her that draws the eye, even in an old photograph like this. And a laughing baby – a toddler really – on her knee. There is a half smile on her lips, like she is trying to smile for the camera, but it doesn't reach her eyes.

'This is you? With your mum?'

He nods. 'Meet Rose Lee. Used to be Rose Lee Wellington, but she changed her name when she moved to Brighton. Just before I was born.'

'She looks so young.'

'She was twenty when she had me and thirty-seven when she died, almost a year ago.' He grips my shoulders. 'You see, this is why. I have to find out. I have to find her, wherever she is now, and make her tell me what really happened. But I can't do it alone. I've tried.' His eyes are intent on mine. 'Will you help me?'

There are so many reasons to say no. But held in his eyes right now, all I can feel or think is that he is in pain, that he needs help – my help. How can I refuse?

'Yes. OK, I'll do what I can to help you.'

'Thank you,' he says, and he sweeps me up close to him, his arms around me, and as he does I feel off balance, like I'm tumbling, falling. That I should have run as far and as fast as I could, and now it's too late.

He pulls away. 'Don't forget, this isn't just about me. It's for you too, so you can reach Molly.'

I break gaze, turn to face the sea. 'So what next? What do we do?'

'I've got a few ideas. Meet me tomorrow morning? Train station. At ten. And get a ticket for London.'

'OK.'

33

Echo

She said yes: three words that I repeat, over and again, in my mind as I walk. There is almost a spring in my step as I consider options.

She said she'd help me – yet at the same time I felt her uncertainty. It wouldn't take much to make her back away.

Kashina could have wrecked everything. What was she playing at? Did she make up all that she said or was there something real behind it?

I need to go slowly, carefully, with Liv. I've come up with something that will scare both of us – difficult for me with my fear of heights and for her with claustrophobia, but not actually dangerous.

It won't be enough to reach Mum or her sister, I know that. But it is a place to start.

34

Liv

I'm walking home from the promenade, each step slower than the last.

Echo was so happy when I said I'd help him. And then as soon as we got the bus back, he said he had to go do something, almost like he was afraid I'd change my mind if we spent any more time together. Who uses 'go do something' as an excuse? You'd say, I have to go to the dentist, I have chores, homework, a sick friend to visit – anything else, really.

What have I got myself into this time?

You are at a crossroads between what is safe and what is not: unbidden, Kashina's words, the way she said them, are in my mind. The way her eye moved and seemed to focus on something only she could see is all coming back to me now, and a shiver goes up my spine.

I don't believe in that stuff.

Do I?

Well, I believe in ghosts. Obviously. But I don't believe Kashina or anyone else can hold my hand and know stuff about me or my future. It's rubbish. It just threw me because she knew my name, but Echo explained that.

Echo's pain was so real, it felt like it was mine. To lose his mum is bad enough, but to not know if it was an accident or if she meant for it to happen? And if she did, *why*. Even if there wasn't anything he could have done to stop it, that would be hard for anybody to deal with, even someone less . . . *intense* than Echo.

Despite the slow steps I've reached our street.

Mum's car is out front, no sign of Rod's, and there is a sinking feeling. Did he leave because of what I said? What if they break up and it's my fault? I actually almost kind of think Rod might just be OK, that it might be all right if he stays around.

And Mum was upset with me, with what I said – and I just walked out. What if something happened to her? What if that was the last time I saw her?

I go up the steps, unlock the door. Hear the radio on in the kitchen.

She looks up from paperwork all over the breakfast bar when I open the door.

'I'm sorry,' I say. And the raw emotion of the day – all of it, Molly and Bowie and then Kashina, Echo and his mum – is too much, all at once. Mum is holding out a hand and I'm there, her arms around me in a hug, and I'm crying. Now Molly is here, too, her arms around both of us.

'What's wrong?' Mum says.

'I'm sorry – I didn't mean what I said.' Well, I did, kind of, but not what she thought I meant – it had nothing to do with Rod.

'I know. It's OK. I was a teenager once too, you know – I remember what it's like. Some of the things I said to my parents – well, I'd tell you, but I don't want to give you ideas.'

'Is Rod OK?' I hesitate. 'He didn't leave because of what I said, did he?'

'He had to go to work unexpectedly – some kind of emergency, nothing to do with you. And you know what? We talked about it and he agreed with you. Said I shouldn't have called Bowie's mum like that without clearing it with you. So I'm sorry, too.'

'Should I call him and apologise?'

'No, it's all right. He was totally cool with it.'

'Maybe that's because he remembers being a teenager, too – even better than you, because it was more recent?'

'Ouch. Liv is back.' She laughs. 'Seriously, you know if there is anything worrying you, you can talk to me, right?'

'Right.' Sort of. If not related to boys, Molly, or anything important.

'So. Is there? Anything worrying you?'

I hesitate. Maybe this is something I do want – *need* – to talk about. 'Well, it's a friend. His mum died last year and he's having a tough time. She died in a car accident, and the thing is, they're not sure if she did it on purpose or not.'

'Oh my God, Liv. That must be so difficult to come to terms with,' she says. 'Wait a sec – you said *his* mum. Who is he? Is he the reason you've friend-zoned Bowie?'

I roll my eyes: typical, out of all that, that is the one detail she focuses on. 'Friend-zoned? Seriously?' I glare.

'OK, I get it. I'll try to stay out of your love life. So, truce?'

'OK. Truce.'

She holds out her hand to fist bump and I roll my eyes again, but go with it.

'So, tomorrow is Monday, first day of half term. Do you have any plans? I could take the day off. We could go out for lunch?'

Yay! says Molly.

'Um, sorry. I'm meeting that friend I mentioned – going to London for the day.'

You better not be meeting goth boy, Molly says, a hand on each hip.

At the same moment, Mum says, 'Does this *friend* have a name?'

I roll my eyes at both of them, yet again. 'Echo. His name, is Echo.'

Are you completely crazy? Molly shouts in my ear, then disappears in the mirror over the table.

35

Echo

As the day wears on, the euphoria I felt earlier recedes. Maybe Liv said yes just to make me go away. Maybe she won't turn up tomorrow, either because she changes her mind after thinking about it and what Kashina said, or because she never really meant to help me in the first place.

There's not much I can do about that right now, but there is something else I can do: find Kashina and ask her why she ambushed us like that. There's no way she just chanced to set out her blanket where she did. She heard the phone message; she knew Liv would be somewhere around there if she hadn't given up and gone home before I arrived. Kashina must have deliberately set out to find us and say those things to Liv. But *why*?

The more I think about it, the more I want to know.

I head back to the promenade first, where Kashina was earlier. I walk all around, from where she was to other places she sometimes shifts to find more punters: no sign of her.

I walk up the hill to her flat, but she's not home, either.

If she made a decent amount of cash today there's really only one other place she'd be: a pub.

There are a lot of pubs in Brighton.

I start with the ones closest to her flat and spiral out. Some I can dismiss without even looking inside – anything busy, trendy or full of tourists wouldn't suit her. She takes drinking seriously.

By the time I get to pub twenty-four, I'm thinking of giving up. It looks the right sort of place from the outside: small, shabby. I go through the door; the lights are dim after the sunshine. There's a half dozen solitary drinkers sprinkled about, and there, at the bar? Kashina.

'You took some finding,' I say.

She turns slowly, sighs. 'You again? What do you want?'

I see the guy behind the bar looking over at us – probably wants to know if I'm old enough to be in here.

'Can we go somewhere else?' I say.

She sees where I'm looking. Laughs. 'You're used to me, aren't you, Tommy?' she says. 'Better give us the rest of the bottle.'

He who must be Tommy clunks a nearly empty bottle of whisky in front of Kashina, then goes off to wipe some tables.

'Why did you come looking for Liv?' I say.

'I had to see what girl would be crazy enough to phone you,' she says, not even bothering to deny it.

'Thanks. And?'

Kashina shakes her head. 'You should leave her alone.'

'I should, should I? And why is that?'

She tilts her head to one side, pours another shot of whisky into her glass. Knocks it back. 'She's in a mess of her own, already. You can only make things worse for her. All you need to do, Echo, is remember. Not what you want to have happened, but what really did. Liv can't help you do that. No one can.' Sadness crosses her face, her eyes. She pours another shot and reaches for it, but I put my hand over the glass.

'If you know so much, why don't you just tell me?'

'I have tried. So many times. You don't – *can't* – listen.'

She reaches up, cups my face with her hands. 'Try, Echo. Try to remember.'

I shrug her off, head for the door. Tommy and the other drinkers were listening – noticing all that was said – but not looking at me directly, like they don't want to know.

I kick the door on the way out.

Kashina talks in so many bloody puzzles. She makes it sound like remembering or not remembering is up to me, but I've tried – so hard. Again and again. The only thing I've managed to remember since I came back here is which way our car was heading – towards Brighton – when the accident happened.

Tired of wandering around – tired of the sunshine and happy faces by the seaside – I head back to Kashina's. Lie down on the sofa, curtains drawn.

Kashina thinks I can remember. I know she often knows things I don't, that nobody knows. My memory leading up to and following the accident is fractured, frayed – as if something unravelled inside of me. But I'll try.

That last day, we'd gone back to that graveyard – the one I took Liv to the other night. There was something Mum was working on there? I frown, concentrate.

Fear: she needed fear to try to reach someone there. She said me being there would help, I don't know why. Something about me being her son, she said.

Fear of losing me. That was it, wasn't it?

A lost girl; she was trying to find what happened to a lost girl. That's it!

And Mum was upset – very. She was pretty calm most of the time, considering that dead people followed her around regularly, telling her things, like how they died – often not pretty. Stuff mostly hidden from me, but I picked up bits and pieces now and then, overheard from Mum and Kashina.

But, for some reason, this missing girl got to Mum.

And then . . . ?

Nothing. I don't remember leaving the graveyard, getting in the car, anything.

OK, Kashina, I tried. Again. And failed. Again.

I'll have to do this my way. With Liv.

36

Liv

It is the next morning before Molly deigns to appear and say hello. Then she insists I tell her every single thing that happened with Echo the day before. She listens, then makes me sit and listen to her whether I want to, or not. She has ways.

Let me get this straight. You've agreed to get terrified together to see if that helps convince his mum's ghost to say hello.

'That is pretty much it.'

You do spot the flaws in this plan, don't you?

I can think of many. What I say is, 'Which do you mean?'

Think about it. What am I?

'A ghost.'

Why am I here?

'Usually I ask you that,' I say, and Molly glares.

'All right,' I say. 'I'll try. At first, you stayed to stop me from crying.' She nods. 'And then . . . you just stayed because you wanted to. You stayed because I needed you.'

Exactly. She was his mum – of course he needed her. If she wanted to be with him, she would have stayed. And she's not with him.

'Maybe she didn't know how. Maybe she needs an "Oi! Over here!" to come investigate and say hello.'

Molly snorts. *But what if it works? That could be even worse.*

'What do you mean?'

Think about it. What if she really did kill herself on purpose and didn't care she was leaving him behind? How does he live with that? Better off not to know.

'Maybe. But he knows that is a risk, so isn't it his choice?'

You're missing the point. What about her choice? If she chose to die, to go, to leave him, she doesn't want an 'Oi! Over here!'. She might not want to remember. She could be really, really pissed off.

I shudder. A pissed-off ghost is something you can do without. I should know. Molly sticks out her tongue and vanishes in the mirror.

'Molly? Please. There's something I want to ask you.'

She looks back out through the mirror. *What?*

'There was this fortune teller at the beach.'

Did you have your fortune read?

'Sort of. She said something that freaked me out a little: that there was one from the other side who always stays close to me. And when she said that, she was looking past my shoulder, as if she could see someone there. Were you there?'

Molly shrugs her shoulders. *Maybe I was, maybe I wasn't. But if you are at a crossroads between what is safe and what is not, it sounds to me like goth boy is the unsafe option.*

I roll my eyes. 'You *were* there.'

OK, I was. But I scarpered when she looked in my direction with that weird eye.

Do you think she could see you?

I don't know. Her eyes didn't look the same direction at the same time – maybe it was a random wandering eye. Or not. But as far as that crossroads thing? You should definitely listen to her. With that she disappears back into the mirror.

Huh. I'm not believing any weird fortune told at the beach.

130

But apart from that, OK, Molly did have some valid points. But I said I'd meet Echo today: I can see what happens, and back out any time I want, can't I?

Downstairs there's a note from Mum – and, yay! – her credit card: 'Have fun, see you tonight x'.

I slam the front door and run to the train station. Echo wouldn't say what we were doing, just that we're going to London. We'll see what happens. How bad could it be?

37

Echo

I get to the station early. It's not busy mid-morning like this, and I settle myself where I can watch the entrances. Tell myself she'll come, don't worry – it's not even twenty to ten yet.

Fifteen minutes to go.

Then ten.

Five, and I'm pacing, looking all around. Past anxious and heading for upset and angry. She never meant to even try to help me, did she?

Someone taps me on the shoulder and I spin around. Smile widely, relieved, when I see it's Liv.

'You snuck up on me. Thought you weren't going to make it.'

'Sorry, got stuck in the ticket queue.'

We get on the London train just as the last whistle sounds. 'We've cut it close,' I say.

'I like to live dangerously.'

'Do you?'

'You don't look convinced. Ask yourself: where am I? Who am I with? Where are we going? All I know is that it's going to be scary.'

I tilt my head, thinking face. 'Hmmm, well I suppose you have a point.' But I get that this isn't Liv, who she is – not usually. She's taking a chance, maybe for the first time, and she's doing it for me. And – well. That's amazing.

I take her hand in mine. 'Thank you for coming,' I say.

'Are you going to tell me where we are going?'

I shake my head. 'I want it to be a surprise.'

38

Liv

How bad could it be?

Pretty bad.

'Are you serious?' I crane my head back and look up. To me they are teeny tiny airless prisons with no way out; to Echo they are torture chambers that go impossibly high into the sky. To everyone else they are the pods of the London Eye, a giant enclosed Ferris wheel with views.

'I thought it would be a good place to start as it should scare both of us.'

Yeah. It should. I sigh. He grins and takes my hand, pulls me towards the distressingly short queue for what they call flights.

'What if I say no?'

'No way! Not allowed. We're here, so come on.'

I look at one of the pods. Completely sealed. Shut in. No chance of a window you can open, or any way out. My stomach is flipping into butterflies, blood draining from my face.

I tug on Echo's hand.

He turns. 'Try not to flip out on the way in. They might stop us from getting on.'

'I don't want to go.'

'Come on! You said you would. You said you'd help, remember?' He pulls me closer and closer.

'Really they're quite big inside,' I whisper to myself. 'Not small. They must have ventilation, right?'

We are near the front. 'Can you get the tickets?' he says. 'I'm kind of broke.'

I get the tickets on Mum's card, hands shaking.

'You can do it,' Echo whispers into my ear. 'Come on.'

Another worryingly short queue. When we get to the front, Echo half drags me into a pod when we're waved forward. Me and another dozen or so people – happy, excited, smiling tourist faces with a variety of accents. Will we all be able to breathe in here? I manage to pull my hand free of Echo's and turn to run out just as the doors sweep shut with a neat mechanical whoosh. Fluttering whorls of panic are starting to rise inside. I am breathing, in, out, in out, too fast and people are giving me curious looks.

And we're off. I watch Echo and that is what makes me calm down. He stands right at the end of the pod, looking down, through the glass by his feet. Second after second we climb higher, just a little bit at a time; actually, we are moving so slowly it is almost hard to tell unless you watch something close by and see that it gets further away.

Echo's face is deathly white. He is always pale but now he looks like he is going to faint dead away. Thinking about Echo and how he is feeling makes me stop thinking about myself so much, and my breathing comes a little easier. This isn't like a lift. Lifts are tiny in comparison, and in them you can't see where you are. Here the whole of London is spread out around us.

I take Echo's hand and pull him towards the big bench-like seat at the centre of the pod. He doesn't resist; his eyes are almost glazed. We sit next to each other while all around there are clicks and flashes of phones and cameras as the other passengers go from side to side to see the view from all angles and capture it on digital.

'You're even worse than me,' I whisper.

He shakes his head. 'Stay with it. Don't evade the fear; feel it. Think of when you were locked in that washing machine. Be there, in that place.'

I sigh. Close my eyes and imagine being trapped, surrounded, suffocated. But that wasn't the washing machine, really, even though that had scared me. This is far, far worse: the womb where I killed my sister. Waves of pressure, again and again, crushing me from all sides.

I can't breathe, everything is fading, disappearing, even my panic.

Molly . . . ? Where are you . . .

Silly girl, come back. Come on.

Molly . . . ? Everything is grey, bleeding into black.

You have to breathe, you know. Or you'll be like me. Oh, bloody hell: if you won't do it, I'll do it for you.

She slips inside. No resistance or thought of it from me. I am too far gone to stop her even if I tried. I gasp and cough as air rushes into my lungs all at once. I/Molly opens my eyes.

No one seems to have noticed anything. The pod hasn't moved that far from where it was the last time I looked, Big Ben drawing all the happy snappers to one side. Echo is still sitting next to me, pale, eyes straight ahead, not looking down – so much for his talk of being as scared as possible.

Typical bloke! Molly laughs, inside but separate still, not taking over, just making me breathe, slowing my heart rate.

'Thanks.'

It's OK. Now you see how stupid this stuff is, don't you? Would passing out and being rushed off in an ambulance have been fun? Think how worried Mum would have been.

'I'm sorry.'

'What for?' Echo looks at me and I realise I've been speaking out loud. Again.

The pod is nearly back to ground level.

'Uh, sorry it didn't work.'

Molly slips out and laughs. *It did so work. You just summoned the wrong ghost.*

With that she disappears.

39

Echo

'We could try climbing the dome at St Paul's?' I say as we lean back on a bench looking over the Thames. We'd stumbled off the Eye, then wandered around the South Bank until both of us were more our normal selves.

Liv shrugs. 'We can go to St Paul's if you want. But it wouldn't scare me: a nice big open space. I've done it before.'

'Head home, then.'

'Why not stay for the afternoon? We could do anything. Don't you have grandparents to visit? Where do they live?'

'South Ken, and no way.'

'Don't get on?'

'You could say that,' I say, not wanting to answer the curiosity I see in Liv's eyes. They may have taken me in, but barely acknowledged my existence when I went to stay with them after Mum's funeral. Looked through me rather than at who I am, and I know it's because of history that has nothing to do with me – Mum left their son before I was even born. But they didn't want to know.

'I suppose London is dull for you because you used to live here,' she says.

'If you are tired of London, you are tired of life.'

'Are you?' she says, and I wonder which she means – London or life – but answer neither.

'What about you?' I say. 'What do you want to do? I bet you like shopping designers at Bond Street.'

'Sometimes.' She shifts foot to foot uncomfortably. 'But that is more my mum's thing. She drags me along and decides what I can and can't wear.'

I eye Liv up and down. As pretty as she is, she somehow doesn't seem comfortable in her own skin, her clothes. She squirms under my scrutiny, a flush working its way up her neck and face.

'Who are you?' I say.

'What do you mean?'

'Is any of this you? All of this' – I gesture at my black jeans, T-shirt – 'is me.'

'Not Kashina's eyeliner, then,' she says, and I laugh.

'If you could alter something about yourself, what would it be?'

'I'm not sure. I'd just like something to be different.' And she tells me how she does a birthday photo shoot every year with her mum; how her mum decides what they'll both wear and how to do their hair so it is just the same.

'Your mum sounds like a control freak.'

'She's not, not really. I think she just focuses a lot on me since I'm all that is left. It's been better since she got this new boyfriend.' It's always feast or famine with Mum: suffocating attention, or none at all.

'You need to rebel.'

'Do I?'

'Refuse to wear what she wants, or don't show up for the photos at all.' She doesn't say anything. 'But you won't manage it, will you? You'll do exactly what she wants you to do.'

She narrows her eyes, annoyed. 'You make me sound like a total wimp.'

'Aren't you?'

'I just went up the London Eye, didn't I?'

'True. But only because I made you.'

She stares back at me, denial on her face at first but she says nothing. She knows I'm right. But then her head tilts to one side and she smiles.

'What? You look like you may be having an actual thought of your own.'

'I have an idea.'

40

Liv

Three hours later I am staring at myself in a mirror.

A girl stares back at me, and I don't know her. Her hair is short, and not just shorter than it was: properly short. A pixie cut. And the colour: wow! Platinum, it said on the colour card – so pale blond it is almost white.

This girl is edgy, she has attitude. She isn't a mummy's girl, and she isn't Echo's girl either: this isn't what goth boy would have picked at all. Molly will probably instantly copy it but she hasn't seen it yet, so now, just for this moment, it is all mine.

This girl is her own person. I like her.

'Happy with it?' the stylist asks.

'Oh YES.' I beam.

'You've surprised me, Liv,' Echo says on the train home.

'Do you like it?' I ask, tilting my head yet again to look at my reflection in the window. I can't stop myself.

He raises an eyebrow. 'You're the same person inside, no matter the outside.'

'That sounds rather philosophical for a boy in black eyeliner.'

'Connection?'

'You obviously care how you look or you wouldn't bother with the whole *Night of the Living Dead* wardrobe.'

He shrugs. 'I dress how I feel. But I wasn't talking about your hair when I said you surprised me.'

'What, then?'

'Meeting me. Going on the London Eye. The whole day. I was sure you'd wimp out at the last minute. I didn't think you had it in you to really go for scared.'

'You'd be surprised,' I say, even though I had kind of surprised myself.

'I hope so. I've been thinking, though, about today. We were both scared, but it wasn't going to work on the London Eye, was it?'

'Why?' I ask, keeping my face neutral. The obvious answer being that using fear to try to contact his mother was totally daft and could never work.

'A few reasons. I'm sure it being daylight and there being other people around didn't help. But mainly this: even though what we did tapped into both of our fears, it was too controlled, too sterile. It wasn't actually dangerous, and some logical part of our brains always knew there was no real danger. How scared could we get? We need to up the stakes. How about we—'

'No. It's my turn to pick.'

Echo looks startled. Then a slow smile crosses his face.

41

Echo

The train gets in. As we cross the station, Liv is looking more and more nervous – as if she expects her mum to jump out in front of us and scream when she sees her hair.

She did more than I thought she'd manage today. But Liv-the-rebel is new. She's just trying it on, to see if it fits. And I'm not sure of her – not at all.

'I need to go home and face the music,' she says. 'It's my hair, right?'

'Right. Channel your inner goth and you'll be fine.'

'I'm pretty sure I haven't got one.'

'You do! Being a goth isn't a fashion choice, it's a state of mind. It's being yourself.'

'Sure.' She doesn't look convinced.

'Have you decided what we'll try next?'

'I think so. I just need to work out some details.'

'Tomorrow?'

'Tomorrow night. When it's dark.' She widens her eyes in mock terror, then grins.

'Excellent,' I say, but I'm nervous to let her out of my sight for that long. 'Want to meet up in the afternoon?'

She shakes her head. 'I'll be busy with Mum.' She rolls her eyes. 'Let's meet by the pier – about midnight?'

'OK. See you then.'

I watch her go until she's nearly out of sight, torn: can I trust her to turn up tomorrow?

If she decides not to come – or her mum stops her going out that late – how will I find her? She's got Kashina's number but I don't have hers. It's term break so I wouldn't even be able to find her at her school. I need to follow her, see where she lives, despite the risk of what might happen if she spots me.

I'm careful. I keep well back, use other people as cover in case she turns or stops suddenly. Her new hair makes her easier to follow from a distance.

Is this her street now? Rows of terrace houses, cars parked all along.

She walks past a dozen or so houses, then stops, goes through a gate – tries the door. Locked. Searches through her bag for a key, then goes inside.

42

Liv

Mum's and Rod's cars are both on the road. There are hooks on the wall in the entrance way and I'm hoping what I want is still there – yes. The hoody I sometimes wear for running when it's cold. I get my jacket off in a hurry and pull it on, hood up and covering my hair.

'Hi Mum,' I call on the way in. 'Hi Rod,' I add when I spot his head next to hers on the sofa.

I needn't have worried. She is so busy cuddling with Rod in front of some lame DVD that she doesn't even look up.

I start up the stairs.

'Bowie called,' Mum says. 'Do you need some dinner?'

'Had it,' I lie. 'I'm going to my room.' I start up the stairs.

'Liv?'

I pause. 'Yeah?' Mum has turned and is looking towards me now, but if she clocks the hoody she doesn't launch into a did-you-really-wear-that-in-London-all-day fashion lecture.

'Don't forget, photos tomorrow, I'll take our clothes and stuff and meet you there at two.'

'Yeah. OK.' A few stairs, a few more, down the hall, door open, then shut behind. Safe.

It's not like I am scared to let her see me, exactly. Well, maybe I am a little. Though it'd probably be better to do it when Rod is in the house: she is unlikely to get too insane with him as witness. But it's more that I'd rather wait until it's too late for her to do anything about it for tomorrow's photos. The closer the train got to Brighton, the more visions – of being tied to a hairdresser's chair, dyed my natural colour and having extensions added until you couldn't tell the difference – had started to flit through my brain.

I pull the hoody off and stare in the mirror. Rebel girl is still here, hanging on. Sort of. She looks more nervous than in control.

Molly peeks at me from the mirror.

Wow.

'Do you like it?'

She circles me. *I think so*, she says, but she doesn't sound convinced.

She stops very close in front of me, eye to eye. *Was this Echo's idea?* She frowns.

'No! It was all mine.'

We have to talk, she says, arms crossed, her hair still the same, long and dark as before. Interesting: no copycat.

'I've got to call Bowie,' I say and reach for my phone. Take it off silent and see the missed calls, texts, all from Bowie.

That can wait.

Surprised, my hand drops. 'Sure.'

You have to listen to me.

'I'm listening.'

No, I mean it! LISTEN.

'All right.'

That boy is trouble.

'Bowie? But I thought . . .'

She rolls her eyes. *You know very well that I mean Echo. Look at*

146

what happened to you today. You weren't breathing. Why?

I shrug, uncomfortable. Not answering and carefully not thinking about where I'd gone in my mind.

Molly disappears. That was easy. Too easy?

I pick up my phone and start to text Bowie when a cold shock hits my spine and slams into the back of my skull.

'Molly, no!' I try to push her out but she is too far in to make it easy. I drop my phone. Fall to my knees on the floor, nausea slamming through my body.

My day starts replaying through my mind for Molly's viewing pleasure.

'Get out, please!' I whimper.

No. This is what happens if you try to keep secrets from me.

She gets to the part where Echo said to imagine myself in my place of fear, but I hadn't gone where he thought.

Darkness, warmth. Pressure building, up and up until I want to scream, and I kick again and again at what encloses and strangles, but there is no escape. Waves of pressure pass through my body, each squeezing harder than the last; panic rises with it.

Molly suddenly leaves me and I gasp and cough on the floor.

You stopped breathing again. Don't do that.

I stare at her in shock. She drapes herself around me, making soothing noises as if I just had a nightmare – even though she's the one who caused it, right here and now while I was awake.

'What the hell was that?' I finally say.

I think when I was in your mind the other day, you somehow plucked that memory from me. It isn't your memory, it's mine.

'But why did I stop breathing? Tell me.' I ask the question but I'm afraid I already know the answer.

147

That is when I died. That is my memory, not yours!

Molly is angry. Angry ghosts are not a good thing to have around.

But I'm angry too. 'Stay out of my head if you want to keep your thoughts yours and my thoughts mine!'

What would have happened if I hadn't come this afternoon? You weren't BREATHING for chrissakes! Don't count on me helping you like that again, not if you want to be with that freak. When you're with Echo, you're on your own.

Molly disappears back into the mirror and I pull myself up, sit on my bed. Wrap my arms around my knees and try to stop shaking.

Molly's death wasn't as she's said before when I've asked – like falling asleep and not waking up. It was struggle, pain, fear. Something *I* caused by being bigger and stronger than her. And somehow it is all tied up with my own fear – being enclosed, unable to breathe.

It feels like the walls of my bedroom are closing in, the ceiling coming down to pin me on my bed. I get up and open the window wide, stand there half out of it, breathing in again and again and gradually start to calm.

My phone beeps and I retrieve it from the floor. A text from Bowie: just a question mark?

Ah, I'd accidentally sent a half-finished text when Molly got me.

I finish it now. Hi B, sorry – was in London today. I glance at the mirror. My face is so pale it almost matches my hair. I've got a surprise, want to meet up tomorrow? Before 2 as doing something with Mum then.

A pause, then a reply drops in. We must be overdue for fish and chips on the beach.

Yaaay!!

We arrange a time, place. I glance again at the mirror across the room but there is no ripple on its surface, just white-faced me staring back.

43

Echo

I'm back, watching Liv's house, early the next morning. I couldn't sleep, couldn't stop myself from coming, even though I know I shouldn't be doing this. Not just because it is – well – seriously creepy. But also because if Liv spots me watching her house, she might refuse to help me or even speak to me, and maybe that is fair enough.

But I need to be close to her. I'm gripped by, what – growing anxiety? Panic? Something is going to happen; it's going to be soon. I can't change it or myself. I have no choice. But I need her to be close to me when it does.

I can't even say why I'm so sure that Liv is bound up in all of this; I just know that she is. Is it just because of how being near her makes me feel – like there could be light in the darkness and pain? I don't know.

Is it not sleeping that is making me think all these things? I don't know how long I can go without sleep. It's bound to be impacting on my feelings, my judgement, but no matter how I try, I can't.

It's still early when the front door opens. Liv's mum steps out and with her is the man I saw her with when they went out for Liv's birthday dinner. They kiss each other. Get into separate cars.

Going to work? But didn't Liv say she was doing something with her mum today?

Liv will be alone now. Is she still asleep? I imagine her lying there, gently breathing, eyes closed.

What is her room like? I bet it's mum-decorated in little-girl pink.

Maybe Liv will decide to paint it a different colour to go with her rebel hair – I could help her?

There won't be enough time for that.

Maybe her window is open. I could look in – just look.

My feet are walking down the road towards her house without me making any conscious decision to do so. I'm almost there before I regain control, turn around.

Watch. Wait. That is all I can do.

44

Liv

There are dark smudges under my eyes, my face pale and anxious after nightmares kept at me all night. Looking at this waif in the mirror, it is hard not to wonder if the change in look was a big mistake: not so much rebel girl with attitude, more like heroin chic. And those dreams: was it leftover dredges of the day, or did Molly cause them?

I wouldn't do that. Not on purpose.

'Sure. I believe you,' I say as I dot concealer under my eyes, blend it in.

She clocks the make-up. *Where are you going?*

'If I tell you, will you promise to behave if you come?'

Are we meeting Bowie?

'*I* am meeting Bowie.'

She claps her hands. *What are we going to wear?*

'We?' I roll my eyes, grab some jeans, a favourite red jumper, put them on. Look in the mirror, shake my head, start again. A half-dozen changes later I settle on black – 'Not goth,' I think in case Molly is listening in to my thoughts. Black just looks the best with my hair.

I'm heading for the door, barely on track to be on time.

So tell me: why did you spend so long deciding what to wear?

I don't answer.

Obvious, isn't it? It's for Bowie.

'No! It's my hair, all right? I'm worried how it looks. That's all. Now be quiet or go away.'

45

Echo

It's late morning when Liv comes out of her front door. She's wearing jeans, a fitted long-sleeved black T-shirt. I don't think I've seen her in black before – it suits her, especially with that hair. She's frowning, seems to be saying something to herself as she starts walking down the road.

I follow, trying to stay far enough away that if she glances over her shoulder she won't see me, even as I'm fighting wanting to get closer to her.

Now she's smiling, waving, and . . . it's him. The blond boy who went on her birthday dinner. But she said she was busy with her mum?

Maybe they just ran into each other, they'll say hello and then she'll go meet her mum somewhere.

They stop, sit at a bench. He's looking at her hair – she looks anxious about what he thinks.

Then they're up again, walking together. I'm following still, not being as careful as I should be – she'll see me if she turns. I almost want her to.

They stop at a takeaway. They're getting fish and chips? And walking to the beach.

They match. Don't they? Her blond head so close to his, but it's not about hair colour. Seeing them together, the way she smiles easily when she looks at him, and he when he looks at her.

Pain twists hard in my gut. She's not with her mum like she told me she would be.

She lied.

46

Liv

'Well, aren't you going to say what you think?'

'About what?' Bowie says.

I punch him in the arm.

'Ow.'

'It's bad, isn't it,' I say and slump on the beach next to him.

'No way! If you'd told me about it, I wouldn't have been sure. But honest, you look amazing.' He gets me up to do a twirl, then wolf whistles.

I hit him in the arm. Again. 'Are you sure it's not too short?'

'It's not too short.'

'It's shorter than yours, now.'

'It is seriously cute,' he says and ruffles my hair, and his smile is warm and does something strange to my toes. Like a trail of heat that starts in my stomach has spread out until my toes almost curl.

'What does your mum think of it?'

'Ah. Well, you see, she hasn't actually . . . that is to say . . .'

'She hasn't seen it yet?' Bowie laughs. 'Isn't it your photos this afternoon?'

'Yep. I'm going there from here.'

'Good thing we got extra ketchup.'

We sit down again. After skipping dinner last night and breakfast this morning, I'm famished. Fish and chips on the beach with too much ketchup is just what I need to get through an afternoon with Mum and Charley, not to mention whatever antics Molly might dream up.

Lunch is soon gone. I lie back on the beach next to Bowie. The sun is out, just; clouds are gathering.

And right on cue, here's Molly.

Bowie seems to like your hair. Of course, Bowie likes us, so he would, wouldn't he?

I ignore her. She curls her body along Bowie's. *He likes me better than you, though*, she says. Trying to get a reaction I guess, but it won't work.

I can prove it. Resistance is futile, she says in her best dalek impression.

And it is, of course. If I try to resist her in public it'll look like I am having a seizure.

Molly slips inside me: side by side together just now, neither of us in charge. I close my eyes to make internal conversation easier.

'Don't do anything,' I warn her.

Or what?

'Please.'

All I want is for you to stop ignoring me.

'OK Molly, you're in, you're not ignored. Don't do anything. Please.'

'Liv, are you all right?' Bowie.

I open my eyes. 'Sorry. Zoned out a bit; couldn't sleep last night.'

'Worried about your mum and hair-gate?'

'Something like that.'

I am up on my elbow next to Bowie but it isn't me looking at Bowie *that* way: eyes half open, lips parted. His hand steals upwards, his finger traces lightly down the side of my face and I shiver. There is a question in his eyes.

'Please Molly, no,' I whisper inside, and she slips away.

I sit up. 'I better get going, or I'll have to add being late to my list of sins.'

As I walk across town to Charley's, I realise: Molly is right. Bowie likes her better than me. It is only when she is there that he shows that kind of interest. It was really just me that prompted him to give the 'let's be friends' line the other night. And I can't even tell if I like him as more than a friend, or if it is Molly muddling me up.

But one thing is for sure: it can't happen. I'm not letting Molly mess us around, not like that.

47

Echo

I thought he was going to kiss Liv. I was frozen, watching, unable to make myself look away – caught in an agony of jealousy, wanting to be the one who kissed her. Then she said something, got up, left.

So maybe she's not sure about him; maybe he doesn't matter to her, not like that.

Even if he does – it shouldn't matter to me.

It *doesn't*.

She lied. She can't be trusted. But it doesn't matter who she meets for lunch, not so long as she still shows up tonight.

At least that's what I tell myself. But I know that I'm lying too.

48

Liv

No hat, no hoody, nothing. I square my shoulders and open the door.

Charley's assistant looks up from her desk. 'Is that Liv? Oh, my. I love your hair!'

As if her words release a double jack-in-the-box, Mum and Charley appear around the corner at the same instant.

The colour drains from Mum's face. 'Liv? Is that you?'

'Of course it is.'

She looks at me from all angles. Silence. Not good.

'How could you!' she says. 'How could you do this?' Molly is sat on the desk, laughing and swinging her feet. Charley and his assistant have melted off to the side.

'Hang on a minute here: I haven't murdered anybody. It's MY hair! I can do what I like with it. I could shave it off if I want to.'

'You've done this to ruin our photos. You never want to do this one thing for me, the one thing I ask; you wouldn't even wear the white dress.' She pauses to draw breath.

'I'm here, aren't I?'

'You told me if I let you have the black dress you'd go along with everything else. The photos will be ruined!'

Charley reappears and gives Mum wine. 'He has even opened some of the good stuff,' his assistant whispers to me, 'that he usually saves for wedding planners.' She draws me away to the back room with her. 'Give him a minute,' she says and winks. 'He's a magician.'

By the time we go back, Mum is all smiles. 'Well, hurry up and get changed.'

Molly tells me that Charley said that the photos would be even better now; that he had wanted to suggest we get opposite hair colours and styles to go with our opposite black and white dresses but wasn't sure what we'd think; that this was beyond perfection and could he possibly use a photo of us for his portfolio?

He pokes and prods us into poses again and again, and for once I don't twitch or complain. Molly prances around behind the camera making silly faces to get me to smile when I am supposed to; jumps out all scary when I am supposed to be in serious mode.

'You're not off the hook for this,' Mum says as we leave.

'I thought Charley said the photos would be divine, the best ever?'

'That isn't the point. You should have consulted with me, first. Oh, dear,' she says, and runs her hand over my hair. 'It's so very short, isn't it?'

My face falls. 'You don't like it?'

'That isn't what I meant. It's just . . . it's so . . . sophisticated. You look older, more grown up. And you've been going off and doing stuff without me.'

I give her a hug; Molly joins in for a three-way.

Don't know how you managed to get away with this one.

49

Echo

There are so many hours to get through before meeting Liv tonight. I could go back to Kashina's but I can't sit still and wait. Instead, I pace around Brighton as the afternoon wears on. Watch the sun get lower in the sky, darkness falling, filling in the edges away from the light.

It's busy still – people going out to dinner, to pubs, or going home. Aimless, I follow one, then another.

Finally it's getting close to time. I head back to Liv's house, watch it from the shadows.

Every second that ticks is an agony: both slow, as I wait for her, and rushing faster and faster to some end I can almost taste and feel, but when I grasp for it to see what it is, there is nothing.

I didn't see her come in so I don't even know for sure if she is there. Her mum's car is out front and there are lights on downstairs. The door opens – it's her mum, putting some recycling in their bin.

Later the lights go out downstairs, then another goes on upstairs – is that her mum's room? Maybe Liv's room is darkened already; she's gone to bed for the night, either for real and she isn't coming, or for pretend – for her mum – and she'll slip out to meet me.

After a while the upstairs lights go out.

It must be near midnight by now.

Please, Liv: don't let me down.

50

Liv

What are you doing?

'Who, me?'

I pull a black hoody over T-shirt and black jeans, hold my boots in one hand and creep out of my room and down the stairs, taking care to miss the third step from the top: it creaks.

You're meeting him, *aren't you?*

'If you mean Echo, then yes, I'm meeting him,' I say to her in my thoughts. I open the front door, step out.

In the middle of the night? Alone?

I pull the door shut behind us carefully, quietly, and walk down our street. The clouds that were pulling in earlier must have settled and stayed: the moon and stars are hiding. Without streetlights I wouldn't be able to see a thing. I pat my pocket to check that my torch is there.

Molly walks next to me up the road.

'If I remember correctly, you said if I was with Echo, I was on my own.'

You are! I'm just keeping you company in case he doesn't show up.

I walk fast; it's chilly. The pier is a shadowy bulk on dark water and my eyes search all around for Echo.

'Liv!' a voice calls out. I turn and there he is, walking towards me. I start to give Molly an 'I told you so' look, but she is already gone.

'You came,' he says when he reaches me, and his face is transformed by one of his rare smiles.

'Of course!'

He tugs at the hem of my hoody. 'Hey, you're starting to look like me.'

'Just dressing to not stand out in the dark.'

'So, where are we going?'

'To start with, we're getting the night bus.' I glance at my watch. 'Should just catch the next one. Come on.'

There are a few other people waiting at the stop. The bus comes soon after and we get on.

'So, it's midnight and we're on a night bus dressed in dark clothing,' Echo says. 'Where are we going?'

'Give up, you won't work it out.'

We get off at the last stop, a dark road near the sea.

'Well? What next?'

'Come on. It's a bit of a walk.'

I take the torch out of my pocket, turn it on, and we walk along a stretch of the coastal footpath, houses above.

'OK, I'm not liking the path, but it's not close enough to the cliff edge to totally freak me out, so there must be something else involved. What is it?'

'Wait and see.'

After a while we leave the coastal path for another footpath that goes up between houses, then leave that one to go right on a narrow lane. There are a few big houses between us and the sea murmuring in the darkness below.

When we are nearly at the end of the lane, I turn off my torch and stop by the last house. Calling it a 'house' is an exaggeration:

it's a construction site. I'm relieved to see it looks as if it hasn't progressed since the last time I was here.

It belongs to one of Mum's ex-boyfriends. They'd got to a certain point in construction when there had been a small landslip to the beach, far below, under part of the foundations. Architects, engineers, safety inspectors and insurance adjustors were arguing about whose fault it was and what to do about it. Everything was put on hold and had been for months. By the looks of things nothing has changed.

'Now what?' Echo asks.

'Now we find a way in.'

We follow along the fence, dim light through trees from a house above just enough to pick our way. Hopefully they are far enough away that if anyone gets up in the night and passes a window, we shouldn't be seen.

We scramble along rocks and through bushes down one side of the house. The metal fence is in square sections, the ground rocky and uneven so there are gaps underneath. The further down we go the steeper, so the bigger the gaps.

'Let's try here,' I say finally. He pulls up on the fence with one hand and I lie on the ground on my back, shimmy along under the gap. Stand up on the other side. 'Easy,' I say.

'Maybe for you,' he answers and tries to follow, but no matter how hard I pull up on the fence, it's no good. He is simply too big to squeeze through.

'I could try to climb over?' he says.

I put the torch on and shine the light at the top of the fence: triple rows of barbed wire. 'That could hurt. I'll see if there is a better spot to get under.'

I follow the fence along to the back, taking care on uneven ground, circling or going over rocks, piles of wood and bricks. The torch light is flickering a little but I shake it and the beam is steady again. Even with the torch I go slower and slower, stepping over and around junk and construction materials. Then the fence ends against the side of the house. No good.

I sigh. If Molly were here she could do a quick survey and tell me if there is another way in.

I head back, but when I get to where I left Echo, he isn't there. I'm sure this is the right place?

'Echo?' I call softly. No answer. Where is he?

My torch flickers again, then goes out. I shake it, but nothing.

Now I am starting to freak out. Where did he go? Has he just left me here? The stars and moon are hidden by clouds; the light from the house above is faint. Too faint really to risk walking around this mess.

'Echo?' I call again, louder. There are sounds along the ground – something scratching, scurrying. Giant rats are in my mind now and I want to move, get away.

I walk the other way by the fence, slow, one hand along it to keep my place in the dark. Maybe I wasn't at the right spot. But the gap at the bottom of the fence, tested with my foot, is getting smaller, not bigger.

Then the lights from the house above go out and it is completely dark – no amount of staring is giving any vision at all. I'm trapped inside a fence, in the dark in the middle of the night, with potentially murderous rats. Nobody knows where I am.

No one will hear if you scream, Molly whispers, right in my ear.

I jump. 'Oh my God, you scared me!'

'Sorry,' Echo says, suddenly next to me, and I'm startled again. Molly vanishes.

I'm breathing in, out, in, out, heart beating fast. Shaking. Get it together, I tell myself,

'What happened to your torch?' he says.

'Stopped working. Maybe the batteries are flat?' I take it out of my pocket and give it another shake; this time it flickers. It sounds like the batteries are a little loose; I wind the casing up tighter and it comes on and stays steady. 'How did you get in?'

'There's a bigger gap on the other side.'

'How did you even find it without a torch?'

'Eyes like a cat, me. What do we do next?' he says, and I can see he is right into this, not knowing why we are here or what we are going to do.

Me – I'd be happy if I could blink just now and be home, safe. 'I don't know, maybe this isn't a good idea.'

'No backing out! What is the plan?'

I hesitate. 'To climb the frame of the house.' I shine the torch that way and he turns to look. It isn't closed in yet. There are foundations and basic framed walls and beams for the roof, and that is mostly it. Two stories high.

'That is scary, but not that scary.'

'If there's no point, let's call it a night.'

'No way, you got me here now. Let's check it out.'

I shine the torch on the ground so we can pick our way. We step through what would be a door if there was a door, and walk across the foundations, through rooms without walls to the other side.

'Careful now,' I say. 'One trip could be your last.'

168

When we reach the back, even I hang on to a bit of frame before leaning out and shining the torch down.

The torch light doesn't stretch far enough to see beyond the first bit of drop. Rather than see, we can hear and feel, and fill in the blanks. Down below, far below, is the sea, and between here and there, a steep cliff. The part I don't tell him, though, is that hidden by the darkness is a wide grassy ledge before the cliff. Falling from here might hurt but wouldn't be fatal.

'This is where double-height windows are meant to be for panoramic views,' I say.

Echo looks down, holding tight as he does so.

'That is, until there was a landslip under the house, right where we're standing. They decided it was too risky to continue construction until they surveyed and underpinned and did whatever. But that was months ago, and here it still stands as it was. Must be too dangerous. The whole thing might slide down the cliff into the sea at any minute.'

Echo steps back. 'What now?'

'I thought we could climb up the frame.' I point the torch up and rest one hand on a crosspiece of wood. It has got a little slimy from exposure to the elements. 'It's a bit slippery.'

'Are you coming, too?'

'Somebody has to hold the torch. But I'm not scared of heights. I can go first if you like.' I hand him the torch and he doesn't argue.

I'm good at climbing, I remind myself, having been abseiling with the Mountain Man, as I used to call him: Mum's crush last summer, until she worked out the outdoor lifestyle wasn't really her thing. And I have good balance from years of gymnastics when I was younger. Despite all that, I still feel uneasy, standing here in the dark and looking up at what I'm about to do.

'Give me a boost up,' I say to Echo, and he gives me a hand up to the first crosspiece of wood. It is hard to feel under my boots. 'Might be easier with shoes off.'

'Quit stalling.'

I reach up and pull myself to the top of the window. This isn't like abseiling. There is no rope tethering me to safety. On cue, as if to remind me how far down it is, the wind picks up off the sea. At least my hair isn't all over my eyes now that it is so short. I pull myself up to the ceiling frame of floor one.

'Pass me the torch, then you climb up,' I say, and reach down. He slips it into my hand. 'Are you scared?'

He doesn't answer.

Much taller than me, he swings himself up to where I'd needed a lift. He sits there a moment, arms wrapped around the wood, then eases himself to his feet, climbs up next to me.

'Next level,' I say, and with another boost from Echo, I reach the next crosspiece and climb up to the top of the second floor. He hands me the torch, but then, instead of climbing up, he moves along to stand on the frame in the space where the upper part of the panoramic windows were meant to go.

'What next?' he says.

'Reach up with one hand, then the other, and pull yourself up next to me.'

A moment passes.

'Echo?'

'I can't seem to let go.'

'Yes, you can. Or you'll be there for ever. Even to go down

you have to let go. It'll be fine, just do one hand at a time so one is always holding on.'

He pulls himself even closer to the frame. Rigid. I can feel rather than see that he's trembling. I shouldn't have brought him here. This is stupid. But it's what he wanted, isn't it?

'Echo, how about you go back down now?'

He doesn't answer, his eyes are closed. And I see he is in the fear, reaching for it.

Suddenly he lets go with one hand, but instead of reaching up with it to join me or down to climb down, he leaves it hanging by his side. The wind plucks at his hair, waving it around his face, so pale, almost a ghost himself in this light.

'Echo, what are you doing?'

He lets go with the other hand.

'Echo, don't! Give me your hand,' I say. 'Reach up.'

He is motionless. Feet standing on a thin crosspiece of wood, balanced, high above his worst nightmare. Eyes closed, pale face and hands picked up by the weak torchlight but the rest of him lost in darkness. Fear slams into my gut as if I am channelling him.

I shake my head. I'm not afraid of heights, I remind myself, and push the fear away. 'Echo, you need to hold on. Reach to the side or up with one of your hands.'

Is he frozen with fear? Can he even hear me? No recognition or response crossed his face when I spoke. Maybe if I reach out, hold him, it might bring him out of this trance or whatever it is.

I balance the torch on an adjacent beam, then lie down on the one I'm on, hooking my feet around it for stability, then inch forward, bit by bit until he's just beneath.

'Echo? I'm going to touch your shoulders,' I say, not wanting to startle him.

I slip my hands against the front of his shoulders and hold him towards the building. But if he loses his balance and I hang on, we'll both crash down. I can't support his full weight.

I can tell now that he isn't as still as I thought, not at all. He is swaying, just slightly at first, then a bit more, and a bit more. Swaying towards the building, then away from it. I try to hold him closer to the frame with my hands.

'Echo!' I scream his name this time and his head moves, tilts back so he's looking above at me. Eyes open, pupils dilated.

He looks uncertain, like he doesn't know for sure who I am, where we are. Anything.

'Reach to the sides with your hands and hold on.'

He looks down and that's when it happens. He wobbles. Loses his balance.

'Echo!' I scream, grabbing at his shoulders, but they are gone.

The torch falls off the beam; it seems to hang in the air as if time is slowing down, then lands below and points to the night and Echo.

His body, stiff, awkward, like a puppet, is falling. His feet slip off the crosspiece into the house, his legs crash against it and the rest of him flails into air and darkness, and surely he must be dragged out and over the side. I'd convinced myself the grassy ledge would save him if he fell, but would it? Or would momentum take him over it to the rocks and the sea far below? There is a moment – it must be a fraction of a second but feels far longer – when he is almost in balance and I don't know which way he will go.

'Echo!' I scream his name again.

Does that wake up some instinct inside him? His body jerks, convulses, and his upper body swings up, tipping the balance so he falls back inside the house. The torchlight goes out.

51

Echo

I groan with pain: the pain of failure. It is so all-encompassing that I can't feel or think of anything else. No matter how I reached for the fear and called out to Mum to come to me, it didn't work. And I don't know if I can get any more scared than I was.

There are scrambling noises above me, air movement and someone dropping down near me.

'Echo?' It's Liv. Of course it is. 'Are you hurt?' she says and now she is running her hands over my head, arms, legs, until I grab them in mine.

'Stop it. I am intact . . . more or less. Just give me a moment.' I move, sit up. Something hard underneath me? I reach for it – it's the torch. I flick the switch and the light comes back on. 'Could have done without landing on this, though.'

Tears are spilling out of Liv's eyes.

'What is that for?' I say.

'You, you big idiot! I thought you were going to be hurt, or worse.'

'Still here,' I say and she slumps down next to me. We sit there, silent, and I can feel her trembling and take her hand.

'So, did it work? Any sign of your mum?' she says.

Still twisting with failure, I can't answer.

She persists. 'You were scared like you said you had to be. Did anything happen?'

I sit up straighter and sigh.

'No. I went with the fear as much as I could. But I knew I wasn't scared enough, that I had to let go, not hold on. Perhaps I imagined it, but it felt like something was pulling at me, making me sway.'

She shudders. 'Maybe that was a ghost: a ghost who likes company and wanted you to fall to your death. See how stupid this is now? Give it up.'

I hold the torch up to my face. Not smiling. 'No way. It's my turn now.'

'Your turn?'

'To come up with a dare for you.'

We squeeze ourselves back out under the fence. Walk back along the lane and footpaths to the road and bus stop and wait for the night bus. Neither of us says much, there or on the bus back to Brighton.

Liv's reaction – her tears – when she thought I was going to fall down the cliff to the sea? Maybe I got her wrong. Maybe, she really does care for me – even enough to up the stakes on her fear. Though I can tell that right now, what she most wants to do is run home and hide.

But if she does care for me, then why did she lie to me to meet with blond boy? I almost ask her; I want to and have to bite it back. She'd know I was following her, watching her, if I do.

Anyhow, what would asking her achieve? If she's lied to me once she could easily do it again.

The only thing that matters is what we do next.

The bus pulls in by the promenade in Brighton. I follow Liv

out the side door to the pavement and touch her shoulder. She turns back towards me.

'Liv? Meet me by the pier tomorrow. 11 a.m. Dress warm and bring your torch. I think I've got an idea.'

52

Liv

I walk up the road alone, having said no again when Echo wanted to walk me home. Our house is still reassuringly dark. Keys out, I carefully, quietly, unlock the door. Open it, step through and close it slowly; it only makes a faint click when I lock it.

Then the lights come on. I spin around.

'What time do you call this?'

Mum. Sitting on the sofa. And next to her? Molly. Positively smirking. If I didn't know Mum couldn't see or hear her, I'd swear she dobbed me in.

'Let me help you,' she says, and peers at her watch. 'It's nearly 3 a.m.'

'Sorry,' I say, and start taking off my boots before she notices how muddy they are. I tuck them away at the back of the mat.

'Where have you been?'

'Out.'

She rolls her eyes. 'Obviously, but I need a little more than that.'

Molly claps her hands. *Go on, tell her what you've been doing, and who with.*

'Why? Can't I go out with my friends without checking in, first? You do it all the time. Half the time I don't know if you'll come home at all, or if you do, who with.'

177

'This isn't about me!' she says. 'You're only sixteen.'

'So?'

She picks up her phone. 'Don't you dare move.' She's making a call? 'Hi. She's home. Yeah, seems fine. Thank you.' Ends call and puts her phone down.

'Rod has been out looking for you.'

'What? Why?'

'Just *listen*, Liv. A few hours ago, a girl was walking home on her own from a party when someone tried to drag her into the park at the bottom of our road. She only just managed to get away. Rod was working late because of this. He came here after and when he told me about that, I went to check on you, and you weren't there. I've been so scared you went out for a late run or something, and . . . and . . .' She doesn't finish the sentence but all the worry and fear is there, and guilt twists inside of me.

'I'm sorry I worried you. I didn't know about that.'

'I know. But you shouldn't have been out that late regardless. Go to bed and we'll talk more in the morning.'

I head up the stairs.

'You might want to tell Bowie you're all right,' she adds when I am halfway up. I stop and turn.

'What did you say?'

'Bowie. I called him to see if he knew where you were.'

When I get into my room, I'm shaking. Whether from the encounter with Mum, everything that happened with Echo, or both together, all mixed in with that it is 3 a.m. and I haven't slept much the last few days. And now she's added Bowie into the mix too.

I get out my phone. I'd put it on silent, not wanting it to ring loudly when we were busy trespassing. And there they are: missed calls and texts from Mum, starting at about one-thirty. Half an hour later, also from Bowie.

I bite my lip and fall back on the bed.

Molly sits cross-legged on my desk. *Whatever are you going to tell him? And Mum?*

'I don't know. Anyhow, it's too late to call him now.'

Chicken. Text, then. He might be worried.

'Fine.' I play around with words, back and forth, less and more, and finally have this: Hi B, sorry mum bugged you. Everything is fine, I was just out with a friend. Lx

Molly peers over my shoulder.

'All right?' I ask.

It'll do.

I press send.

'Wish I could just send Mum a text.'

Go on – give it a try.

'Do you think so?' Mum is confusing. She morphs back and forth between cool friend and suffocating mother so fast that it is hard to keep track. Maybe it would help.

More playing with words. Finally I settle on this: I'm really sorry you were worried, and for what I said. Love you xx. Molly nods and I hit send.

Too wired to sleep, I head for the quickest of showers.

Back in my room, Molly is sitting on my desk. *Your phone has been vibrating*, she says. She finds no end of frustration that she can't look at my messages when I leave it screen down – precisely why I do so.

There are two.

179

Bowie: obvs you owe me cake for keeping me awake – tomorrow afternoon – 3 ok? Bx

Mum: Love you too, sorry I was mad xx

I turn out the lights, try to sleep, but every time I close my eyes, I see Echo falling, feel the certainty, the fear, that he will crash on the rocks below and die. I turn again, punch my pillow.

Liv?

'What.'

You do realise what all this means, don't you?

'What?'

You've got TWO dates tomorrow.

'Trust you, Molly, to think of that.' I can't help myself. I start to giggle, more and more. Hysteria?

Whatever, it must do me some good. Not long after, I finally fall into a dark, dreamless sleep.

53

Echo

I don't go back to Kashina's. Instead, I walk along the seafront as the night wears on. There's a sense of waiting, of pressure, of a storm coming, both inside and out.

Finally the sun fights its way out of darkness and blood-red streaks slash the sky. Wind whips up the sea to frothy violence against the beach.

How long can I go without sleep? I don't know, but there is no point in even trying. Every part of me is on alert – almost vibrating with anticipation. Something is about to happen, good or bad, and there is nothing I can do to stop it.

54

Liv

Despite saying we'd talk in the morning, Mum didn't wake me before she left for work. Perhaps it was the text I sent? When I crawl out of bed not far off ten, I find her note: 'Be home this evening by 8 p.m. Or else.'

Or else what? Molly says, looking over my shoulder.

'Who knows?'

Time for tea and toast. The radio is on and I'm only half listening when something in the news makes me sit up and listen. It's about that girl Mum told me about – it was only eleven in the evening when it happened, too. People are worried whoever it was will try again. There's mention of that other girl, a few years ago, who disappeared at night in Brighton and they never found out what happened to her. There is speculation that it's a serial thing – though apart from the one a few years ago, they have to go back another five years for a similar sounding missing person.

I feel bad that Mum was worried. But what am I supposed to do: stay home and hide? Be escorted everywhere I want to go? When that girl disappeared a few years ago, it was like that for a while – everyone too scared to let their daughters out of their sight. I mean, I understand wanting to keep us safe. But that's not living, and it makes me angry.

Just try to not freak Mum totally out again, OK?

'I'll try.'

I dress in layers with a waterproof – it's not raining but it's windy and the sky says it might. I find keys, phone.

Are you sure about this? Don't go. Molly leans against the front door.

'Why not? Get out of the way.' It's not like I can't unlock the door with Molly leaning against it; it bothers me more than her to put a key through her stomach and turn it in the lock.

She sighs and slips through the door to the outside. *He'll want to top last night. Are you up to that?*

'I don't know. But just because he dares me to do something, doesn't mean I have to do it.'

Yeah, right.

55

Echo

I think about going to watch Liv's house again, to make sure she comes out when she should. But somehow, this time, I'm sure she will show. That she's part of this now, caught in the same irresistible rush to what is coming that I am.

The minutes are counting down. I concentrate on Liv, on bringing her towards me. As if I've drawn her in my imagination, there she is.

'Hi,' she says.

'Hi.'

'Look. Last night was stupid. I'm sorry I took you there.'

'It wasn't—'

'I mean it. Nothing like that again, OK? Scared is OK, almost dead isn't. I never thought it could go that way. I don't want to do anything even a little bit dangerous again.'

'Gotcha.'

'So, I want to know what you are thinking of us doing today. Tell me, and then I'll decide if I want to come along.'

'Isn't it more fun if you don't know?'

'No! Well, maybe. But no. Tell me, or I'm not going anywhere with you.'

'OK. We're going to get a bus to a beach. Explore the beach. Then come back.'

'Huh. Somehow, I don't believe that is all there is to it.'

56

Liv

We get off the bus and walk down a rocky path to a cove.

There is a sandy area, rock pools. A few families braving thin October sunshine and wind with buckets and spades and picnic lunches on blankets.

'This way,' Echo says and smiles. We walk along the beach and out along the curve of the bay, then clamber over rocks to the next cove.

'Why are we here?'

'You'll see.' We continue along the curve of the cove. 'Are you ready?'

'For what?'

He turns and faces the cliff. 'For this.'

There are overhanging rocks from the cliff above, shadows beneath. Echo bends forward and ducks, and I began to understand.

Caves. My skin crawls, my feet involuntarily start to back away.

'Are you coming?' He turns, peers back from under the rock.

OK. The cave can't go back that far, can it? It is wide open at the entrance. These are the things I repeat over and over in my mind, as I step towards Echo and under the tons of rock and earth of the cliffs above.

Cliffs, like the ones that collapsed under the house we were in last night.

One step. Then another.

My movements are jerky and I try to control them, to calm down. I have to bend down to go through into the cave proper to join Echo, but once I do so the roof of the cave inside is higher and I can stand upright. Here it is instantly cold, much colder than on the beach. Echo can't quite stand straight and is bent at an awkward angle.

'Well?' he says.

'I don't like being in here. But I can turn and still see the light, the beach. It isn't that bad,' I say, trying to convince myself while all the while I can feel the pressure of all that rock, a whole cliff, right over my head.

'Just you wait. Torch?' he says, and I get it out of my pocket.

'Shine it back this way,' he says, pointing to the back of the cave, a little to the left. 'We're going back as far as we can. Or you are, at least.'

With the torchlight, now I can see that the roof of the cave drops lower but the opening continues. The cave goes back further than the light can reach.

'Are you serious?'

He grins then, for the first time today. 'Oh, yes. If this won't entice Molly to come help you, nothing will.'

'What if nothing will?' I counter. Of course I know Molly won't come. She said she wouldn't and she is even more stubborn than me.

'Go on, I dare you.'

I stare back at him and somehow he must see what he wants in my eyes: acquiescence. Like Molly said: he dared, I caved. Literally.

He nods. 'Probably take your jacket off?' he says. 'It might get caught.' Too tight a space for a jacket? Hands shaking, I unzip my anorak and hand it across to him; he takes off today's black jumper. Puts them together up on a rock. The cold and damp cut in.

I hold the torch, bend down and shuffle further into the cave. Echo follows just behind. The ceiling drops as we go; we are bent more and more until we have to drop to crawl on hands and knees. On damp slimy stones that slope down, sharp, awkward. My breathing is all I can hear; panting, like I am running instead of barely moving.

'Easier to crawl if you let me hold the torch,' he says. 'I'll stop here and shine it forward.'

I look back the way we came. The entrance to the cave is not visible any more – we've cut in at an angle – but there is faint light still from that direction. Echo is twisted awkwardly, his longer limbs and bigger shoulders have come almost as far as they can. I toss the torch back to him.

'This is far enough,' I say.

'No. Look.' He shines the torch forward again, over my shoulders. 'See that rock that juts out, where it narrows? Get past that. There is a bigger chamber beyond.'

'How do you know? It's not like you'd fit.'

'I've been here before. Years ago when I was a kid.'

'If I go past that rock, to that chamber, we're done. Right?'

'Right,' he says.

Echo shines the torch and I wriggle forwards, not quite on hands and knees now: there isn't enough space. There is water dripping all around, soaking into my clothes, my skin soon so numb I can barely feel the sharp edges of rock.

I get to the place Echo pointed out.

I twist my head to look back. 'I can't go any further. It's too narrow.'

'Yes, you can. Go on your side and you can twist around.'

'I don't want to.' The panic I've been trying to stuff down is rising, waves of fear that I can't control. Echo isn't next to me now; he can't even reach far enough to touch my ankle to hurry me along. The torchlight barely reaches me and beyond it is black.

'No!' I say. 'I can't do it.' I'm shaking. Breathing faster and faster. Hyperventilating. I try to inch backwards but I keep getting caught and panic even more.

'Liv, listen to me. If you get past that rock, it opens up and you'll have more space, you can collect yourself and turn around to come back out. It's harder to crawl backwards. Trust me.'

Tons of rock are pushing on all sides, compressing. Air, where does air come from? The way we came, but my body is almost blocking the way. I can't breathe.

Go forwards. How? Sideways. Yes. That is what Echo said. I can hear his voice somewhere behind me, making encouraging sounds, but I can't make out what he is saying. Somewhere inside I find some will, some fight, and I do it: scrunch around on to my side. It's so narrow, I turn my head sideways and use my feet to push myself forwards, around the rock. I can only breathe shallowly now and I'm panicking even more. I'll be crushed, I can't do this. But I use the fear to push as hard as I can with my feet, and then, finally, something gives. My body is around enough of the rock that I can breathe all the way in, and all the way out, slowing down, bit by bit.

I inch forwards, and like Echo said, once I'm properly around this jutting rock the space opens up again. I can sit, lean against the wall of the cave, and just breathe. It's completely dark. I can't see at all but sense air movement, space, above me. My heart is still beating too fast. I'm trembling, hysteria coming back in waves and I need to calm down, to think, to focus on *something*. My senses: it's dark. Wet, the floor of the cave is wet. Cold. There are little faint scrabbling sounds up above. Something scurries in the dark places.

This place feels *wrong*. I shouldn't be in it. Wrong how, I don't know, but cold and old and awful. I am scared to be here and scared to think of crawling back out of it. All I want to do is roll in a ball and howl, never move again.

'Liv? Come on, crawl back out.'

'In a minute,' I manage to say, still trying to catch my breath, to breathe normally and not gasp. If I stop breathing again, what if Molly doesn't come? It's not like they can get teeny, tiny paramedics to drag me out. Panic starts rising again: I can't go back through that narrow space to get out of here, I can't. My mind is playing tricks, spinning around.

Kashina – that old fortune teller. She said I was at a dangerous crossroads, and here I am. Then there is something else. In this space with me. Voices, whispering – not Molly – and fear is taking over and the voices are getting louder but I'm pushing them away, not listening.

'Liv, come on!' It's Echo again. He says my name again and again, louder, and I start to feel confused. How long have I been sitting here?

There are whispers in the darkness, too faint to hear, then

getting louder. *Please stay, don't go. Why won't you talk to us?*

I'm hearing things because I'm scared. Nothing is here. I'm leaving and I'm going to do it now. You can do it, I tell myself, since Molly isn't here to say it.

I turn around to face the way I need to go and feel the opening with my hands. There isn't enough space. There just isn't.

'I can't. I'm stuck,' I wail.

Laughter – all around and inside my head. *Then you will stay with us for ever.*

I can hear Echo shuffling – trying to get closer?

'You got in there, didn't you? Come back the same way. Arms first,' he says. 'Come on. Go sideways, arms out. Push against the wall behind with your feet. I can reach your hands if you do that and I'll pull you out.'

There is more water on the bottom of the cave now. It slopes down: is it flooded when the tide comes in? I'm soaked and shivering.

'Come on Liv, you can do it. Hands first, come on.'

Crushed, I'm crushed, breathing in and out too fast, everything going grey and misty. Dark shadows loom behind in the cave: terror. Laughter echoes in the rocks.

I need to get away but I'm frozen – too scared to stay, too scared to leave.

But then – all at once – I'm filled with calm, soothing, gentleness. A familiar presence inside me. The chorus is silent and there is just one voice: *You can do this*. Molly.

Molly joins inside me and the shadows are pushed back.

Take your jumper off – it'll make it easier.

Why didn't I think of that? I pull it over my head, leave it behind. Move along sideways, pushing with my feet. An inch, another inch, reaching out with my hands.

Finally Echo's hands clasp mine and I cry great gulping sobs. Molly slips away.

'We've got to get out of here, now,' he says. 'Get a grip!'

Anger returns somewhere inside.

He's a total asshole.

'You total asshole!' I shout, Molly's thought and my words coming at almost the same moment.

'That's the way. Come on, help me, push with your feet.'

He pulls and I push with my feet and gradually the space is bigger, until finally I can get on my hands, knees, go a bit further, then half stand. There: light!

I scramble out into the air, half laughing, half crying, then, suddenly weak, collapse. He helps me up.

'Oh, thank God. I thought I was going to be trapped in there for ever. You did this to me, you jerk!' And I punch him, hard, in the arm. He barely reacts. He is looking across the beach, at the point, the way we came.

I turn. Waves are hitting high on the rocks.

We're almost cut off.

57

Echo

We run. I push Liv to go first and she starts to clamber up the rocks, gets up over the first few but then slips, falls, cold waves plucking at her legs, and she's scrabbling at the rocks for grip, falling further, but then the waves fall back again. She finds a toehold, heaves herself up higher and then over to the other side – to the cove where we started. She falls to the rocks, cries out, but when I drop down next to her, she gets up, starts running up the beach. It's deserted now.

I catch up to her. 'Are you OK?' I say.

'NO! I'm not anything like OK.' She pushes me in the chest, hard. 'That cave sloped down – it was dripping wet. It floods when the tide comes in, doesn't it? I could have drowned in there, or we could have been cut off in that cove by the tide. You *knew*, didn't you?'

'I didn't think it would take so long for you to get out.'

'I told you this morning that I didn't want to do anything dangerous. But you didn't think to tell me what the risks were, did you? You – us – this is it. We're done. You can play your scary little games by yourself. I'm through.'

'Liv—'

'Just. Keep. Away. From. Me.'

She turns, marches up the beach, doesn't look back. Reaches the path to the road, the bus. I want to run after her, say

I'm sorry, promise that if she stays my friend I'll never scare her again.

But I'd be lying.

58

Liv

I'm angry like I've never been before – a hot fury – but it slowly bleeds away, and I want it back; it was keeping me warm.

Have you learned your lesson? Go on, say it.

'OK, fine. Molly, you were right. Are you happy?'

I'm shivering wildly now the wind is picking up. Fat drops of rain start to fall to take care of the few parts of me that aren't already soaking wet.

Call Mum or a taxi.

I feel in my pockets for my phone – thunk myself on the forehead. No phone. It was in my jacket pocket, presumed washed out to sea from the cave. I say a few words that would have all my pocket money in the swear jar if Mum heard.

Excellent vocab. You've got to move around to stay warm until a bus comes.

I'm marching back and forth on the spot, and the anger relents enough to make me realise: Echo must have got soaked too. Is he still on that beach? Is he all right?

Molly sighs, guessing before I ask. *I'll go look.*

'Thank you.'

She's gone a while and I'm worrying more and more. Why didn't I keep my phone in my pocket? Though if I had, it would have got soaked or smashed and probably wouldn't work anyhow.

She's back. *He's not there.*

'Where could he be?'

I thought maybe he took the coastal path and is walking back. But I looked along it quite a way and couldn't see him anywhere.

There's a horrible feeling inside me. 'He didn't . . . he wouldn't . . .'

I looked in the sea, too. That's why I was gone so long. No sign.

'You're worried, too.'

Maybe.

The bus appears in the distance. I wave it down.

The doors open. I step in.

The driver looks at me and it mustn't be good. 'Are you all right, love?'

'Got caught by the tide, and—' I'm just about to say, call the RNLI, the coastguard, get them to look for Echo, when I glance down the bus and see him slipping in through the side door.

59

Echo

Liv sits by the driver at the front, eyes forward. Sitting upright and rigid. And no matter how I will her to turn to meet my eye, nothing.

She's really angry. Isn't she?

When we get to Brighton she's the first out the door. When I get off, I watch her, walking away as fast as she can. But I don't need to follow her this time.

I know the end is coming. I know she will be there, with me, when it does. I can feel it rushing towards us, and there is nothing either of us can do to stop it.

60

Liv

I don't head for home. Mum is at work and I don't want to be alone. Am I scared of Echo – that he might follow, of what he might do or say if he does? I examine the question as if from outside of myself. Maybe there is enough reason to be at least nervous of him, but that isn't why I'm heading for Bowie's.

Why, then?

'I've had a shite morning and he's my friend; I want to see him. Is there something wrong with that?'

No. Anyhow, your house keys are in your jacket pocket with your phone.

'Oh, yeah. That too.'

Some people walk past. Going by the glances, I'm not looking normal.

No. You're a mess.

'Thanks.' I'm having second thoughts about going to Bowie's, but just as I'm thinking of maybe turning around, the skies open again. Beyond heavy rain, it's like standing in a shower set to freezing. I'm so cold that I'm numb.

You need to get out of this.

And now I've reached his street; we're almost there.

I knock on the door. Bowie's sister, Tina, opens it.

'Liv?' she says, eyes wide. 'Christ, you're soaked. Get in.'

She yells, 'Bowie,' up the stairs. I'm shivering, violently.

'At the risk of sounding like my mother, what were you doing out in this weather without a coat?' she says.

'L-l-long story.'

She looks closer. 'You're bleeding.' A scratch, I remember now, when I slipped on the rocks. I was too busy panicking at the time to pay much attention. I touch the side of my face and flinch. Now Bowie's coming down the stairs.

'Ah, hello, I didn't order a drowned rat. And wasn't cake meant to be later?'

'Do you want me to get a friend to run you home?' Tina says.

I shake my head. 'Thanks, but no. Haven't got keys. I sort of lost them.' Tina's phone is ringing in her pocket – she goes to answer.

'I'm guessing there is a story behind all this,' Bowie says, and I sneeze.

I wrap my hands around a mug of tea, feel the heat ease into them. Wet stuff off – Tina lent me some of her sweats – a blanket wrapped all around. A plus of short hair I didn't appreciate until now is that instead of a cold wet weight down my neck and back, it's almost dry.

'So, where were you last night?'

'Oh, yeah. That. Really sorry if you were worried.'

'Just a little.'

'I was out with a friend – well, sort of a friend. Maybe he isn't any more.'

'Oh. I see.'

He thinks you mean boyfriend.

'No, not like that,' I say, and can feel my face getting hot,

198

and why am I denying it, anyhow? 'It's a bit of a long story.'

He doesn't say anything, waits while I gather my thoughts. And it's like he's trying to keep his face neutral but it isn't really working, and I'm not sure how much I want to tell him.

Do it – run it all past someone rational and see what they say.

'OK, here goes. It's going to sound mega bonkers. Do you remember on my birthday, there was this goth boy at the cemetery who freaked me out talking about ghosts?'

'Yeah?'

'I met him again a few days later, outside of school.'

Like you just happened to bump into each other? Why don't you tell Bowie that he was watching your school to find you?

'Be quiet,' I hiss at Molly, silently.

'His name is Echo. His mum died in a car accident almost a year ago. Her car went off the road up the hill, past the marina – it crashed down the cliff. The police think it was suicide but he doesn't agree. He's trying to work out what happened to her.'

'God, how awful for him,' Bowie says, with real sympathy in his voice, concern on his face. 'But what can he find out about it now that the police haven't managed?'

'Well, this is the bonkers bit. He wants to ask her. I mean, his mum.'

There's a pause while Bowie takes that in. 'What, like have a séance?'

'Not exactly.' I explain Echo's theory: that fear at an extreme level opens the veil that is normally there between the living and the dead.

'That's a freaky theory. But what does all this have to do with you?'

'He heard me talking to Molly's headstone. On our birthday. He thinks I want to reach my sister, just like he wants to reach his mother. That we can help each other.'

'Do you believe all that?'

I shrug, not sure what to say. 'I didn't,' I say finally. 'But something really weird happened today.' I go through where we went, the cove we clambered across to. The cave under the cliff.

'Seriously? *You* went into a *cave*?' He knows I'm claustrophobic, won't even get into lifts.

'Somehow, yes. It got narrower and narrower.' I describe what it was like, and, as I do, all the fear is coming back. I'm still cold but it's like this blanket wrapped around me is smothering me and I push it away.

'Why put yourself through that?'

'Honestly? I don't know.'

'So what was the weird thing that happened?'

'It was like I could hear voices. Laughter. All around me in the deepest part of the cave. Just when I was the most scared.' More scared than I can remember ever having been before.

'Maybe it was Echo winding you up?'

'I don't think so – it wasn't coming from his direction. Anyhow, once I got out, it stopped.'

It must have stopped when I came, Molly says. *I didn't hear anything like that.*

'Was it in the cave that you got that scratch?'

'No, that was later. When we got out of the cave, the tide was coming in. Only just made it over the rocks – waves caught me.' I shudder. They were pulling at my legs as if they were alive, wanted me to fall.

200

'What were you thinking? You could have been seriously hurt, or worse. Where were you last night?'

'Echo is afraid of heights. We went to this building site, climbed the frame.'

'All right. So, let's see if I've got this straight. You've met a weird guy and went somewhere dangerous with him late at night and again this morning, without telling anyone where you were.'

'Hey. Calm down. That might not have been the best move, but he's not weird. Well, OK, maybe he is a bit different, but not dangerous. He's a friend.'

'Sure. What did you say before – a sort of a friend? One you've known for, what, a week?'

'Look, if I want a lecture, I'll talk to my mum.'

'Sorry for being worried about you. You're not going to do anything like this with him again, are you?'

Now I'm getting really annoyed. I'm about to tell him to mind his own business, I'll do what I like, but then Tina comes in. 'Zahra is out front. We're heading out – want a lift?'

'Yes. Thanks.'

'Thought you didn't have keys?' Bowie says, then looks at Tina. 'And I thought you were grounded.'

'This is a special occasion: the first time Zahra's brother has let her borrow his car since she got her licence.' Tina blows him a kiss. I get up, grab my bag of wet clothes. Grimace as I put on wet trainers.

Bowie follows us to the door. 'Call me, Liv. Please. *Before* you do anything else.'

'Can't. Lost my phone.' And I shut the door in his face.

'Ooh, tension,' Tina says. 'Lovers' spat?'

'We're not!'

She laughs. 'Never mind.' She opens the back passenger door. 'Get in.'

'Belt up – I'm potentially dangerous,' Zahra says. 'Where do you want to go?'

I get them to drop me at home and tuck my bag of wet clothes behind a tree by the door. The sun is just about breaking through.

Why didn't you tell Bowie that you already told Echo to leave you alone?

'I don't know. I just didn't, that's all.'

I don't think that is the last you'll see of Echo. He's not going to just give up. Is he?

'I don't know.'

And why didn't you stay with Bowie – what are you going to do now? Sit on the step all afternoon?

'I've had just about as much of listening – to Bowie, to you – as I can take in one day.'

That's because we're the voices of reason, Liv. And you're not being reasonable.

Huh. There's only one sure-fire way to tune Molly out. I'm wearing sweats, right? It's time for a run.

61

Echo

I get the bus and ride it for hours, back and forth, back and forth. Past the place where Mum died. Finally I convince myself to get off. Walk – pace – along the stretch of road and think. Struggle to remember. I know what happened, and if you're told something often enough you can start to convince yourself you can see it. Driving fast down the hill – hit the chain fence at such a speed that the car kept going, over the cliff. Somehow just before that, I jumped out of the car. But I don't *remember* any of that.

Later – seconds, minutes, I don't know – I opened my eyes on the side of the road. Dazed, confused. Struggled to my feet and saw it below – the wreck of our car on the rocks.

Apart from that? My memory won't come. It's useless.

The only one who knows what really happened is Mum. I know her, love her, trust her. She would *never* have crashed the car with me in it on purpose. But the voices of doubt are too loud. I have to prove them all wrong.

When it hits me, it's so obvious I can't work out why it didn't before.

This is where it happened. This is where it will finally work – it must. It has to.

When? How?

I begin to work on a plan.

Tonight: I'll try it tonight.

62

Liv

I've run fast enough, far enough, to leave Molly behind. I'm tired, drained, and hungry too.

What I need is fish and chips and too much ketchup on the beach – with Bowie.

Why am I such an idiot?

He just wanted to listen, to try to understand, to help. In short, be my friend. Molly was right.

I'd text him if I had a phone. Mum is going to freak when she finds out I lost it. Keys too. At least I've got lunch money in my pocket – but now I thunk myself in the head, too close to where I banged it on a rock earlier, and wince. I *had* money, but it is in the pocket of my wet jeans in a bag by the front door.

I sit for a while on a bench but start to get cold. Get up, wander around. I'm walking near the pier when I think I hear someone call my name, and turn.

'Liv? Is that your name?'

It's Kashina – Echo's Mum's friend. The one who freaked me out staring at me with her scarred eye and talking about dangerous crossroads. Maybe I should have listened to her.

I nod. 'Yes, that's me.'

'Is everything OK?'

'Just peachy. You?'

'Oh, you know, can't complain.' She hesitates. 'Have you

seen Echo? He hasn't come by for a few days.'

'I thought he was staying with you?'

'He comes and goes.' She shrugs.

'I saw him this morning, not since.'

She hesitates, then fixes me with her good eye. 'Some people can't be helped. Can't be saved. He's no good for you, Liv.'

Late that evening I'm staring at the ceiling. I'd watched for Mum's car and timed arriving at the front door just when she did, so she wouldn't realise I didn't have any keys. I wasn't up for all the fuss, so pleaded a headache and went to my room soon after dinner.

No sign of Molly, then or now. She must still be annoyed, and I'm feeling guilty about how I dumped her, went running, after she'd come and helped me in the cave.

I can't stop thinking about Kashina – what she said, the way she said it. She's beyond weird, no doubt. But there is something about her that makes me think she's for real. She really meant what she said.

So that's Molly, Bowie and even Echo's family friend, Kashina, all telling me to keep away from Echo. Something I'd already decided to do anyhow, so why is it so annoying? I can't stop thinking about him. Worrying too. What might he try next? What if he tries some stupid stunt and falls, and no one is there to help?

Is it true what Kashina said – that some people can't be helped, can't be saved? Maybe, instead, it's that no one is there for them when it counts.

★

It's late – almost midnight – when the landline rings. Mum gets there first, yawning. Answers. 'It's for you,' she says. 'It's Bowie.'

I shake my head, not ready with what to say, hissing for her to tell him that I'm not here, I'm asleep, anything.

'She says to tell you that she's not here and/or asleep.'

'Mum!' Cringing with embarrassment, I take the phone. 'Hi.'

'I won't keep you, Liv,' he says, his voice cold. 'Just checking if you know where Tina and Zahra were going? She hasn't come back and she's not answering her phone. My parents are getting worried.'

'Oh. They said something about going for a drink? I don't know anything else. Hope she's OK. And about earlier – I'm sorry.'

'Yeah. Me too. Liv, just promise me you'll tell me, or somebody – anybody – if you go anywhere with Echo again.'

'I promise. But I won't—'

'Bye, Liv.' There's a click and I put the phone back on its base. Turn, and Mum is still there, standing on the stairs.

'Why didn't he call your mobile?'

I could tell her the battery is flat. But I'll need to face this soon, won't I? And just now it seems less important. 'Well, I kind of lost it.'

'You lost your phone? Not again. Where do you think it may be?'

'It, well, it kind of got swept out to sea. With my coat – it was in my coat pocket. Along with my keys.'

'Honestly, Liv! I told you when your last phone went through the washing machine that I wasn't going to get you another if you were that careless again.'

'I know. I'm sorry.' What does it matter? No one wants to call me.

'Why was Bowie calling so late?'

'His sister, Tina. She and a friend of hers dropped me off this afternoon. She didn't come home and they don't know where she is.'

Worry crosses Mum's face, annoyance at my phone forgotten.

'I bet she's fine,' I say. 'She's been arguing with her parents and been grounded and stuff. She's probably just staying out late to get back at them.'

'You wouldn't do that, would you, Liv? Promise me you'll never disappear. I couldn't bear it.' Her arms are around me now, a warm hug, and instead of pushing her away, I'm holding on.

63

Echo

The wind is picking up. Pressure is building inside me, like I'm in a plane coming in to land and my ears won't pop as we descend. The pressure builds and builds until I want to scream from the pain.

It's dark, clouds covering the stars, moon. I can smell the sea down below. What is stopping me from stepping off this cliff? Falling, landing in a tangle of broken bones below. Dying where Mum died. I'm on the edge of the cliff now and a knife's edge too: live or die. Take one last step forwards, or don't. Even now the fear that I feel is not enough.

What else can I do?

Kashina seems to think I can remember if I try hard enough. And the closer I get to the anniversary of the day, the more it feels like what I need to know is getting closer, that it's within reach. But when I try to grasp it, it slips away.

I sit down, then lie back on the cold rock and mud. Close my eyes. But instead of reaching for what I want, I let my mind drift as it will. Random images, words, from the weeks leading up to the accident.

One place keeps coming up again and again: the graveyard where I took Liv. My thoughts keep veering back to it. Mum went there many times – she often took me with her. Each time she seemed more upset when we left. She wouldn't tell me what was going on – I just knew she was trying to find a missing girl. Elsie was her name. There must have been a ghost there that knew something, something they didn't want to tell her, but she kept trying.

We were there, weren't we? That last night. I'm sure of it now! Whatever happened – she was angry, absolutely furious. She wouldn't tell me why. She said one of those typical Mum things, without explaining what it meant: something like that if things never change, why bother?

And then . . . . and then . . .

That's it.

That's all I can remember – as far as I can go.

I'd tried to convince myself I didn't need Liv, that I should try without her. But the fear I should be feeling – it's somehow muted, even in this place that I fear more than any other.

Is that because Liv isn't here?

Or maybe it's because the anniversary of Mum's death – the day, the hour – hasn't yet come.

It's getting closer.

I need to wait, but waiting is hard. There is a need, a hunger, and it's growing.

64

Liv

There is a spare key by the kettle when I finally come down, just after noon. And a note: 'We'll go shopping tomorrow and get you a phone. One the size of a brick, so it can't get lost.'

Great.

In the meantime, it's term break and I have nothing to do. Nothing. And not in a good way.

'Molly? Are you there?'

Still no answer. She's cross with me. Why not? Everyone else is.

Then she's looking at me from the mirror over the table.

Well? I'm waiting.

I'm so relieved to see her that I'd say anything. 'I'm sorry.'

And?

'You were right. AGAIN.' I flick the radio on, fill the kettle. 'So, what do you want to do today?'

Ooh, you really ARE sorry! Um . . . I know! Let's go on the zip line across the beach – and do it tandem.

Tandem, as in Molly will come inside for the ride. I guess I owe her. 'Your wish is my command.'

The radio has gone to the news now. The kettle is starting to whistle and I can only half hear over it, but was that something about a missing girl? I turn it up.

'. . . was reported missing last night, raising concerns that it was connected with the attempted abduction of a teenage girl in Brighton just days ago. However, we have good news just in from police that she was found safe and well at a friend's house.'

Was it Tina that was reported missing last night but has been found? I need to call Bowie to make sure Tina is OK but I don't know any numbers. Who does when they're always in your mobile?

Mum phoned his parents – she must have their landline. I hunt around for her address book, finally find it. Flip through and there it is.

Dial. It rings twice. 'Hello?' It's Bowie's mum.

'Hi, it's Liv. Bowie called last night about Tina – has she come home?'

'Hi Liv. Yes, she's fine. Said she told Bowie she was staying at her friend's, not that he remembers it. They were at a party late and her phone went flat. Do you want to speak to Bowie?'

'No, thanks. Just wanted to check she's OK.'

I'm relieved. I'd got worried again when their mum – who would usually be at work – answered the phone.

Maybe after staying up late worrying, she needed a day off.

65

Echo

It's coming. There is blue sky above now, but a bank of heavy gloom is getting closer, circling all around. The pressure both inside and outside of me is building even more.

It's late afternoon. I can't wait much longer. Just when I'm thinking I'll have to try to find an open door or window to slip through, the front door opens and out steps Liv.

I follow her, taking care to stay well back. Ready to duck down and hide if she begins to turn.

She walks to the beach, then along to the queue by the zip line that goes across it. Maybe she was thinking of that to be her next dare for me? Before she told me we were through. The zip wire isn't that high up, not really – tens of metres at the highest point. Enough for a jolt of fear, but that's it; fits her scary-but-not-dangerous criteria, but useless for mine.

But maybe, just maybe – it is just what I need to help me today.

I walk around the long way – to make sure she doesn't spot me – to the end point of the zip. Keeping out of sight but glancing around now and then to see who is being strapped in next. They're given instructions, then fly hurtling along – some laughing, some screaming – to stop abruptly at the end. Unstrapped and step or fall to the ground. There are two zip lines next to each other and most of those taking part seem to have a friend, a relative, fly at the same time next to them. What if Liv was meeting someone? Having someone with her could make it more challenging. What if it is blondy boy? If she told me to go away so she could meet with him . . . I clench my fists, gripped by hurt and anger inside.

But there she is – Liv. And on the other line an older woman, not her mother – and the anger eases. They don't seem to be chatting, either, so likely not together. Good.

Final instructions. Liv looks nervous. And then they're off – flying across the shore. Now her head is back, she's laughing. God, she's beautiful in the sunlight.

It's just seconds and it's over. She's so close now. Chatting to the boy who is helping her out of the harness. Feet on the ground again, a smile that lights her up inside.

She turns, sees me and her eyes open wider.

'Hi, Liv.'

She hesitates. 'Hi.'

'I'm sorry about yesterday. I went too far.'

'OK. But I meant it – no more dares. I've had enough scary stuff for a while.'

I raise an eyebrow. 'Is that why you just went on a zip wire?'

Her smile is coming back. 'Well, it wasn't that scary – it was fun! You should try it. But that isn't a dare,' she hastily adds.

'Well, it kinda sounds like one. But I need something scarier than that.'

She sighs. 'Echo, I'm really worried about you. Can't you let it go?'

I shake my head.

'I get it. Not knowing if your mum meant to take her own

213

life must be unbelievably hard. But maybe it's something you will never be able to know. Maybe you need to look ahead, think about your life, and move on.'

Pain is twisting through me, then anger. She doesn't understand, she doesn't know the rest of it – the part I don't want to say out loud. Though . . . maybe that is what I have to do now to make her see. But I don't know if I can, and now I'm turning, walking away.

She follows. Puts her hand on my arm. 'Echo?' she says, concern in her voice and now her eyes when I turn and meet them.

'Let's find a place to talk,' I say, and I take her hand. She doesn't pull away. We walk further along the beach, find a spot away from other ears.

We sit down, facing each other.

'There are some things I haven't told you,' I say. 'About the night of my mum's accident.'

She nods, waiting.

'The night it happened, we went to that graveyard I first took you to. Mum was working with the police – as a psychic. Advising them. She'd reached a ghost at that graveyard who knew something about what happened to Elsie – the missing girl – but wouldn't tell her what it was. She tried again and again. That last time we went there, something she found out made Mum beyond angry and upset – she was in a state when we left, in a way I'd never seen her before. She said something like, that if things never change, what is the point? And she really was normally the queen of calm – nothing ruffled her. But this did.'

'Do you know why?'

214

I hesitate. 'A bit. Things I'd heard and picked up rather than was really told, you know? But I think Mum had been abused by her boyfriend. She ran away before I was born to get away from him, which was why we were in Brighton. Something about Elsie really got to Mum – maybe because of that.'

Shock in Liv's eyes. Nothing like that in her family tree, I'm guessing.

'Anyhow. It . . . it's so hard . . . to talk about.' I swallow. 'It's just . . . I was there. In the car when it happened. I jumped clear, before the car went over the cliff.'

Her eyes, wide. 'Oh my God. That must have been terrifying.'

I shake my head. 'I can't remember. One minute we were leaving the graveyard, driving back to Brighton; the next I'm lying by the side of the road. I need to know: was it just a freak accident – maybe because she was so upset, she was driving too fast – or did she mean to do it? Because if she did, she must have meant to take me with her. And that's why I can't leave it alone.' I'm saying the words the way I need to say them to get Liv to understand, to get her to help me again, but I don't believe it – I *don't*. I tell myself again and again. Mum didn't mean to die. She didn't mean to take her with me. I have to hold on to that.

There are tears in Liv's eyes. One slips free, traces a path on her cheek. I reach out, a wondering finger, and lightly touch her cheek to wipe it away. She comes closer, goes on her knees and wraps her arms around me. Holds me close and I'm burying my face in her shoulder. I didn't know I could cry any more, but now my whole body is shaking, racked with dry sobs.

Something is breaking, deep inside, something I need to

215

keep whole. I fight for control and push her away. Hold her hands in mine.

'Liv, that is why I'm going to try again tonight. One last time, that's all. If it doesn't work – well, that's it. No more. Will you help me?'

66

Liv

Before I can even process what he's saying, what he's asking, he raises one hand – holds fingers lightly across my lips a moment, and I vibrate to his touch. I want to hold him, keep him safe. Not let go.

'Don't answer,' he says. 'I know you said you were out – no more scary stuff. If you want to stay with that, it's fine. But let me hope in the meantime.'

'What are you going to do?'

'I'm still working out some details – where to get the equipment I need. But if you want to help, meet me tonight, around ten. By the road, where we got off the bus that first time – where Mum's car crashed.'

I bite my lip, searching for the right words to say – the ones that will stop him from doing whatever reckless, dangerous thing he is planning to do. 'Echo, I—'

'Not another word. I'll either see you tonight, or I won't.' He gets up, walks away. Doesn't look back.

67

Echo

She thinks she won't come.
I know she will.
All I have to do now, is wait.

68

Liv

I stay at the beach. Looking out as if I'm studying the waves, the horizon, but I'm not even seeing what would usually soothe me.

Molly is next to me. 'You've stayed quiet,' I say.

Yeah. I was just – you know. Shocked.

'Me too. But the question is, what should I do?'

Don't go. He's dangerous.

'But mostly just to himself. And maybe, he's right – that it could actually work, if he gets scared enough. That he could talk to his mum. Those voices I heard in the cave – were they ghosts?'

I don't know. Maybe you were so scared you were hearing things that weren't there.

'Maybe that is the same thing.'

The sky is closing in, wind picking up. Goosebumps on my neck and arms make me shiver.

Let's go home.

Mum is attempting to cook dinner. Rod is coming, she says, and I volunteer to help.

The radio is on, she's got a glass of wine and is singing to Ed Sheeran's latest while I chop veg. Molly is next to me on the counter, swinging her feet. Something is boiling over, something else is approaching charred under the grill. Her phone rings.

She answers. 'Hi. Ah, OK. No, it's fine. I understand. Bye.'

'He's not coming?' I say.

She shakes her head. 'Working late. He'll come after but said not to wait dinner. And just when I went to such an effort to ruin food, so he'd know to never let me cook again. Takeaway?'

The pizza is mostly gone. The wind has picked up, rattling the windows. We're watching some creepy movie together – I can't remember the last time we did something like this. Mum has fallen asleep – I pull a blanket over her shoulders.

Look at the clock. It's nine-thirty. Half an hour to go.

I can't stop thinking about Echo, what he said, the pain he was in. How I would feel if it was Mum who died like that.

'What if it was Mum,' I say to Molly, silently. 'We'd do anything to find out what happened to her. Wouldn't we?'

No no no! You're not thinking about going, are you?

'Do you think Kashina was right – what she said? That some people can't be saved?'

I don't know. Please *don't go. You said you were done with him.*

I'm trying to think this through, to hold Molly away from my mind so I can work this out without her interference. But no matter how many times I try to convince myself otherwise, what else can I do but go and try to help him? I don't know if Kashina was right, but I do know that there is something that draws me to Echo in a way I can't understand. Even if I believe what Kashina said, I have to *try* to stop him, try to save him. I get up, moving carefully, quietly, to not wake Mum.

You promised! No more scary stuff.

'I'm sorry, Molly. It's just something I have to do.'

A piece of paper. I write a note for Mum: 'I had to go out. Love you. xx.'

I put it on the kitchen table, get shoes. Borrow Mum's waterproof since mine is in the sea.

You promised Bowie – didn't you? That you wouldn't go anywhere with Echo without telling him.

I hesitate; she's right. I get the phone and go back to the kitchen, close the door carefully, find Bowie's number again.

It rings once.

'Hello?' It's Bowie's dad.

'Hi. It's Liv,' I say quietly. 'Could you give Bowie a message for me? Tell him I'm meeting Echo tonight. That's it. Thanks. Bye.' I hang up. 'OK, I told him. Are you happy?'

NO! DON'T GO. Molly is really upset.

I'm easing the front door open. The wind almost takes it but I manage to shut it quietly.

If you do this, you're on your own. I'm not going to come help this time! Even if you beg me to.

She dives through the window and disappears.

69

Echo

The wind is wild. It's dark. The minutes are counting down. I don't need a clock; I can feel it coming, throbbing inside me.

Will Liv come?

She'll come.

Why does it matter so much?

I don't even know. But somehow, I need her.

70

Liv

Even for seaside Brighton this weather is something else. Mum's too-big coat is flapping wildly, threatening to make me lift off. But it turns out that there is another bonus of short hair: it stays out of my eyes. In this wind, no hair band would have had a chance.

When the bus finally comes it rattles and sways as we creep up the road. It's almost empty; there are few cars. Is there some megastorm coming that I missed hearing about? I automatically reach for my phone to check – duh. It's lost at sea, not in my pocket.

I'm watching the road. At night it's hard to pick the place that Echo had taken me. I think it was just before Rottingdean? I ring the bell when I think we're close.

The driver stops, opens the doors. 'You sure you want to get off here?'

No, I'm absolutely not sure in any way whatsoever. 'Yes, thanks,' is what I say.

When I step off the bus it feels as though the temperature has dropped during the short journey; the wind may be even worse. At least it's not— oh. Now it is: heavy drops are whipped into a frenzy by the wind and sting when they strike my face.

The bus disappears up the road.

I cross to the other side, trying to keep my hood up and the

223

jacket close around me. There's a flash – distant lightning – a brief chink of light in the darkness, and I scan all around but can't see Echo.

It's darker than it should be. The lights of Rottingdean have gone out – there must be a power failure. No stars or moon – masked by clouds, it's completely black. Dangerous to walk when I can't see – the rain driving in from one side makes me feel unsteady on my feet.

'Echo?' I call out, but my voice is swallowed by the wind and rain. Louder: 'Echo!'

Did I hear a reply?

71

Molly

Wake up! I'm shouting at Mum, knowing she can't hear me, but unable to stop myself from trying.

She said Rod was coming – he'll wake her, they'll see the note. They'll worry, won't they? Go look for Liv?

Then someone is ringing the bell. Mum stirs, stretches. The bell – it's ringing again and again.

She yawns, goes to the door. Opens it and is surprised – it's not Rod. It's Bowie.

'Is Liv home?' he says.

'She must be upstairs. I dozed off—'

He almost pushes her aside to get in through the door and runs upstairs to Liv's room – of course it's empty. Bathroom too, and now Mum is calling him.

'There's a note,' she says.

He rushes down the stairs – she has Liv's note in her hand, shows it to Bowie.

'What does she mean, she had to go out?' Mum says. 'At night, in this weather?'

'Liv'll go spare, but I have to tell you. She's been meeting up with this guy – all I know is he dresses like a goth, his name is Echo. They've been doing some stupid dares – scaring each other, risky stuff. I was worried, made her promise she'd tell me if she's going to meet him again. She called and left a message

225

with my dad that she's meeting him tonight but didn't say where. I was coming over here anyway, was nearly here, so when Dad called and told me, I ran the rest of the way to try to stop her.'

Mum's eyes open wide, all traces of sleepiness gone. 'You think he's dangerous?'

'Yes. And that's not all. Echo told Liv that his mum died in a car accident in Brighton almost a year ago, but I checked news online – I couldn't find any mention of an accident like she described when he said it was. I think he's been making stuff up. That's why I was on my way here – to tell Liv.'

'She told me about a friend whose mum died. Nothing about dares.' Phone out, she calls Rod. Gives him the gist of what Bowie said.

Rod is there minutes later. He gets Bowie to repeat what he said and I'm hopping around: *go, go, go – look for her.*

Rod calls to get the police to check for any records of a boy named Echo, or an accident where a car went off the cliff a year ago.

'Any idea where she might have gone?' Rod says.

Bowie is shaking his head. 'I've never met the guy. I just know what she told me – which wasn't much. But I can't see why she'd bother leaving a message without saying where they were going? Unless – it was something she didn't want to say to my dad but thought I'd figure out.'

'Tell me again what she said about what she and Echo were doing.'

'Dares – to scare each other. Liv is claustrophobic, he's scared of heights. They went to a cave last time, so it'd be something up high . . . Of course. I think I've got it! Liv said it was nearly the

226

anniversary of Echo's mum's death – off a cliff. Maybe they're going there, where it happened? I don't know exactly where, just that it was up the road past the marina – towards Rottingdean.'

'Let's go look,' Rod says.

'I'm coming,' Mum says.

Rod shakes his head. 'You need to stay here – she might come home or call. All right? Try not to worry. I'll find her. The second I know anything, you'll know.'

72

Echo

I see Liv, outlined for a split second by a flash of lightning. The intense joy that she came is mixing with the fierce agony of this day, making me feel unbalanced, drunk.

'Liv!'

She turns to my voice and now we've found each other. I grip her hand, stare at her in the darkness, and now that I'm touching her, it's as if her skin has a luminescence – of life and hope – that I can somehow see.

'You came to help me! I knew you would. Thank you.'

'That depends. What is the plan?' As Liv speaks, lightning once again splits the sky – lights up her pale face, wet hair and then is gone. Thunder crashes loud a few seconds later. 'Flipping heck, that's getting close,' she says. 'What are we doing out here in this weather?'

'It's a surprise. Come on.'

We head back across the road towards Rottingdean, and I feel her relief that we're leaving the cliffs behind.

Not for long.

'Don't suppose you've got a torch?' she says.

'No. You?'

'Huh. Mine – and my phone – are either in a cave or swept out to sea during our last adventure.'

'Oh, yeah. Sorry about that.'

Car lights sweep up behind us, carry on, giving enough light to orient myself. Down the road, a lane.

'What now?'

'I've arranged to borrow some stuff from a friend.'

Another flash of lightning – a house, a garage. 'They said there's a key under a rock to the left of the door.' We both feel around under rocks; she finds it first – holds it up.

'This is definitely *borrowing*, right?' she says.

'Of course. How else would I know where to find the key?' She's unsure. 'Trust me.'

She unlocks the door, I step inside, feel my way around. 'Here it is. Help me get this down.' Something bulky, wrapped in canvas.

'What is it?'

'You'll see.'

We leave, Liv locks the door, replaces the key.

Lights come on all around us – the power is coming back? It wavers on, off, on another moment, then is gone.

The rain is slackening off a little as we cross the road, go over the fence. Her steps are more hesitant now.

She stops before we get close to the cliff. Puts down the kit.

'That's far enough. Tell me what you're planning to do.'

'OK. It's tonight: the anniversary of Mum's death. This place, this time – it will work, it has to.'

'What will work?'

'I'll reach her. No other place could scare me more.'

'What are you going to do?'

'I'm going to fly. Well, glide – paraglide – so we borrowed this paraglider.' It'd taken me ages, staking out the houses all around, watching. To find one we could get to easily.

'Have you ever done that before?'

'No.'

'So, you thought tonight, in the dark, in the middle of a storm, would be a good time to give it a try?'

'Yeah. Isn't it a great idea?'

'No. I won't let you.'

'Try to stop me.'

She's walking away now, towards the dark road. I hurry, catch her. Grab her arm and spin her around. 'I need you to help me.'

'No way. You can't do this. Not in this weather. You want to learn? Take lessons somewhere on a nice sunny day.'

'It has to be tonight.'

'Why?'

'It has to be tonight, that's all. And you have to help me.'

I've got her arm still. I'm pulling her back, away from the road. Car lights are coming up and she's struggling to free herself as the lights sweep over us, but the car doesn't slow.

She was trying to get away from me. Trying to get them to see, maybe, to get someone to send for help?

There's pain inside.

Then a cold knot of anger. She has to help me. She *will*.

73

Liv

The rain slashes my skin, Echo's fingers are digging in my arm.
I shouldn't have come. He doesn't look right – he's not just a lost
friend who needs saving. He's something else, something
dangerous. Another flash of lightning; his eyes are wild. I'm going
to have to pretend to help him until I can get away.

'Echo, I'm sorry – of course I'll help you.'

But his grip doesn't loosen. He's dragging me and I'm dragging
this kit that we borrowed, if that is what we did. I'm shaking so
with fear I can hardly move. A scream is building up inside and
I need to not lose it, I need to try to calm this down, but the fear
is taking over.

This is nothing like vertigo on a zip line.

It's all fun if you're safe, but nothing tethers me to safety now.

This is real.

74

Molly

Rod and Bowie are just getting into Rod's car when his phone rings.

'Yeah. What, seriously? When was that? Yep. Thanks. Bye.' He swears.

'What?' Bowie says.

'There was a fatal accident about the right place, but it was thirty years ago. A woman and her son died. His name was Echo.'

'What the hell? Is someone impersonating someone who died years ago?'

They're talking about it as Rod starts the car, but I'm tuning out, thinking:

I could never say why Echo made me uneasy. What the problem was.

I couldn't see him anywhere when I went to look for him on my own. I could only see him when Liv did.

She could hear voices in that cave; I couldn't.

Kashina: she said to Liv, *You can't tell the worlds apart.*

Echo isn't what Rod and Bowie think he is — some nut pretending to be someone long dead. Is he?

Panic twists inside me and then I rush through the night to Liv.

75

Liv

'Stop, here,' Echo says. 'Unpack the paraglider.'

'Please, Echo, no. This is mad.'

'Do it now,' he says.

The rain is pounding down harder again, the wind pulling and plucking at us, like we might fly off the cliff even without a paraglider. I'm frozen and scared, my fingers numb, and I'm trying to undo the ties around the kit when I can't even see what I'm doing.

Molly, please come. Help me. Tears on my face.

Another flash of lightning and it's playing tricks with my eyes. Echo looks . . . different. Not just angry and desperate, but . . . I don't know. Something else – something wrong.

Exactly what Molly said. But I didn't listen.

We've got the paraglider out now – the harness and seat, straps, the parachute or wing or whatever it's called. It whips around in the wind, getting tangled.

'Help me put this on,' he says, trying to work it out but it's impossible in this wind.

Liv! What are you doing?

'Molly. You came.' I'm crying. 'He's going to paraglide, he'll die—'

He can't die.

'What?'

233

'Who are you talking to?' Echo says.

'Molly. I'm talking to Molly.'

'Your sister? She came?' Now he's smiling, eyes shining. 'I was just scaring you, you see, so she'd come. Now it's my turn – to reach Mum.' I see him now, as he is: half glowing in the dark, part translucent.

He is of the other world. Why can I see that now when I couldn't before?

He can't die . . . because he's already dead.

He died in the accident that killed his mum – Rod found out. It was thirty years ago. Rod and Bowie are coming to look for you. Keep him talking until they get here. He's dangerous. But he doesn't understand that he's dead.

'Echo, listen to me. Getting scared to reach your mum won't work.'

'It worked with Molly, didn't it?'

'No, no. She has always been here with me. All along.'

'What?'

'She's always been with me – since I was a baby. Like an invisible friend.'

'And you didn't tell me? After what we've been trying to do? Didn't you think maybe that is the kind of thing I needed to know?' He's hurt – angry: it's a visible thing – red fury, swirling inside him.

A strong gust of wind pulls the glider towards the edge of the cliff, Echo with it, and I'm caught up in it, being dragged with him, losing my balance. Molly is screaming. Echo's arms tighten around me as we're whipped off the side of the cliff together.

76

Echo

We're flying! Terror grips and trembles inside me, more than anything I've ever felt before, but this time it's not just from being so high above the world. It's Liv in my arms, screaming. I don't want her to die. No matter what she did or said or didn't say: I want to save her. I *need* to save her, more than myself.

The wind is too wild, we're going up, up, the wing is flapping and whipping around us, tangled. There are car lights from the road lighting us up and then we're falling.

Down, down, down . . .

'Mum, I need you – I need you now. Where are you?'

But there is no answer.

We slam into the sea, get sucked under, dragged by the wing of the paraglider. Liv – she's bleeding, her face? She's fighting to untangle herself, to leave me behind. I can't let her drown. I help her get free. She kicks to the surface, leaves me behind.

'Mum! Help me! Where are you?' I'm howling, anguish, pain, held under by the harness. Soon I'll drown – and still, she doesn't come.

Then all at once – I *remember*.

Mum was upset, angry. Driving too fast. She smashed through the chain fence – over the cliff. The car flying into the night – down, down. The crushing impact.

Bleeding, dying. *Both* of us.

235

I . . . died?

I'm dead.

I die again, this time, this place. Every year.

No. *No* – she didn't, she wouldn't. I'll never believe it. Never.

A howl of agony swirls through me and around me until I disappear.

77

Liv/Molly

Pain – *agony* – my face, my eye. It's taking over every thought, every sense, until that is all there is. But still I'm fighting to surface, to breathe. To snatch a quick lungful of air before another wave pushes me under.

So tired. So cold. It's starting to numb the pain . . .

Fight!

'Molly! You came back. It's no good. I can't . . .'

You have to. They saw – Rod and Bowie – they called the coastguard. You have to stay alive until they come.

I fight to the surface, breathe in once, then again – just as a wave hits my face. Now I'm coughing, water coming in, coughing, I can't breathe . . .

Stay with me, Liv!

And I try, but time is weird, slowing down.

I've been here, cold, wet, in pain – struggling to the surface to breathe – for an endless time . . .

Too long. I want to let go. Leave this world, with Molly . . .

Liv! It's OK! They're here! To rescue you!

Molly is shouting inside me. I want her to go away, I want to sleep . . .

Then there's a wrenching, deep inside. I'm ripped open and don't resist. Molly can have this moment, if she wants it. Everything fades to black.

★

The RNLI boat is bobbing on the angry sea, getting closer. A light on the water – they've seen us.

Now that I'm in Liv's body, I'm feeling as she did – the cold, pain, exhaustion – the will to struggle, to live, almost gone . . .

Stuff that. I didn't die over sixteen years ago for us to give up now. I *fight* – somehow find the last bit of energy in Liv's body, kick up. Breathe in a gulp of air but water comes too, and I'm coughing, coughing . . .

They throw a life buoy towards me, but it's swept to one side, too far. One of them is yelling to hang on, they throw it again. I reach it, try to wrap an arm around it, but I'm too weak, tumbling in the water. It floats away.

The boat is closer. One of them is in the water now, arms around me. Pulling me towards another in the boat – they have me between them. Pull me up and on to the deck.

'Hey there, beautiful, I'm Jason. What's your name?'

His face above me fractures into two, one fading. Can't talk. Coughing, on my side. Water – vomit – coming out.

Things fade away, then come back – they're tucking silver blankets all around me to keep me warm, telling me I'm going to be OK. A bandage is being wrapped around my head, my eye.

Jason is asking my name again – asking if I'm Liv.

I manage a half smile, a thumbs up. I'm Molly – I'm Liv – I'm both. Bound tightly together, for ever.

But it's not an equal partnership. Is it?

I pull away, let Liv take over. Return to my half life of shadows.

78

Liv

It's dark, cold. So cold. Movement – I'm moving, or the world is moving around me.

'Liv, Liv,' a voice, insistent, repeats my name and I want it to go away, let me sleep. 'Liv, say something or open your eye if you can hear me.'

I try to speak but no sound comes out. Watery – lights – flashing. My head hurts and my eye slips closed again, to comforting darkness.

'Stay with us. Listen to my voice, Liv. We'll be at the hospital soon.'

His voice ebbs and flows around me, as if I'm slipping in and out of this world. Molly is next to me, talking to me – trying to make me focus on her so I don't drift away, but all I can think of is Echo.

The worlds, I couldn't tell them apart. Now I understand: the living, the dead. That's what Kashina meant.

Echo's fear and pain were all for nothing. He was already dead. Why does he still suffer, after so many years?

Molly saved me. I don't deserve her; I didn't listen.

Why didn't she let me die?

Her love is wrapped all around me, cradles me inside as I cry for Echo.

I'm slipping, falling, lost.

79

Liv

I open my eyes – my right eye, that is. There is dull pain in the left and, when I reach up a hand, there are bandages. I'm in a bed, an IV in my arm. Hospital? Why am I in hospital? I try to move, to look around me, and groan.

'Liv?'

Mum. She's here, holding my hand. Molly holds the other one.

I'm confused. Why am I here?

Then it's all rushing back and I'm gasping to breathe – thrashing, tangled in the glider, underwater—

There's a buzzing noise, footsteps.

'Hush, baby,' Mum says. 'You're all right now. You're safe.'

I focus on Mum, her words. I'm all right. I'm safe. Gradually calm, sink back to the bed. Peace is flooding through me: something in the IV? I slip away.

80

Liv

I open my eyes. Correction: eye. Something woke me? I'm still in a hospital bed. Curtains pulled all around.

Mum is asleep in a chair next to me. Molly is on my other side and she sits up as I do.

It's still, quiet. But there are goosebumps up and down my spine, dread in my gut. Something is wrong. I can feel it.

Then – a faint sound. Thud, thud. A pause. Thud. Thud, thud.

'Can you hear that?' I whisper, and Molly nods.

It's not even and regular enough for footsteps – more, shuffling, as if something is being dragged across the floor.

'I'll go look,' she says, slips through the curtain, back again in a moment. Confused. 'I couldn't see anyone. I don't know where the noise is coming from.'

Thud, thud.

It's getting closer.

Is someone there?

I'm staring where the curtains are pulled together. Did they move, just slightly? There's a pinch of fear in my gut.

Mum? I try to say, but not even a whisper comes out. I can't speak, can't move.

The curtain. It sways slowly, side to side, fluttering, as if there were a breeze – but we're inside.

Then it is yanked to one side. Molly gasps as I do.

A man stands there, face ashen. He lurches through the curtains, half falls on to my bed and as he does, I see the back of his head – it's pushed in, collapsed, a mess of white bone and dark clotted blood and worse.

Help me, you've got to help me, please, he says, his hands gripping the blankets, trying to grab on to me, Molly shrinking behind and I can feel her fear with my own.

Darkness is swirling around him now and he screams – but Mum doesn't wake up, no one comes running. The darkness is growing, coming up his legs and he's trying to brush it away but it's all around him, closing in. I'm frozen – can't move away, can't call for help . . .

The darkness wraps around him completely. His scream cuts off when he disappears into the centre of it. It contracts to a point and vanishes.

And now I'm screaming – not frozen any longer – lights are coming up, footsteps, Mum, her arms around me.

81

Liv

Hello.

I open my eyes. Mum is gone; Molly, too. The curtains are pulled back to the wall, light coming through a window, and there's a little girl, four or five years old, staring at me intently. Thumb in her mouth. Otherwise my hospital room is empty.

'Hello. Where did you come from?'

Mummy brought me. I fell asleep and when I woke up, she was crying and wouldn't talk to me. I want to go home.

I'm about to push the button to call the nurse when she moves a little, the light shifts. Her skin – it's translucent. As I watch, it changes. Light shining through her more and more.

She turns. *Nanny?* she says and holds up her hand as if someone is there, taking it. The light brightens and I can't look at her directly, like the fiery edges of an eclipse. She vanishes, leaving only afterimages behind.

My head feels weird, light. I'm staring at the place where a moment ago there was a child, but now, there is nothing.

Did that really happen?

I wrap my arms around myself. I'm awake. It wasn't a dream. Last night maybe could have been: the fear, being frozen – the darkness. I desperately want it to have been a nightmare. What the hell is wrong with me?

There's a light knock on the open door: a doctor, a nurse, are walking in towards me. At least, I think that's what they are, and that they're alive. But how can I be sure?

'Good morning, Liv. How are you feeling today?'

Like I nearly died. My friend did die – well, OK, he was already dead – but he left. And a screaming guy with his head kicked in that no one else could see or hear got dragged to hell in front of me. Followed up by the not-as-frightening-but-just-as-freaky disappearing little girl.

Not knowing quite how to articulate any of that, I say nothing, turn to face the wall. They check some things – blood pressure, blood oxygen with a gizmo on my finger, and pulse rate. They change the dressing on my head – gentle hands, but it hurts, and when it comes off and they're about to fix the new one, all I can see with my left eye is blur and light.

They ask me if I need pain relief. This time I answer: yes. Tablets and water are found and finally they go, but when I hear their footsteps going the other way, I almost cry out: don't leave me.

'Molly?'

No answer. She's probably with Mum. They'll come back soon, won't they? I don't want to be alone. Fear and panic are swelling inside me, a scream is building up. I don't understand what has been happening—

Breathe: in, out, slowly. Repeat. Gradually my heart rate comes down. I need to stay calm. To focus, to work things out.

Molly is a ghost, but I've always known this. Or is that even true? When I was small she was a friend I played with, as real as anyone else. Maybe it's more accurate to say that it's something I worked out when I got a little older.

Echo, also: he was a ghost. I didn't know it, but he was. Somehow Molly worked it out before I did, that he wasn't just intense and troubled – he was also dead. But even now that I know it, I still can't believe it. And what about all the things we did together? If I was the only one who could see and hear him, did it look to everyone around us that I was talking to myself?

That man last night, the little girl this morning: also ghosts. Again, I didn't know, couldn't tell – not until they crossed to wherever they had to go after they died.

Ghost or not, Echo's suffering was real. I had to try to help him; I almost died in the process. But I failed. And right up until the end, he was as real and solid as anyone else, and I was so drawn to him. Being with him made me feel more alive than I ever have before, and he was dead. What does that say about me?

Echo didn't know, either. He thought he survived that car accident and that it only happened last year – but Molly said Rod found out that it was thirty years ago. Is that because he can't accept that his mum deliberately killed both of them?

The pain and distress he went through. I don't know where he went, if he'll ever appear in my life again. But for now at least, he's gone. And I can't tell who is real, alive, and who isn't.

Mum comes back later, Molly alongside but hanging back, quiet. When Mum hugs me, I hold on to her tight, afraid to let go. Afraid she'll leave again and I'll be alone.

Finally she pulls away. 'I've got a few things for you.' She reaches into her bag. 'This' – she holds out an envelope – 'is from Bowie.'

Tears smart my bandaged eye. 'He hasn't run a mile in the other direction?'

'Somehow I don't think he'd do that.'

'How about Rod? I'm sorry about him getting dragged into my mess.'

'He's fine. Concerned, of course. Listen to me, Liv: don't worry about other people. Focus on *you*. On healing, and sorting out whatever is going on in here.' She lightly touches my head. 'That's all that matters right now.' Another hug.

'And there is something else I have for you,' she says. 'A new phone. Same number. And it's all charged up and set up from your account in the cloud. So you can text me whenever you want.'

She hands it over and it's the latest model, not the promised brick. 'Thanks. But can't I come home with you now? Please. I just want to come home.'

'I want that too, but they need to keep you a little longer. To make sure you're OK, that you won't do something like that again. But I don't understand. Why, Liv?' Pain, bewildered pain, and she's shaking her head. 'You told Bowie you were meeting someone. Rod and Bowie raced there, worried the boy you told Bowie about might hurt you, but they saw you go off a cliff in a storm in the dark, on a glider, completely alone. No one else was there. Why did you do this?'

Something slots into place. The way Mum was last night and just now; the doctor today, the words he used and the way he said them when asking me how I was. If no one else could see Echo, do they think I made him up? Do they think I jumped from the cliff on purpose . . . that it was an attempted suicide?

246

I'm shaking my head. 'No, no. I didn't want that – to die. I wouldn't – no.'

'But then why?'

But I can't tell her. Can I? She'd never believe me – how could she? She'd think I'm lying, or worse – that I've lost my grip on reality completely.

Maybe I have. Maybe that has always been the case and I invented Molly – she was never with me. Her sitting there now, on the foot of the bed? A delusion. And Echo too: all made up. Seeing visions at night, likewise. I'm psychotic. That's it, isn't it?

I belong in a hospital, locked away.

Molly scowls, breaks her silence. *I am not a figment of your imagination, thanks very much.*

My dinner comes and I'm surprised to find I'm hungry. Mum supplements it with chocolate chip cookies – made by Rod, she says – and they are yummy.

Mum goes home when visiting hours are over. I want to plead with her to stay but it's obvious she needs to sleep, and not just in a chair. Anyhow, that first nightmare last night – or whatever it was – came when she and Molly were right there, so Mum being with me isn't going to change anything.

But Molly stays. She's sitting, knees up, in the chair that Mum was in. 'Why so quiet?' I say.

She shrugs. *Wasn't sure if you wanted to hear from a figment of your imagination.*

'Sorry. It's just . . .'

She waits as I struggle to find words.

'It's kind of like this. I don't want to believe what happened last night, or this morning, or that Echo wasn't real. But if none of that really happened – if I was seeing and hearing things that weren't there, why would you be any different? If you are real, it's like all the other scary stuff must be too. And why all that now when it hasn't happened before?'

She tilts her head to the side, thinking. *I don't know,* she says finally. *What happened this morning?*

I show her the memory – the little girl.

Wow. First the guy last night, sucked off to darkness. Then a little girl leaves with her nan in a blaze of light. Is it like heaven and hell?

'Or something like it? I don't know. But what about Echo? Where did he go? What happened to him?'

I don't know. I was too focused on keeping you alive.

'I know. Thank you.'

Just remember you owe me one!

'I do.'

There is something about what happened that you might have been too freaked to notice. It wasn't Echo who dragged you off the cliff; it was the wind catching the glider. He tried to stop it going over but couldn't, so he went with it, held you tight, tried to stop you from falling. And under the water he was trying to help you get free and to the surface.

There are tears in my eyes. 'All he was going through was tearing him apart. And OK, he made me help him – but then tried to save me?'

Molly nods. *As much as I hate to admit, it's true.*

'You never liked him. You always said something was wrong with him, but never what it was.'

She nods. *It isn't so much that I didn't like him. He made me, I don't know, uneasy. But I didn't know what he was, either.*

'But you knew when you came to the cliff. You told me, and

248

then I could see it, too. How did you work it out?'

Remember when I went looking for him at the beach and couldn't find him, and then he appeared at the bus? I couldn't work out how I missed him. And it just hit me: maybe I couldn't see him unless you could.

'But why?'

I don't know. Maybe it's a bit like how I can sense your thoughts most of the time, or we can show each other memories — sort of like you're streaming live, and I'm watching.

'So that would mean that I can see ghosts and you can't. Even though that is what you are. But if you're with me you see what I see?'

Yeah. I think so.

'Maybe that is why — last night. When you went to see what was making that sound, you didn't find anything. Because I couldn't see it yet.'

She shudders. *He was a sight, wasn't he? And all that black stuff that took him away, too.*

'But again, you only saw him when I did. That gives me an idea. Maybe that is the way I can work out who is dead and who isn't?'

You mean, if I can't see them when you aren't looking?

'Exactly.'

Sure. We could try that the next time a head-kicked-in-dead-guy appears. Though with him, the injuries kind of said it all.

My turn to shudder.

Let's do something to take our minds off all this. She gestures at Bowie's card.

I'd saved it to open for when I was alone.

You want me to go?

'No! I meant until Mum was gone.' I take it out of the envelope now, and smile. I wonder where he found it: fish and chips with a mountain of ketchup on the front. Inside blank, and he's written: 'Whatever is going on – when you're ready for fish and chips with too much ketchup on the beach, I'm here.' And he's signed it, 'Bowie xxx.' I show it to Molly.

Unlike Echo, I'm pretty sure Bowie is alive. Why don't you give him a chance?

I don't answer. It's always been Molly and Bowie, the way she means; he's my friend.

Call him.

I put the card on the side next to my new phone. I could call him, but should I? He's bound to ask what has been going on – if not now, then later – and I can't begin to work out how to explain all this to him when I can't even explain it to myself. If I try, he's going to think I'm either lying or crazy. I couldn't bear it.

A tap on the door – a nurse. I quickly avert my eyes to check. *She's still there*, Molly says.

'Hi, Liv. I've got your pain relief. Also, the doctor has authorised sleeping tablets if you want them?'

'How do they work? Like, if I take one, and something happens, would I still wake up? Or would I sleep through anything?'

'Well, they mostly help you fall asleep. You can still be woken up – you'd probably just be a little groggy.'

I think a moment. 'I think I'll pass, thanks.' If any of the undead are planning to pop by, I'd rather not be startled awake, confused. Anyhow, both times it happened before, my eyes were shut. I'm keeping them open.

'OK. If you change your mind about the sleeping tablet you can buzz for me, OK?'

'Thanks.'

Mum left magazines also, and a few novels. I try to read for a while, but reading with one eye makes my head ache, and I keep reading the same paragraph and not taking anything in. Now and then someone walks past my room, or a phone rings down the hall or a buzzer sounds, and every time I'm on alert. Waiting to see if anyone or anything appears.

It's ten . . . then eleven.

I'm trying not to but I can't stop thinking about that man – his ghost, or whatever it was – last night. And the girl this morning. And what they must mean: that I can see dead people. Not just Molly and Echo, but generally. Did both the man and girl die nearby in the hospital? Then it was like there was a delay before they went . . . er . . . beyond, wherever that is, and somehow they found me. Knew I could see them, maybe help them?

I don't want this. I don't want to believe it's real.

Molly comes to sit next to me on the bed, hurt in her eyes. *Am I part of what you don't want?*

'Of course not. Stop eavesdropping on my thoughts.'

Maybe it would help if you could find a way to back up what has happened – so you know it must be real.

'How?'

Me first. She points at the novels Mum brought. *Open one at a random page. Don't look at it.*

'Ah, I get it. OK.'

I pick up *Slated*, an old favourite, open it randomly and hold it where I can't see it and Molly can.

251

OK, here goes. She reads a few paragraphs, then I turn it around – it's just as she read it.

Could a figment do that?

'I guess not. But if I'm delusional, I might just *think* that happened.'

She rolls her eyes. *OK, how about the two hospital ghosts?*

'If I could get information on who died in the hospital, I could see if it ties in with what I saw? But I'm guessing if I asked someone who died here recently and what they looked like, they might think it's a bit strange.'

And maybe against privacy laws to answer.

'Though that man, last night – the injuries he had didn't look like they could have been accidental. Maybe there is something in the news?' I make myself remember last night, every detail of him that I saw, even though just thinking about it directly makes my fear, revulsion, come back.

Phone out – local news.

It doesn't take long to find it.

'Look. It's him. Isn't it?' A photo – it's from CCTV, not that clear. Police are appealing for information about the identity of a man found with horrific head injuries in Withdean Park yesterday evening. He died a short time later at hospital.

It's not clear enough to be completely certain, but it looks to be the same man. The story adds up.

Molly looks over my shoulder. *That's him*, she says.

There are goosebumps up and down my spine. Is this for real? If it is . . . *WHY?* Because apart from Molly – and more recently, Echo – this has never happened before, and surely other people have died in my vicinity; they're bound to have.

Can you find anything on that little girl?

I do more searches but find nothing on her – not expecting to – it'd only turn up if the cause of death were suspicious, I guess, and even if it were, maybe not straight away. She didn't have any injuries I could see.

She was so small. Her family must be in pieces. If I could tell them – that she's gone with her nan – would that help?

If I did, they wouldn't believe me, would they? It would only be distressing.

Now it's heading for midnight.

I keep looking sideways at my phone. I want to call Bowie so much. I want to see him even more. But he must think I was lying to him, losing it. Why would he want to have anything to do with me?

But he did send this card.

It's too late to call. I'll text, instead. What should I say?

Stick to the truth, Molly says.

I think for a moment. Then send this: Thanks for the card, it made me smile L xxx

Seconds later: I'm glad. And also glad to hear from you – new phone? Is it a brick?

No, it's rather swish.

Are you home?

Not yet. Hoping tomorrow.

Are you ok? Then, seconds later: Sorry, daft question – you're in a hospital.

Not daft. Got a bandage on my head and my eye hurts. But apart from that, just being in a hospital is freaking me out. I almost delete the last part. It's freaking me out because sometimes people die

253

in hospitals, don't they? And I'm afraid they'll come by and say hi on their way to eternity.

Don't blame you – the food is terrible and there's no Netflix.

I know! And I can't sleep, either.

Neither can I – I'm here. Keep on texting.

It's not a good night. A hospital is a really bad place to become aware that you can see and hear the dead. It's almost like word has spread. People keep dying and shouting to tell me some critical thing: find something; do something else. I try to tune them out, avert my eyes, but I can still hear them and wish I'd thought to ask Mum to bring my ear buds.

But Bowie gets me through it. Texting nonsense back and forth keeps a thread of reality going through the night, one to hang on to.

But one thing is clear:

I've got to get out of here before I really do lose it completely.

82

Liv

The next morning, the doctor comes to talk to me again. This time, I don't blank him. He asks how I feel. I say sad. That I miss my twin, desperately. That I was confused before, but I understand now that she is gone for ever. And I don't want to die.

I call Mum soon after. 'Good news: bring me some clothes. I'm getting out of here.'

The news about poor mental health provision and bed shortages must be right: after having the bandages on my head changed again, I'm discharged a few hours later without any further questions. We've got an outpatient appointment to check my eye again tomorrow, but psych referral has a waiting list of over a year. Mum is worried, asks about going private and is told that even there the waiting lists are long. But I'm relieved. I feel like I need to sort this out for myself. Talking to someone like that might muddy things up even more.

When we finally go through our front door, it's like a weight has come off me.

'It's so good to be home,' I say.

'You look really tired.'

'Couldn't sleep much – at all – last night.' I don't tell her that was out of choice.

'Duvet day?'

'Sounds good.'

A blanket, the sofa, TV on sometimes and sometimes not. I watch some, sleep some more, and manage to get through the rest of the day without seeing anyone vanish. I guess there haven't been any recent deaths in the neighbourhood.

Bowie texts me later that afternoon. Did they let you out?

Yep! Didn't text when got home as I was mostly asleep – thought you might be, too. Thanks for last night.

No worries. Is it good to be home?

YES!!

Are you up for fish 'n chips tomorrow? I really need to see you – to know you're all right.

I hesitate – look across at Molly curled up in the chair next to me. 'Bowie wants to meet at the beach tomorrow.'

Yay! She looks at me closer. *Tell me you're not thinking of saying no.*

'It's just . . .'

What?

'I really need him to be my friend. No interfering. Promise?'

I thought you owed me one.

'I do. But don't monkey around with my head around Bowie. Please?'

She sighs. *Whatever. I'll stay away.*

'Thanks, Molly.'

Phone in hand, I realise Molly is just one of the problems with seeing Bowie. I hesitate a bit longer, then send this: I'd really like to. But can we not talk about, you know, stuff.

No stuff allowed. It's a deal. Can we make it early – meet at noon? I have to get home to help Tina set up some surprises – parents' anniversary tomorrow.

Sounds good.

See you then.

83

Liv

Mum takes me to outpatients the next morning. The ophthalmologist takes off the bandages, and Mum's sharp intake of breath says it doesn't look good. Molly's eyes are wide when she sees it, too.

'How is it?' I ask her silently.

Pretty impressive.

He covers my right eye, asks what I can see on the chart at the end of the room.

There's a blur of light and dark and that's it. Now I'm starting to panic. 'What chart?'

'Ah. Tell me if you can see anything now.'

'There was a light that's gone off. And now it's gone on again.'

'OK, thank you, Liv.' He takes the cover off my right eye and the room swims back into focus, but with my left eye still open it's weird, like I'm switching from one to the other. He's tapping on a keyboard, making notes on a computer.

'Will her vision in that eye get better?' Mum says.

'It's too soon to know. There is swelling which will settle down, but we don't yet know how extensive the scarring will be, or if we can reduce it surgically.'

I take that in.

'You'll need to be extra careful with your right eye. Wear eye protection, that kind of thing. For now we'll replace the dressing with a smaller one, and—'

'Show me, first – my left eye,' I say. 'I want to see it, what it looks like.'

Hesitation. A hand mirror is found, given to me.

Ugh. There are stitches on the eyelid, forehead; a whole rainbow of bruising all around the eye – a hell of a shiner. And the eye itself: well, it's looking a bit horror-movie-ish.

I'm going to be wearing sunglasses a *lot*.

84

Liv

It takes a while to convince Mum to let me out on my own, but I manage it and meet Bowie by our usual takeaway at noon. We get in the queue. Molly, true to her word, is nowhere in sight.

'I'm liking the pirate look,' he says.

'Especially with the bruises?'

He looks closer, side to side. 'They provide colour and contrast.'

I'd tried to cover it up with sunglasses, but with the bandage there it was too bulky, and the lens of the sunnies pressed against it and hurt. So Mum found a pirate eye patch in an old box of Halloween stuff.

'What surprises do you and Tina have in store for your parents?'

'We're cleaning the house and making dinner – me mostly cleaning, Tina mostly cooking. Then taking the other two out to the movies.'

We order, then walk past the pier with our loot. Find a spot on the beach, sit down and tuck in.

'This is so good after hospital food.' I squeeze the bottle Bowie brought – because they never give enough, even if you ask for extra.

'That's a lot of ketchup. How are you feeling? Or is that *stuff*. If so, I take it back.'

'No, that's allowed. Weird. Tired. Wired. My eye hurts – eyelid, face too. The painkillers are a bit trippy. And I may not be able to ever see properly with my left eye. But I've got a spare, so I guess I'll get by with one. Though I keep walking into stuff, like I can't judge where things are.'

Now that my tummy is full of the yummy stuff, weird and wired are dissipating and tired is making a comeback. Bowie slips an arm around my shoulders and I lean back into him. Solid. Safe. Being here with him is so normal and so right. It makes everything else slip away. I cast around with my mind: Molly has done as she said and stayed away. It's just us.

'I was so scared,' he says. 'When I saw you go over the cliff. Whatever the stuff is, I have to tell you – what you mean to me. How much I care for you. Not just as a friend, Liv. I was kidding myself when I said that before. Can you handle this now? I'll back off if you say the word.'

He's warm, his heart beats a fast beat against my ear and I pull away a little, look into his two eyes with my one. I must look a bit of a freak with this eye patch, but he doesn't seem to mind. I want his arms around me. I want him to kiss me, so much – to push the darkness away. But it's not right – not now. It's not fair to use him like that when I don't know what it means.

'I think . . . I feel the same way. But I'm a mess, Bowie. I need to sort myself out before I can be sure how I feel.'

His eyes stay steady on mine. He nods. 'So, that's not a no. It's a maybe?'

'I guess. I'm sorry.'

'I will wait for you, Liv. As long as it takes. And I'll always be your friend – no matter what. You know that, don't you?'

'There is the *stuff*. You might change your mind, how you feel.'

He shakes his head. 'Won't happen.'

'Just the same, I think maybe we need to talk about it after all.'

'Are you sure?'

'Yes. No. Yes.' I shrug. 'And maybe I can't keep it all in any more. But this is going to sound pretty out there. Can you keep an open mind?'

'Totally open. In fact, so open, the wind is whistling through from one ear to the other just now. I promise.'

'Do you believe in ghosts?'

He's thinking, takes a while to answer. 'I guess what I'd say is, I'm not sure.'

'Echo – the boy I told you about – was a ghost. He was as real to me as you or anyone else; I didn't realise what he was until almost the last moment.' I tell Bowie the whole story, beginning to end; including about Kashina and the things she said. And I tell him about Molly, too. How she's always been with me; how she saved my life.

'Is she here now?'

I cast about again with my mind, but there is no answer when I say her name.

I shake my head. 'No, I asked her to stay away. There's more.' And then I tell him about the man in the hospital – how I found out about what happened to him online. And the little girl. And the others while we were texting the other night. And as I tell him, I'm blinking back tears, trying not to cry – left eye hurts too much to take it – and he holds me. Doesn't interrupt.

'So there you go: the whole story,' I say. 'Now you think I'm bonkers – you want to back away. It's OK. I understand.'

'You're wrong. I don't. But I think for your peace of mind – and mine a little, too – we need to find ways to test this, objectively. See if it is real. And if it isn't, work out what is going on to make you think that it is.'

I absorb that. 'I agree. That's why I wanted to check into that guy in the news.' I think a moment. 'There are some things already. Like stuff that Echo told me – his name, his mum's name, where they died. Years ago, wasn't it? How did I know about him if he didn't tell me?'

'There is one possibility,' Bowie says. 'I was trying to get my head around everything when you were in hospital. I went to the cemetery. Echo and Rose Lee have a plot near Molly's grave, with the usual details: names, dates of birth and of death. And it was thirty years ago, exactly, that night. So even if you don't remember explicitly, maybe you remembered their names from seeing them there? Anyhow, wouldn't Echo's ghost know how many years ago it was?'

I shake my head. 'He was trapped by that event – the same day, time and place every year. He didn't even know he died in the accident.'

'So does that mean he'll be back again next year?'

'I think so. Imagine having to go through the trauma of what happened year after year?' I shudder.

I'm thinking, trying to come up with something else – something about the other night? When it hits me. 'There's stuff I only know because Molly told me, like about when you came to our house before you and Rod went to look for me. That you

263

ran up and checked my room, then Mum found my note.' I tell him everything he did and said that I can remember from Molly's shared memories.

'Though did your mum tell you about that?'

'Not in that detail. Also, Molly was with you and Rod in the car when he got that call about Echo.' Again I tell him every bit she told me. 'I wouldn't know that if Molly hadn't told me. I haven't seen Rod since then, and even if he told Mum about it and she told me, once again it wouldn't have been in that much detail. You could check that with them? To be objective.'

'Though asking would be weird, unless you've told your mum about all of this already?'

I shake my head. 'Do you think I should?'

'You know her better than I do. But it'd probably be a good idea.'

'I'll think about it. Thank you. For listening. The thing that is bothering me about all of this – well, one of them, anyhow – is that first there was only Molly. Then there was Echo too – though I didn't know he was a ghost until the end. Why would I suddenly be seeing more and more?'

'I don't know. Has something changed maybe?'

When it occurs to me, I'm so surprised I didn't think about it before that I sit back upright. 'I think I've got it. Kashina – the psychic, who said I couldn't tell the difference between the worlds? She could see and talk to Echo too, and saw Molly. Anyhow, Kashina is blind in one eye. Like I am now.'

85

Liv

It doesn't take me long to find Kashina, her fortune-telling stall set out on a blanket. When she sees me – the patch over my eye – her reaction. Well, it's fair to say she couldn't have looked more surprised if a small spaceship had landed in front of her and a miniature army of minions trooped out of it.

'I need to talk to you,' I say.

'I'm busy right now.'

I look side to side; no one is even nearby. 'Yes, I can see you have quite a queue.'

'Don't be cheeky. I'm working.'

'So work for me.' I sit down on her blanket, put some coins in her hat. 'Please.'

She sighs. 'Your hand?'

She takes it in hers, then seconds later pushes it away as if afraid of what she saw. 'Go. I can't help you.'

'Please,' I say again. 'I need to understand. Echo is gone. Will he be back next year, before the anniversary?'

'You worked that out?' She sighs. 'Yes, every year. I have tried so hard to get him to see the truth, year after year. He never could – he can't accept that Rose would hurt him.' Real pain crosses her face.

'It's my eye, isn't it? The one that got hurt. Is it why I am seeing ghosts more now?'

She nods. 'Not everyone who damages an eye will have that happen – it only enhances the sight if you have it to begin with. Usually the sight is sporadic, unpredictable; enhanced by strong emotions or fear, like Echo was trying to do. If one eye is blind, it makes the gift – the curse – clear, so that is unnecessary.'

'Echo showed me a photo – of him and his mum. Her eyes looked normal?'

'Yes. That is why she had to use fear to communicate with the dead. Now that is enough questions – go. On your way.'

'Why are you so hostile? This whole thing has been impossible. I didn't understand. I was thinking – as was everyone – that I was losing my grip on reality, going crazy. That I could see things no one else could, didn't know what was real. Why don't you want to help me?'

'Hostile? Me?' She sighs again. 'I tried to help, to train one person, who became a dear friend – and she's dead. Her son is dead, too. I'm not dealing with that again.'

She gets up, starts gathering her things and I stand, help her fold her blanket.

'Please, Kashina. You said before that I couldn't tell the difference between the worlds. Is there a way?'

Her face softens. 'Now you are two-eyed – one for this world, one for the other. It makes it clearer, but you will suffer. I'm sorry. Though it was long ago, I do remember how frightening the sight can be when it begins. This is what you do to tell them apart. Close your normally sighted eye. If you can still see them, they are dead. And it doesn't matter if you wear an eye patch over the other eye or even close both eyes: you will still see them. It is beyond normal vision.'

I watch her as she walks away. She's so matter-of-fact about it all, which makes it seem more real. I mean, it has been real enough when it has happened, but all along I've been looking for some kind of way to get out of it – to the point that even thinking I was imagining things seemed better than what was actually happening.

She said she remembers how frightening it was when it began. How many years ago was that?

It's like a life sentence to something I never wanted, didn't ask for. Can't get away from.

86

Liv

My phone beeps when I'm walking home – alone. Still no sign
of Molly. I sigh. Is she sulking because I didn't want her to come
to meet Bowie?

A text: it's Bowie. Did you find Kashina?

Yes.

Helpful?

Not exactly – sort of. Long story. How goes the cooking/cleaning?

Tina isn't back yet grrrrr

I don't ask. I know what he'll say. I text Mum that I'll be late
as I'm going to Bowie's, and divert.

Walk up, knock on the door. He opens it a moment later.

'Liv? What are you doing here?'

'Is Tina back yet?'

He shakes his head. 'Can't believe it – this whole thing was
her idea. She went on about how she wanted to do all this to
make up for all the trouble she's been causing lately, and she's
not here.'

'Let me help.'

'No way – you're recovering. You're not hoovering.'

'Definitely not. But I could dust, or empty the dishwasher.
Not going, so you might as well let me in.'

'OK. Thanks,' he says. 'But stop if you're tired or whatever.'

'How much time have we got?'

He glances at a clock. 'About two hours.'

We dust, tidy, Bowie hoovers, then we head into the kitchen. As we go, I tell Bowie what Kashina said.

'So Echo comes back every year? You were right.'

'Yeah. And talking to her has made it really hit home. That the kind of stuff like what happened in the hospital could happen to me anytime, anywhere, and it may never go away.'

He takes off the rubber gloves and comes close, gives me a hug. I nestle my face in against him despite the smell of cleaners. 'One day at a time for now, OK?' he says.

'OK.'

And I'm wondering why I said maybe instead of yes, why I'm not kissing him, but then there's a knock at the front door and I pull away.

We go through and he opens the door – it's Tina's friend, Zahra.

'Where is she?' Zahra says. 'She needs to be told.'

'Tina?' he says.

'Who else? I waited, waited, waited – kept calling her, but she never answered. Didn't even text.'

'She didn't show for lunch?'

'No. Isn't she here?'

'No. She left just before I did – a bit before noon – told me she was meeting you. Promised to be back by two.' He's glancing at the clock as I do: it's almost four.

'That's weird,' Zahra says.

'I've been messaging and calling her too – no answer,' Bowie says. 'And you know Tina.'

'Yeah, she lives with her phone surgically implanted in her

hand at all times. She might blank somebody if she's annoyed at them, not otherwise.' They're looking at each other, uneasy.

'I couldn't believe she didn't come back to help when it was her idea,' Bowie says. 'Even for Tina, that was beyond. She'd at least have said she was going to be late or something.'

'She even told me she'd have to leave after lunch before two to get back – asked me to remind her,' Zahra says. 'But look, this is Tina we're talking about. She could have got distracted on the way, anything.'

'Yeah. But I'm still worried.'

87

Liv

'You've overdone it, haven't you?' Mum says. 'You look exhausted.'

'I'm OK. Need painkillers now though.'

'Sit.' Mum goes to the kitchen, comes back a moment later with tablets and a glass of water.

'Thanks.' I take them, sigh and lean back on the sofa. Molly comes in and sits across the room, arms crossed, saying nothing. Great. On top of everything else, she's still upset I kept her away from Bowie.

'Is something wrong?' Mum says. I turn, try to focus on her and ignore Molly.

'I hope not. But yeah.' I tell her about Tina. 'They're really worried.'

Molly is next to me now, contrite. *I hope she's OK.*

'Did they call the police?'

'Yeah. Bowie's dad talked to them on the phone – they were going to come by, but hadn't yet when I left. But they said she isn't considered to be a missing person yet – she's eighteen. She could have just decided to go somewhere and not tell them. And there was that other night just recently that they called the police and thought she was missing when she was just staying at a friend's house and forgot her phone charger. I don't think they're taking it seriously.'

'Could she just have taken off, not told them?'

'Sometimes maybe, but not today.' I tell her about the plans Tina and Bowie made for their parents' anniversary. 'Why would she come up with all that, and then not be there?'

Mum gathers me in for a hug.

I'm not very hungry, but manage some pasta that Mum makes that is nearly edible, listen when she says I should go to bed early, even let her come up and tuck me in – something I haven't let her do in years.

Molly is quiet, sitting on my desk. *Are you going to tell me?* she says, as soon as Mum has closed the door.

'What?'

What happened with Bowie. She looks at me closer. *Did you kiss him?*

'No.' But I'm smiling, thinking of the things he said. And I show her my memory of it all.

I knew it! That he's the one. I can't believe you didn't kiss him.

'The one, what?'

Now that we're sixteen. She winks.

'Shut up!' I throw a pillow at her and it sails through her and scatters pens and books off my desk. 'Look, I'm too worried about Tina and Bowie and his whole family right now for this.'

Sorry. She looks at me closer. *You really do need to get some sleep. You look dreadful.*

'Thanks.'

I try, but I can't drift away. I check in with Bowie now and then – nothing still from Tina. It's late now – where could she be?

I hear the door open and close below, voices – it's Rod. I get up, head down the stairs in my dressing gown.

272

'Hi Liv,' he says. 'How are you feeling?'

'OK. But there is something I need to ask you. Do you know anything about Tina Reilly? She's Bowie's sister.'

'I shouldn't talk about cases—'

'I was there all afternoon – I know all about it. Is everyone out looking for her now?'

'She's eighteen—'

'So?'

'Everyone knows what she looks like and are keeping an eye out for her.'

'Is that all? Shouldn't they be going door to door and all that kind of stuff?'

My phone vibrates with a text in my dressing gown pocket.

It's Bowie. Dad posted up about Tina on a neighbourhood Facebook page, and asked everyone to check video doorbells along the way Tina would have walked. Someone found footage of her walking with someone following her – then nothing on the next camera.

I'm just reading this when Rod's phone rings. 'Yes? Yeah, on it.'

'Is that about Tina and the door cams? Bowie texted me about it.'

He nods, just as Mum is coming out of the kitchen with mugs of tea.

'Sorry, love. Got to go.'

I have the tea that was meant to be Rod's with Mum, while I tell her and Molly what happened. Molly drops her mood and comes close, holds my hand while Mum gets on Facebook and finds the page and the videos posted up. It's not that clear but it's definitely Tina.

273

There is a shadowy figure behind her. A man. Tall – very. Broad shoulders, a hat shields his face enough that I'm not sure I'd recognise him if he walked past right now. Is it enough for the police to work out who he is?

And then the next door cam, across a road. Tina would have gone this way, to go where she was meeting Zahra. And nothing.

Mum gets a blanket – we snuggle up on the sofa. Molly, too. We're too worried to go to bed but Mum eventually drifts off. I listen to her even breathing. I'm tired but can't close my eyes. Something about all of this is bothering me; I can't quite figure out what. Then with everything drifting in and out that weird way it does just before you fall asleep, some connections slide into place.

Echo told me Rose was helping the police try to find a missing girl – thirty years ago.

There have been other missing girls now and then since then. Could it be the same person who has taken them? It could be, if he was young thirty years ago – say in his teens, even. He could be under fifty now.

Rose had been trying to help the police find that first missing girl. And Rose and Echo had been at that old church graveyard. After they left, they had the accident that may have been suicide. But what if it wasn't? Maybe someone forced them off the road – to silence her. Before she could tell the police something she'd learned.

Maybe there is something she told the police before this that ties in, would give a clue to what it was. Even if there isn't, if there is a ghost at that graveyard who knows something, maybe if I go back there now I can find out the same thing that Rose did. Help the police, finish what Rose started – and maybe this will lead to Tina.

I pick up Mum's phone – unlock it with her finger. She's stirring, starting to wake up as I call Rod. It rings and rings.

'Yes?' he says.

'It's Liv. I may be able to help find Tina.'

88

Liv

'Let me see if I have this straight,' Rod says. 'You've recently become aware that you can see and hear ghosts, and it was somehow enhanced by your eye injury. The ghost of Echo Lee, who died thirty years ago, told you his mother, Rose, a psychic, was working with the police and trying to find a missing girl named Elsie, and may have learned something from a ghost in a graveyard. You want us to check records of anything Rose may have told the investigation, as well as go to the graveyard and attempt to contact the same ghost that Rose spoke with.'

'Yes. But I'd have to do that last bit.'

Rod is nodding in a noncommittal sort of way. He must talk to a lot of people with a shaky grip on reality, and he's developed a way to deal with them. And now, me.

'You don't believe me. Do you?'

'It's not that I don't believe what you are saying is completely true to you, Liv.' His voice, face, are kind.

'Can you at least check to see if there is anything Rose said to the police thirty years ago?'

'I can, but I don't have to. I'm involved in the line of inquiry looking for any connections between missing persons in the area, going back over thirty years. I've read all the case notes. There was no mention of Rose Lee, or any other psychic – I'd remember that.'

He has to go. Mum goes with him to the door and I can hear their low voices, but not the words. The door opens, then closes.

You tried – you did what you could.

'It's not enough. Why wouldn't he believe me?'

I guess it's the kind of stuff a lot of people would have trouble believing.

'What about Mum?' I have visions of her locking me up and throwing away the key.

I don't know.

Mum comes and sits next to me, takes my hand in hers.

'Why didn't you talk to me about all this before?' she says.

'I guess I was afraid. Worried what you would think. But because of Tina – I had to.'

'Please, Liv. If you have a problem, if anything is worrying you, anything at all – come to me. I'll always listen. You know that, don't you?'

'I guess. But this isn't usual stuff.'

'No, I suppose not. But all the more reason to talk it through. And you've reminded me of some things I haven't thought about in a long time. I'm not sure if telling you will help or not. I'm pretty sure if I spoke to your doctors they'd tell me to keep it to myself. But there's a few things about my family that I've never told you, and I think it's time that I did.'

I'm surprised. What could this have to do with them? Mum was born here but her parents are Irish, and they moved back to Ireland when she was in her twenties. We visit them there once every few years and Mum always seems glad to get back home to England.

Then a penny drops. 'Do you mean a history of mental illness?'

'Not that there's anything wrong with that, but no, not that I know of – at least, not officially. It's about my Granny Brogan – your great-gran. The source of your middle name. She passed when you were small – you probably don't remember her.'

'I think I do. She was tiny, wasn't she? Funny glasses. Didn't she say something that upset everyone?' I frown, trying to remember.

'You were only about two the last time you saw her; I'm surprised you remember. She was tiny, about five foot nothing, and yes to the funny glasses. She'd had an accident as a girl that damaged one eye. And Granny Brogan was always saying things that upset everyone. One of which, was that you have the sight, same as her.'

'What? Seriously? Did she? Have it herself, I mean? And she had a damaged eye, too. What exactly did she say?'

'Well, she kind of cornered your dad and me. This was our first visit with you – so the first time she'd met you. And she said that you had the sight, could see and hear things others cannot. The next bit was what really set your dad off. Granny Brogan said that Molly was with you. Your dad was furious that she mentioned Molly like that.'

Molly's eyes are as wide as mine.

'What about you – what did you think?'

'I said I didn't believe it. But I was uneasy – there were many family legends about Granny Brogan saying things she'd have had no way of knowing and that turned out to be true. And a few years later – do you remember this? – you were four. I was asking about your imaginary friend—'

'And I said it was Molly. You were so upset, I never told you again.'

'And then a few days ago, when I first got to the hospital, you were delirious – kept calling for Molly. As if she was in reach. Was she? With you, there?' She hesitates, tears welling up. 'Is she here, now?'

I nod, tears slipping from my eyes, hers now, too. She takes my hand in hers, then holds out her other hand, trembling. Molly takes it.

'Molly?' Mum says. 'I've never stopped loving you.'

Tears would be streaming down Molly's face now if she could cry. Mum gathers us both together – the one she can see and feel, and the one she cannot. She holds us close.

Later I'm staring at the ceiling, trying to get some sleep. Even after what she said to Molly, I'm not sure how much Mum really believes. It's almost like, emotionally she does – or she wants to – but when she stops and thinks about it, I don't know if she'll talk herself out of it. But she did tell me about Granny Brogan, even though she wasn't sure if she should. And the last thing she said was that she trusts me. She knows I'll work it out for myself.

And that's just – wow. She can be more amazing than I give her credit for sometimes.

Maybe Granny Brogan was telling the truth: she had the sight, it skipped a few generations, and so do I. Or maybe . . . she had a mental illness. And so do I.

But what I come back to, again and again, is this: I *can't* believe I made up Molly all these years. She is here, next to me.

Quiet just now but she is real – a part of my life. And if she is real? It stands to reason that the rest of it is, too.

What now?

'I have to go to that graveyard. See if I can find out whatever it was that Rose did all those years ago.'

Not on our own. Get Bowie to come with us.

'I'm not sure I should.'

Well I am. Why not?

'I told him all about this, and it seemed like he had an open mind. But what if he doesn't really believe it? He'll think I'm freaking him out about nothing just when his family is freaking about something real.'

Show me what he said.

I replay the whole conversation.

OK. He wants objective proof, does he? Let's give him some.

89

Liv

I text Bowie, asking him to call if he's free. My phone rings soon after.

'Hi. Any news?' I say.

'Nothing. The police are taking it seriously now at least.'

'Bowie, I've been thinking. There may be something we can do that might help find Tina.'

'What is it?'

I explain about Rose, the graveyard. That the missing persons might be linked and there might be a ghost at that graveyard with an answer. That I want him to go there with me tomorrow.

He's quiet a moment. He doesn't know what to say, does he?

I can see him because Molly is looking through his bedroom mirror and is sharing what she sees. A place it turns out she's been before. I wonder how often she's gone there to watch him?

'Don't answer yet,' I say. 'Remember how you said I should try to look for ways to prove things objectively? Molly is with you now. Show her something or do something or whatever you can come up with that I'd have no idea about. She'll tell me, then I tell you what she said. Then you'll know it's for real.'

'She's here? Right now?'

'Yes.'

Molly flits back a moment later, laughing. *He's making faces. Looking all around. Tell him where I am.*

'OK. Molly says you're making faces and looking all around. She's actually looking through your mirror if you want to address her.'

His eyes are open wide.

He waves at the mirror. Hesitates, picks up a notebook. Writes something on it and holds it up to the mirror and Molly shows it to me here.

'OK. Llamas? Really? So you've written on your notebook, "Hi Molly! Thirty thousand flying llamas with minions on their backs are on their way to the moon."'

He's pale. 'Flipping heck, Liv.'

'Are you in?'

'Yes.'

90

Liv

Bowie is waiting when I get to the bus stop the next morning. It's a grey day, cold, which makes it easier to cover up school uniforms; today was meant to be the first day back after half term.

'Thanks for coming with me,' I say. Even though I'd decided I had to try this, I was nervous. Actually going looking for a ghost in a graveyard? Who knows what might happen.

He nods. 'If there's even a chance that this could work, I had to come.'

'How is everyone?'

'A mess. I keep hoping Tina will walk in, grinning and apologising and wondering what all the fuss is about, like she usually does. But somehow I don't think that is going to happen this time.'

'I hope it does, too.'

He hesitates. 'Is Molly here, now?'

'Yeah. Hold out your hand?'

He does and Molly takes it.

The bus comes. We get on and we're soon lumbering up the road. After a while we change to the second bus. Along the way I tell Bowie what Mum said about Granny Brogan. As I do, I can see him trying to reach for belief, for hope, that we'll find out something – anything – that will lead to Tina.

We get off the bus, take the short walk past a few houses, then go up a lane to the church. In daylight it lacks the fear factor of the night I came here with Echo. Birds are chirping in the trees, the sun is trying to break through clouds. We hold hands as we walk through the gate, up the overgrown path. Old graves, some illegible with age, tilt at odd angles near the church. Further along, towards the crumbling wall where I sat with Echo, are newer graves.

'Anything?' Bowie asks.

I shake my head. 'Maybe let me wander around on my own a while?'

'OK.' Bowie goes to the wall, leans against it, Molly next to him. I walk on alone.

The sun is peeking through now, but it is like its warmth doesn't penetrate the air of this place and I shiver.

A faint sound – rustling – laughing? I spin around – nothing is there. Silence. I walk on a few more steps and hear it again.

'I know you're there,' I say, but I'm only answered by silence. I turn slowly.

A child – a girl – is peeking up over a headstone.

'Hi,' I say.

Her eyes open wider, she steps out. Dressed in old-fashioned clothes – like a long pinafore – and she takes a few hesitant steps towards me. Close your good eye, Kashina said, to check. I do so. The girl is still there – light in darkness.

'What's your name?' I say.

I'm not supposed to talk to strangers.

'That's a good rule. But I bet you don't get many people who come and talk to you.'

No, not for a long time. Curiosity. Then her eyes shift over my shoulder – fear, alarm – she does a spin and vanishes.

You're back. An old voice, cold. I turn – a woman – and I don't even need to do the eye test to know that she's a ghost. Her skin is paper-white, her eyes, dead. *You couldn't see me the last time.*

'No. But I can now. I was hoping you might be able to help me with something.'

She turns her head to one side. *Why would I want to do that?*

'A girl is missing. We need to find her.'

She shrugs. *So many lost girls and boys. Living or dust, what is it to me?*

'Someone came here, years ago – she learned something from you or one like you. But she died before she could tell anyone what it was.'

That boy with you the last time – the dead one. It was his mother, Rose.

'So you do remember her! All I want is for you to tell me what you told her.'

You don't want to know.

'Tell me, then I'll let you know if you're right.'

She shakes her head. *Oh no, I'm not falling into that trap again. Rose was clever, you're not. Girls live, girls die. They die so easily.*

'Did you? Die, easily?'

Her lips tighten, fists clenched. *He didn't mean it. He never means it. Leave him alone!*

'Leave *who* alone? Someone you cared about? Let's see. A boyfriend? Husband? No, they'd be too old by now, wouldn't they. Maybe, your son?'

She shrieks, rushes towards me and slams into me, cold, so cold. It's like when Molly tries to slip inside and take over, but

285

she's stronger than Molly. I fall to my knees. Dimly I hear Bowie calling my name, alarmed. Molly is here now too, adding her strength to mine. Together we manage to push back strongly enough to keep this ghost from taking over my body, but she's showing us her memory:

He was strong – angry. Much bigger than her. He pushed her, slammed her head against the wall. Then raised his fist to her, and she crumpled to the ground. Even as I'm seeing and feeling her fear and pain, I'm trying to take in every detail of him that I can.

Molly joins with me fully and we focus: find the will, the strength, to push back against her as hard as we can. For a moment, it's equal – both sides trembling with effort. Then all at once, she lets go.

She's gone and I collapse on the ground.

Molly slips away. *Liv? Are you all right?*

And now Bowie is here too, his arms around me, asking the same thing. And I look at him, try to answer, but my vision has gone grey around the edges, as if I'm going to pass out. Gradually it brightens, and I breathe in deep.

Finally I nod. 'Yes, I'm OK. I'm OK.'

But I'm full of horror inside.

91

Liv

Once I've recovered enough, I go back in my memory to experience her death again. Molly does, too. We didn't see his face. But the size of him. His shoulders, hands. It feels like there is enough detail there now that I'd be able to recognise him. But how do we find him?

Bowie gets the doorbell cam of Tina up on his phone, and I watch it through again.

'I can't be absolutely sure, as his face isn't clear and I didn't get a proper look at it in the ghost's memory. But I really do think it is the same man. He was really tall, broad shoulders – the way he moves. His build is heavier now, but it's years later. If it is the same guy – if we can work out who his mum is, that should lead to him.'

'I take it she didn't give you a name.'

I shake my head. 'But maybe we can work it out? If her son is the one responsible for girls going missing and Rose found out from her, since Rose died just over thirty years ago, his mum must have been dead then. Because her ghost appears here, I'm thinking she's buried here. From what I saw in her memory, I think her son was something like twenty years old when she died. If she died thirty years ago, he'd be fifty now. If it was fifty years ago, he'd be seventy now – maybe that's too old to be the guy in the video. But say we take a window of time of burials of women between fifty and thirty years ago, note down who they are, when they died. Then the son of one of them is the one that the police need to find.'

We begin in the section with the newest burials, Bowie writing down names and dates of birth and death of everyone that fits our category. I take photos of their headstones too, in case we need to check any details later. Then we hunt all around in case any more recent burials are mixed in with the older ones.

Finally, we have our list: names, dates of birth, dates of death. Seventeen of them.

They have to have been the mother of a twenty-year-old when they died. So we cross out any that were too old or too young to have a son about twenty years old.

Eleven names are left.

We head for the bus stop.

'What now?' Bowie says.

'I'll call Rod and give him the list. He'll have to check them out. Won't he?'

When I look at my phone I see there are missed calls from Mum. I call her first.

It only rings once and she's there. 'Hello, Liv?'

'Hi.'

'So, I gather you're not at school.'

'No. Did they call?'

'Yes. I've been worried, Liv.'

'I'm sorry, but we had to go to that graveyard – Bowie is with me. We found out some things. The man who has been kidnapping girls? His mother is buried here. We've got a list of

288

eleven that could be his mother. Give me Rod's number? And email, too. And I'll give him their names.'

Silence for a moment.

'I'll message both to you. Then come home. All right?'

'Soon. I promise.'

We go back through the gate and leave the graveyard. Each step away from it is easier than the one before, and I'm glad to leave it behind. It's like the sun agrees with me as it has stopped hiding behind the clouds.

Mum's message comes through as we're getting on the first bus, and I call Rod's number. It goes to voicemail. 'Hi, it's Liv. I've got a list of eleven names of women buried in the graveyard I told you about, one of whom is the mother of the man responsible for girls going missing. You have to check it, all right? You can call me back to ask me anything, but I've got your email from Mum and I'll email the list to you.'

I'm part way through tapping the email for Rod into my phone when it's time to change buses. When we get on the second one, I'm soon done and just reading it through to check all the details are correct before sending, when I glance up. We're approaching the place where Rose and Echo's car crashed off the cliff to the sea.

What's this? There's a shadow in the road ahead. Getting darker, bigger. I'm looking all around, but there's no cloud, nothing to cast the shadow. Now it's too dark to be only a shadow, and fear and dread are squeezing me tight inside. A screech fills my ears – a chilling, horrible sound – and the bus disappears. We're surrounded by cold, black, death – it's her, the ghost from the graveyard – gathering us to join her and

I'm screaming, screaming—

The bus swerves. The sun is shining brightly again. The bus is pulling in. The driver walks back to us. 'What the hell is wrong with you? You nearly made me drive off the road.'

92

Liv

Once I apologise to the driver – say I fell asleep, was having a nightmare – he goes back to his seat, muttering. We continue to Brighton. My heart is pounding as I tell Bowie what I saw. Molly was so scared she left. She's only just back as we're getting off the bus, an echo of my fear in her eyes.

I send the email on to Rod. I try calling him again: voicemail.

'Do you think he'll take this seriously?' Bowie says.

'I don't know. Do you take it seriously?'

'Well, you either have a helluva overactive imagination or you really saw what you said, both in the graveyard and on this bus. Would it be trite to say you looked like you'd seen a ghost?'

'Trite and true.' To even think of it makes me shudder, feel sick with fear. 'That must be why Echo and his mum went off the road back there – I'm sure of it. I mean, if I'd seen what I did and I'd been driving, there'd have been no hope. Anyhow, as far as Rod goes, I'll ask Mum to get on his case too.'

I call her, again – explain.

'I'll try, Liv. But I can't promise anything.'

'Try really hard, OK? Text me how it goes. Thanks.'

'What else can we do?' Bowie says.

'I don't know. We could try the names in telephone directories or online, see if we come up with anything. But I'm thinking it might be worth talking to Kashina again, to see if she has any ideas about all this – she must understand all this psychic stuff better than me. Maybe she knows a way to find out this ghost's identity.

She's not out where I've seen her before, telling fortunes near the pier. We start asking around all the other sellers and small shops in the area. People shrug, say she comes and goes, that there's no real pattern as to when she is here.

Then one of them says, if she's not here then she's probably in a pub. But he shrugs when we ask which pub, then points to someone selling wooden carvings on a blanket, says he may know.

We go over to him. 'Hi. We're looking for Kashina. Do you know which pub she goes to?'

'Well now. There's a few, not sure I can remember.'

'This is pretty,' I say, picking up a small carving of a dolphin. 'How much is it?'

'Five pounds.'

I take out a note, he reaches for it and I pull it back. 'Are you sure you can't remember what pub Kashina goes to?'

'Can't think of the name, but it's close to the train station.'

I give him the money, pocket the dolphin and we set out for the station. My phone beeps with a text from Mum: Rod promised he'll look at the email when he gets a chance.

When he gets a chance, huh. When will that be?

There are a number of pubs near the station, but Molly goes ahead and directs us to the right one.

We can just see Kashina through a dirty window, sitting at the bar.

'We'll get thrown out,' Bowie says.

'Probably.' We go through the door.

Kashina looks up, sees us. Frowns. 'Oh no, not you again.'

'We need some help.'

'Go away.'

'Kashina, this is Bowie. His sister Tina is missing. I have some leads from an unpleasant ghost whose son may be responsible. Please.'

'There is nothing I can do. I told you before, I won't train anyone again.'

Please, Molly says.

'Now I'm seeing double. Your twin, I take it?'

'Yes – Molly. Please listen at least. You weren't responsible for Echo or his mum's death. It wasn't your fault. Let me explain.'

The guy behind the bar comes over. 'Kashina, you know the rules – get them out of here.'

She looks at me carefully a moment, then sighs. Knocks back her drink, heaves herself out of a chair.

'Come on. Outside.'

We step out of the pub, go past the few tables.

'OK, talk,' Kashina says. 'I give you five minutes.'

I tell her exactly what happened in the graveyard, then on the bus.

'If the same thing happened to Rose and Echo – it must have been an accident,' I say. 'Rose didn't mean to kill either of them. And that ghost must be the mother of the man responsible for a number of disappearances, including Tina's.'

She's staring at me as if she can see down deep, inside.

Finally, she nods. 'You might be right about it being an accident with Rose. But it would still be my fault that she went after something like that when she didn't know enough about what she was doing. And *you* – you've got nerve. That was stupid – going to a hostile spirit like that. You must be a tough cookie. Lucky your sister was there to help you.'

I shake my head, still scared to even think about it.

'I doubt Rose had as much figured out as you have now,' Kashina says. 'She struggled, her sight was hampered – she had two good eyes. That doesn't work as well. She had to channel fear and strong emotions instead. If she crashed her car like you said, she must have still been in that state or she wouldn't have seen this ghost. It's not a good way to be. What is it you want from me?'

'We made a list, based on dates, of who the ghost might have been.' Bowie gets out his notebook with the list, written legibly as it was by him and not me. 'I took photos of each one, too,' I say.

'Do the police have this list?'

I nod. Explain about Rod, my connection to him. That I'm not sure he'll look at it any time soon.

'Bah. Typical.'

'So, can you help? Is there like a friendly ghost who'll know who on this list is the hostile one?'

She rolls her eyes. 'It doesn't work like that. But *you* should be able to figure it out, yourself. Most of being psychic is observation, memory, drawing connections where no one else sees them, and intuition too. Look through the photos you took. Does anything strike you about any of them? Think about what you know about this woman and her son. Her memories were inside you when she showed you what he did. She could have let anything slip. Just let your mind wander as you look at each in turn. If that doesn't work, look at each one and tell yourself that it is the one you are looking for – see if that feels right to you.'

'Her memories – they were horrible.' I shudder.

She shrugs. 'Don't bother then.'

I glare at her. 'I'll do it. But I don't see how just *looking* at them is going to tell me anything.'

'That is for you to work out. Now, if you'll excuse me, I'm behind schedule.' With that she walks back into the pub.

93

Liv

We sit on a bench at the nearby bus station. I go through the photos, again and again, trying to do what Kashina said, but nothing.

'It's no good. I've got no idea at all.' I slump against Bowie. 'I'm sorry.'

He gives me a hug. 'Maybe, you're trying too hard. Take a break, think about something else for a while. Then have another look. But I'm thinking our best option is to hope Rod can be persuaded to look into each of them. The police must be able to find out which of them have sons in the area, their addresses.'

'Yeah. I'll try to get Mum on his case again. Speaking of which, I better get home. Come over?'

Bowie shakes his head. 'I should go home, too. In case, you know, there's any word or they need me around. I'll walk you home first, though.'

We walk in silence, holding hands. My thoughts are flying around all that has happened and been said on this strangest of days. And that somehow I'm supposed to be able to work this out myself? I can't get my head around half of it.

We get to my front door and Bowie gives me a hug. I look up into his eyes. 'Thank you for believing in me.'

'Well, now that I've met Kashina, I know you aren't the nuttiest resident of Brighton.'

'Huh. Thanks a lot.'

'Anyhow, I should be the one thanking you – doing things that scare you, for Tina.'

'I'll try again later – with the photos. I'll let you know if I come up with anything.'

'But no racing off anywhere without me. Promise?'

'I promise.'

'Bye,' Bowie says. I watch him walk away. He turns, waves, and I go in.

Mum isn't happy about us cutting school and going to graveyards. 'Please don't do things like this without telling me. I've been worrying.'

'I'm sorry. Just felt I had to do it. And Bowie came, so I wasn't alone.'

'So I saw. And I saw that hug, too. Does that mean he isn't friend-zoned any longer?'

I roll my eyes, then give Mum a less scary version of today's events – and leave out Kashina too. I'm not sure she's ready to hear about her. But even with a downplayed version, I can tell that Mum is having trouble taking it in.

'Please, can you check with Rod that he's looking into the names I emailed him? Somehow I think it'll work better if you do it instead of me.'

'OK, honey. He's coming by later. I'll do it then. He said to go to sleep, though – he'll be late.'

We have ready meals for dinner, then I fake yawning in front of the TV: I need to be alone.

'I'm really tired,' I say. 'I'm going up.'

My thoughts are whirling around. Eleven headstones –

eleven names. I print out the headstone images from my phone, mix them up and lay them all around. Reminding myself what Kashina said, about observation, memory, drawing connections, intuition.

I go through them, one at a time. Not focusing closely, like I did earlier; mind wandering. What strikes me about each headstone, each inscription? I try to imagine the family left behind, the woman who died in each case, as if I can see them from what is said.

The headstones vary from simple – name, dates of birth and death, that's it – to fancy, as if the family wanted everyone to know how much they loved and missed the woman they've buried. Now, that is hard to imagine in reference to this ghost.

Her son killed her – she showed me. Slammed her against a wall. Hit her, hard, once, with his huge fist – that was all it took.

She was small next to him. Was her memory just the way things happened, or something coloured over time? If it was softened, I'd hate to see how it was before. Yet she still wants to protect him, despite what he did. There was no thought of anyone else: as if it was always just the two of them.

He was an only child. As soon as this thought is formed, it feels right, true; he was the only one who meant anything to her. Even if he killed her, she wasn't going to betray him. They were alone in the world.

His dad wasn't around: he either died or left. I'm sure of it.

Back to the images I've printed out. Some of the inscriptions say things like, beloved wife, mother, grandmother, or loving wife and mother. None of these ones are her, I'm certain of it – there are five like this. I put them aside.

Six left. I space them out in a row in front of me.

What else?

I've been thinking of everything from her point of view. What about her son?

If he's still committing crimes, he must have got away with murdering his mother. And she's been buried in a churchyard, not hidden down a well or something. If he wasn't charged or anything and it was just the two of them, he'd be the one who decided what would be said on the headstone, wouldn't he?

I go back in my mind to the graveyard. Everything she said, the images she showed me. Her words, as she said them:

He didn't mean it! He never means it!

If she was right – and he killed her in a rage, never meaning to hurt her – how would he feel? How would that impact the inscription on her headstone?

Trying to get my head into his – when I only glimpsed him second-hand, through his mother – is hard. But if she was right about him not meaning it, he'd feel guilty. Maybe go over the top on the stone to compensate?

Or – maybe she's wrong. Maybe he had no remorse at all, in which case he might do the bare minimum. Small stone, name, date of birth, date of death – that's it.

I go through the six of them again. There are three that are simple like that. And one big, lots of marble. It says 'Devoted mother', name, dates, then, underneath, 'Never forgotten'. Actually, that doesn't say how her offspring felt about her: it just says she was devoted and won't be forgotten. Which isn't necessarily in a positive way.

OK, I'll put that one and the three that are basic into a pile as the most likely ones. But can I be sure I'm right to eliminate all the others?

Kashina said if I look at each, one at a time, and tell myself they are the one, I should be able to tell if they are or aren't by how it feels when I do that. I take the pile of rejects. Look at each in turn with that in mind.

And it's no, no, no for all seven. It's weird how strongly I feel it. How can I be that sure?

So I'm left with the four. And the start of a headache.

Anything on a search of the names on the headstones?

I do a search of each of the four names in turn. Each gives endless pages of hits but nothing that instantly feels important. What did I expect – a story about a scary son whose mum died in strange circumstances?

Maybe there is something on the Ancestry website? Burial records? Church records? I start trying to find out about all these things, but there is an endless sea of information that I don't know how to navigate. If I go to the library tomorrow, I bet someone who works there will know how to make sense of all this.

But somehow it feels like that approach – logical and sensible as it may be – isn't going the right way. And anyhow, I need this answer *now*.

I go back through the searches again, head spinning with information overload.

I keep going back to the images of the headstones. Something is niggling away.

The one that says, *Devoted Mother, never forgotten.* Her name was Margaret Fernsby. She died thirty-two years ago; she was

300

forty-three years old. If her son was twenty, she would have had him when she was twenty-three, so that works out OK. He'd be fifty-two now.

I do what Kashina said. I hold it in my hands, stare at it. Tell myself, this is the one.

There is no internal *no*, like with the others. Just complete certainty that it is the one I seek.

How can I be so sure?

I don't know. But I'll concentrate on Margaret Fernsby for now, see where that takes me.

Fernsby isn't a common surname; there are fewer hits than with the others. Though still way too many to read through.

I narrow the search to 'Fernsby, Brighton.' Nothing comes up that feels even remotely relevant.

Where could I find information on Margaret? What do I really know about her? Well, that she's a freaky scary witch of a ghost. I guess . . . I know what she looks like. I mean, probably not identical to how she looked when she died – she's been busy haunting since then, and that's bound to impact on her appearance – but are there photos of her anywhere I can find?

She was born seventy-five years ago. There was no social networking back then, no endless photos of everyone's life played out online. What kind of stuff gets put online after the fact?

Historical images: things like famous people; groups, maybe – like sporting clubs. Schools?

She was five years old seventy years ago. I search primary schools in the area, check websites to see when they were established to find the ones that are old enough. Some have friends of the school websites, classmate finders . . . *class photos.*

I switch to my laptop for a bigger screen. It takes ages going through every one I can find.

Then finally, there it is. According to the names written underneath, one Margaret Fernsby is seventh along from the left in the second row. It was taken sixty-eight years ago – she would have been seven.

A child of seven to a woman of forty-three at her death. Plus hauntings for thirty-two years or so before I saw her. Will I really be able to recognise her?

I don't count along to find the right child. Instead I let my mind be still, my eyes wander randomly around the faces on the screen. My eyes touch lightly first one child, then another, rejecting each one as I go.

And then I see her. Very pale, thin, long dark hair. There is a little more space around her, as if the other children don't want to get too close. Dark eyes. A smile on her lips that doesn't touch the rest of her. I look into her eyes on the screen: are you who I think you are?

Yes. It's her. It must be – it feels right. I count along. The one my eyes were drawn to *is* seventh from the left in the correct row: Margaret Fernsby. Goosebumps track up my spine and neck. Is this actually working?

Next: I need to track down her son.

Fernsby was her surname, aged seven, and also on her gravestone, aged forty-three. So if she got married she didn't change her name; or if she did, they split and she changed her name back. Either way, her son might have a different surname than her. Or maybe she never married and had a son on her own; then he might have the same surname.

302

My head is splitting – all this screen time with one working eye isn't something I'm used to.

I close my eyes and lie down.

Kashina's assertion that if I just looked at everything a certain way, the answers I need would be there seems to be working out. But it's not helping me find Margaret Fernsby's son.

I cast my mind back, yet again, to standing in the graveyard earlier. Meeting *Margaret*. The memories she showed me – a kaleidoscope of misery. Was there anything hidden in them that will help?

Going through her flashes of memory again makes me wince, want to pull away and hide. I focus, slow them down – to stills of each moment.

Her son's hands.

Big hands – muscular and tanned. Dirt under his nails but his hands weren't dirty. Like work gets it ingrained. Not grease like a mechanic; more like soil – a gardener, maybe. Or a farmer. Or—

Farmer. Wheat waving in the fields, the smell of it after rain. A snatch of memory from Margaret, one she didn't know she shared.

They lived on a farm.

Eyes open again, another search: Fernsby Farm.

A few hits come up with references to Fernsby Farm. It's in West Sussex!

This is it, I know it. There is this strong feeling of complete certainty in my gut.

Where is this farm, more precisely? There is almost no information on it; nothing in directories as to where it might be, or who runs it. Maybe it doesn't exist any more? Even if it does, maybe he doesn't live there now – he could be anywhere.

No. Where else would he go? There were just the two of them. It was a home he could never leave, not after what has happened there.

This won't work, will it? But I try, anyhow: put Fernsby Farm into the map app on my phone, and . . .

There it is.

94

Liv

I look out the window. Rod's car isn't here yet. The house is dark and silent – Mum is probably asleep. Should I call Rod, or wait until he gets here? Insist he goes to check out this place and find this guy?

He's probably not going to listen to me. Even if he does – would he rush over there tonight? Maybe Tina needs help right *now*.

But what else can I do? Go knock on this guy's door myself? Then I might be the next girl to go missing.

Don't even think about it. Molly is back.

What I *can* do – is go there, quietly, carefully. Not knock on the door. Just see if there are any ghosts around – friendly or otherwise – that can confirm my suspicions. I mean, if he's been involved in multiple disappearances over decades, there's got to be a good chance of a ghost hanging around the premises. If I find one and they can confirm what Margaret's son has done, then I'll call Rod. Say whatever it takes to make him come.

You promised Bowie you wouldn't go looking for ghosts without him, remember?

'I know. I'll let him know.'

First, I work out how to get there. The closest bus route will leave a long walk, but it's doable.

Phone out, I send him a link to the school photo I found. Then text: It's her: Margaret Fernsby. I think she lived with her son at Fernsby Farm. I send the map link. I'm going there now.

A reply, seconds later: Oh no you're not.

Oh yes I am. Rod isn't going to take my say so. All I want to do is go there, sneak around a little, quietly, to see if there are any ghosts in the area who can confirm or deny. If confirmed, call the police then.

Do you really think Tina could be there?

Yes.

I'm coming with you.

And then there is Mum. I can't wake her and tell her what we're doing; she'd never let me go. But I can leave a trail. Just in case.

I print off the map. Circle Fernsby Farm and leave it on top of the photo of Margaret's headstone.

I slip out quietly, glad it's not raining for a change. I get to the corner where we agreed to meet before catching a bus, and when Bowie arrives, I'm startled: he's in a car – on the passenger side. Tina's friend, Zahra, is driving.

I get in the back.

'Thought we'd best have a getaway car to hand instead of stuffing around on buses,' Bowie says.

'Hi Liv!' she says. 'Seat belt on, please. I haven't driven in the dark before – if I scratch this car my brother will kill me.'

'So . . .'

'Did I tell her we're going ghost hunting?' Bowie says. 'Yes.'

'Yeah, that's totally wild. And I'd do anything to help Tina. Who knows the way?'

I get the map up on my phone. As we leave Brighton, it must be said that we're going very slowly and carefully.

'Hope there isn't a high-speed chase,' Bowie says. 'We'd be toast.'

'Ha. Great,' Zahra says. 'Thanks for the encouragement.'

Before long we're on back country roads, then single lane.

'Pray no one comes the other way,' she says. 'Reversing isn't my strong point.'

But there's no one. It truly is the middle of nowhere.

'Should we pull over soon?' I say. 'There's only a mile or so more – easier to not be seen on foot. Unless you want to drive with no lights.'

'No way,' Zahra says.

'Or could we just drive by the place slowly – would that be enough for you to check the place out for, er, ghosts?' Bowie says.

'I don't think so. But anyhow, going by the map – we can't drive by. It's a dead end.'

'Nice choice of words.'

Zahra tucks the car into a passing place.

'Let's make a plan,' Bowie says. 'How about Zahra stays here in the car. We'll go there on foot, see if Liv comes up with anything, then come back. It should be, what – about a fifteen-minute walk?'

I check the map. 'That's about right.'

'So, if we're not back in, say, forty-five minutes – and haven't called you to say we need more time – then leave. And call the police.'

'Seriously?' Zahra says.

'Yes.'

I give her Rod's number.

We walk up the road using the light of Bowie's phone. When we get close, he turns it off. There isn't much of a moon but it's almost enough to walk without tripping on anything if we go slowly. I motion to Bowie to stop now and then. Just stand, being still, listening – casting out with my mind – but nothing. Go a bit further, and further again.

The gate to the farm is just ahead now.

'We are not going through the gate,' Bowie says.

'OK. Just here instead.' There's a stile to the side of the gate. We climb over, then cross a cattle grid in the lane. The lane is overgrown, weeds encroaching. Broken fences to one side. Neglect that makes me wonder if the place is abandoned? There are no lights ahead.

'What if there are dogs?' Bowie whispers.

'Dogs? I didn't think of that.'

'We need to stay within a quick dash of the gate. I don't think we should go much further.'

'OK.'

We stand still in the dark shadows. Waiting. Listening. Trying to be still in my mind, but it's hard when panic keeps trying to crowd in.

'Anything?' Bowie says.

I shake my head.

'Let's go,' he says. We walk back to the stile, and I take a last glance down the road.

A girl is walking towards us, shining a little in the dark.

Hello, she says. *Who are you?*

I'm getting better at this but do an eye check just in case. She's a ghost.

'I'm Liv, this is Bowie.'

'Who are you talking to?' he says.

'He can't see you.'

But you can! That's amazing!

'Who are you? We're trying to find Bowie's sister – she's been missing for a few days.'

I'm Elsie. Is his sister's name Tina?

'Yes! Is she all right?'

Elsie is troubled. *She is, but maybe not for long. She's refusing to even talk to him. He's very angry.*

'By *he*, do you mean Margaret Fernsby's son?'

Yes, Oliver Fernsby.

'Where is Tina?'

She's locked in one of the outbuildings. I can show you where.

I've been relaying this, line by line, to Bowie, and get my phone out to call Rod. 'There's no network,' I say.

Bowie checks his also, and curses.

'Where is Oliver?' I ask Elsie.

He's gone night fishing. Could come back any time.

'Can you check? Where he is right now?'

She disappears, comes back a few moments later. *He's not fishing any more, but he's not at the house, outbuildings or the barn, or in-between, either. I couldn't find him.*

I explain this to Bowie. 'We could go back to the car, call the police there if we can, or drive back until we get a signal.'

'But what if he gets back before then?' Bowie checks the time. 'Zahra will call the police in twenty minutes, anyhow. Liv, you go back. I'll try to find Tina.'

'You need me to relay what Elsie says. I'm coming.' And I

309

can see he is torn between the logic of that and wanting to keep me safe. 'You can't stop me,' I say, and finally he nods.

Molly keeps watch all around as Elsie directs us.

We go past the house and a few outbuildings to one at the back. Through a door. Bowie shines his phone light around: it's a workshop by the looks of it. A door at the back.

She's through there, Elsie says, and we go through the door to what looks like a storage room. *At the back – that door. It's locked.*

Molly goes ahead to look. *It's Tina*, she says, a moment later.

I relay this to Bowie and we rush in; he tries the door. 'Tina?' he says, voice low. 'It's Bowie.'

'Bowie? Is it really you?' She's crying. 'How did you find me? Get me out of here.'

I keep talking to her while Bowie looks through some tools. Comes back with a long piece of metal – a makeshift crowbar. Puts his phone down, angled to shine light on the door, then wedges the metal between the side of the door and the frame around it. Both of us heave on it, again and again. There's a cracking, splintering sound. It's starting to give.

We try again. It cracks a bit more. We reposition our crowbar and do it again. Now we can see Tina though a hole in the door. Another go and the hole is getting bigger.

Oliver is coming, he's almost here! Elsie says just as we make enough of a gap for Tina to pull herself through and into Bowie's arms.

'Everyone, quick,' I say. 'We have to hide – he's coming.'

We scatter, duck behind and under things, and Bowie switches off his phone light, plunging us into darkness. Now we can hear a car getting closer. But wasn't he on foot? Maybe

310

Zahra called Rod early and it's the police?

But Elsie said it was Oliver.

The car stops. Footsteps. The door opens, overhead lights come on: bright, dazzling.

Oliver is big, tall – thick arms. He's got a shotgun in one hand and Zahra held in front of him with the other.

The car we heard – it must have been her car. The police aren't coming. Are they?

Oliver sees the wrecked door, pushes Zahra in front of him, keeping a grip of her shoulder. He's looking all around. He's close to where Tina hides now, under a workbench.

Bowie is on the other side, crouched behind a stack of wood. He gets up slowly behind Oliver – then leaps out, swinging the crowbar. Oliver must hear something – he turns and ducks so it connects with his shoulder not his head. He staggers, loses his grip on Zahra but doesn't drop the gun. Now Bowie is too close to him to shoot and he's trying to get a lock around Oliver's neck, but is shaken off. And then – Oliver's fist – it connects with Bowie. He crumples slowly to the ground. Oliver points the shotgun at Bowie's head.

'Come out, Tina. Who is this? A boyfriend? You don't want me to shoot him, do you?'

Tina stands up slowly. 'He's my brother.'

'Anyone else with him?'

'No,' she says.

'You two,' he says, and points at Tina and Zahra. 'Go back through that door.' He gestures with the gun to the door we'd just got Tina out through. They're moving towards it, terror on their faces.

311

I'm sick in my stomach. He doesn't know I'm here, but he won't take Tina's word for it – he'll search the building, won't he?

Run – get out of here! Molly says. *Then you can send help. Go!*

But I'm frozen with fear. He'll hear me if I move, and he's got a gun. Even if I make it outside, it's dark – I don't know the area – and we're miles from anywhere. What should I do?

Let me help. Elsie.

'How?' I answer her, silently.

If you let me in, I can talk to him – he'll listen to me.

'He killed you.'

Yes. But he loved me, too.

I hesitate. This would be dangerous with a hostile spirit like Margaret – Kashina implied I was lucky to get away from her.

I'm scared, Molly says. *Don't do it.*

'Got a better idea? Anyhow, Elsie isn't hostile.'

But what if she won't leave?

What choice do I have?

'OK,' I say.

Elsie settles around me gently, not a full-on assault like Margaret the other day, or even Molly at her worst. I force myself to relax.

Everything blurs, changes. I'm still here but tucked in a corner. What I can see has changed to half-light and shadows.

Elsie is in charge.

95

Elsie/Liv

Elsie stands up. 'Olly, what are you doing?'

He spins around, shock on his face that clears when he sees a face he doesn't recognise.

'It's me, Olly. Elsie.'

'How do you know about Elsie? Don't say her name again.' He's wild — angry — and I fear for her. For us.

'I *am* Elsie. I died nearly thirty years ago but I never left.'

'Shut up!' he says, and his face — it is warring between fury and pain.

'The flowers, you found — all through the woods. Spring flowers gathered and you put them all around me. Tucked in my hair. You cried. Tried to kill yourself then, didn't you? But you couldn't pull the trigger.' As Elsie says the words I see it in her memory: her body, cold and still. A profusion of blooms all around her. What was she — seventeen? I grieve a girl I never knew.

'How do you know all this?'

'I'm a ghost, Olly. I've never left you — I promised I'd never leave you, no matter what, didn't I? So I stayed. This girl — this body — isn't mine. She's letting me use it to talk to you. You have to see reason, Olly. You can't keep doing this. No matter how many girls you bring here, none of them will be me.'

Tears are running down his face. The gun has dropped down,

313

almost slipping from his hand. And even though I'm caught in this tableau as it unfolds, it is all one step removed – as I am.

As Molly always has been.

Elsie promised she'd never leave Oliver. And she didn't. No matter what he did – and it must have horrified her. What did this cost her? What has she witnessed all these years?

She's in pain – so is he. She loved him too – or at least what she hoped he could become. And what made it worse is that she was trapped with him in silence: he couldn't see or hear her. She couldn't do anything to stop the things he did – the other girls he brought to this place. Their deaths.

There's a distant sound – a car? Getting closer. Oliver turns his head – holds up the gun again.

Screeching tyres. Voices.

Whoever it is must see the lights in this building; steps are coming this way.

Oliver is pointing the gun at the door.

'No, Olly – no. Don't do it. Let this end now.'

He goes through the door to the workshop. The lights go out, plunging us in darkness. Molly checks outside – tells me it is Rod and another policeman, getting out of a car. Walking towards this building. They must have seen the lights before they went out.

And Olly is waiting for them in the dark with a gun.

Please, no, no. Not Rod. I want to shout out, to warn them, but Elsie is still inside me and so terrified for Oliver and what he might do that she is frozen.

BANG – so loud it rends the air and takes my breath away. And Molly screams: *It's Oliver – he shot himself*, she says.

Elsie pulls away from me in a rush to go to Oliver. The lonely boy who only knew cruelty and violence – who almost broke free of it, loving Elsie. The man who did so much that was wrong.

Both are gone, for ever.

96

Liv

I collapse to the ground. Elsie's emotions – her agony, when she heard what Molly said – strong inside me still. I roll into a ball, shaking, crying.

Dimly I'm aware of other voices: Rod's, another. Molly is back with me now, cradling me in her arms.

Bowie. Is he all right? Fear lurches in my gut.

I sit up, open my eyes. The lights have been switched back on now. Bowie is on the ground where he fell – unconscious. Tina is with him, Zahra nearby. Rod is telling Tina not to move Bowie, that paramedics are on the way.

I get up. Go to the doorway.

Elsie is cradling Oliver just through it. Crying and saying goodbye.

She kept her promise. She couldn't leave, not until he died.

She's changing: becoming more translucent. Brighter. Patches of light are shining through her.

She looks to me and shares memories: a panorama in an instant. She was brought here over thirty years ago, when she was sixteen – forced to be an unpaid servant by Margaret. Margaret was a bitter, cruel woman; she ruled her son much like she did Elsie. Until one day, in a fit of rage at how his mother was treating Elsie, Oliver had finally had enough. He struck and killed his mother.

And Elsie thought, at last, she was free. But Oliver wouldn't let her go. Months later he lost his temper, struck her. She died, but stayed as she'd promised. Years later he took another girl, then another. Trying and failing to find another Elsie. Tina was the latest.

As to why his mother's ghost was guarding the graveyard and the road instead of her home, Elsie doesn't know. Maybe she couldn't face what she'd done to her son – what she'd made him become.

Elsie says thank you. Tells me where she and the others are buried, then says goodbye.

She is glowing, bright – light shining through her more and more until I'm almost blinded. She has peace at last. And then she is gone.

Ambulances are here now. Nothing can be done for Oliver. He sits up from his body: the darkness is gathering around him, taking him, but he doesn't scream or struggle. He disappears in a point of darkness.

Bowie is groaning, regaining consciousness. They're stabilising his neck, his back. One of them checks me quickly. My wounds aren't physical, but they are deep.

I finally understand so many things that I didn't before.

Molly promised she'd never leave me, too. She is as trapped as Elsie was, and how have I made that easier for her? I haven't. It's all been about me, what I need, want. I have to let her go.

Do you mean it?

'Yes. I love you, Molly. I release you from your promise – you're free. Go.'

I love you, too. Kiss Mum goodbye for me?

317

I nod, through the tears. Like Elsie – and the little girl in the hospital – bright light shines through Molly. She blows me a kiss.

And then, she's gone.

I'm alone.

For ever.

97

Liv

Weeks later, I slip out on my own to meet Kashina. My eye patch and stitches are gone – the scarring and redness are still a bit much. Mostly I wear sunglasses but I take them off so she can see.

'They said they might be able to, basically, scrape some of the scarring off my eye,' I say. 'Not convinced that sounds like fun. Or put me on the list for a corneal transplant.'

'Well, you have to ask yourself: who do you want to be? If your vision is restored, your sight will decline.'

'I haven't worked that one out yet.'

'You are a crazy girl. All of you are lucky to be alive.'

'I know.'

I tell her what happened – the parts of the story not in the news.

It turned out that something I said did get through to Rod. He decided to check into what I'd told him about Rose, and tracked down and spoke to a retired policeman, the one who'd originally been looking for Elsie. He confirmed Rose was helping them; that she often had, unofficially, and her skills had helped them solve cases before. She'd do anything to help girls like Elsie; she had a history of being a victim of abuse herself. Is that why she was so upset about Elsie? So upset that she saw Margaret even with her two good eyes, and had the accident that killed her and Echo.

Rod felt uneasy enough about what he learned about Rose to take what I said seriously – at last. He went to our house to talk to me, roused Mum. They found I was gone and the address I circled. He and his partner went straight to the farm then.

Bowie made a complete recovery from his concussion. Apart from being locked up and terrified, Tina was unhurt. She and Zahra are dining out on it all; Zahra's brother has even forgiven her for the scratches on his car made by Oliver veering into hedges on the way to the farm.

The reported version is that I somehow pretended to be Oliver's long-dead girlfriend, convinced him to give himself up, and at the last moment he turned the gun on himself. They kept quiet that I led the police to where Elsie and the others were buried.

Despite everything, Elsie cared for him. It had been the two of them against his mother before Oliver killed his mother. And then everything changed. Killing his mum changed him. It was as though he blamed Elsie for what he'd done. He'd done it to protect Elsie; that wasn't her fault but he couldn't see it that way.

'I need your help, Kashina.'

'We've talked about this before. Anyhow, if you had asked me – about allowing Elsie in, to do what she did – I would have said no. Never. Yet it worked. Maybe your own abilities and judgement are things that can't be taught.'

'But there are so many things I don't understand.'

'Join the club.' She sighs. 'OK, ask.'

'Why didn't Molly and Echo never seem to see other ghosts, but Molly could see Echo? Why could I see both of them but not other ghosts?'

320

'Before your eye injury, your sight was limited to moments of extreme emotion or fear. You saw Molly to begin with because of birth trauma; she stayed to be with you so you could both see each other still. Most ghosts are not aware of other ghosts unless they are connected in some way. From what you've said before, Molly probably could only see Echo because you did. So when you weren't there, she couldn't see him. But as to why you could see and hear Echo – so fully that you thought he was alive? I don't know. Maybe because in some way you were the one who was meant to help him? There aren't always answers to these questions. Sometimes people who don't have the sight can see or hear – or both – a ghost that is significant in their lives. Maybe it was something like that.'

'But I didn't help Echo. He's still trapped, isn't he? And he'll be back again next year at the anniversary of his death?'

'I expect so. He comes every year.'

'Where is he now?'

'My guess is that he is between worlds – not aware of time passing until it is near to when they died.'

'Next year, at this anniversary – can we somehow explain it all to him so he'll understand, and not have to go through this over and over again?'

'I tried to, many times. It's like this: he can only see and hear what backs up his version of the world. Nothing else gets through or is remembered. For that reason he is unlikely to even remember who you are the next time he comes; he only knows me because I was part of his world before he died.'

'But now that I understand what he is, would it make any difference if it is me explaining all of this to him?'

She hesitates. Finally she says, 'I honestly don't know. But my instinct says it won't.'

'But we know more than you did when you tried before – that it was the ghost of Margaret Fernsby that caused the accident that killed Echo and his mother. Maybe he couldn't take in what you said because you thought Rose caused the accident on purpose.'

Her head tilts to one side. Thinking. 'There may be something in that.'

'Would he have seen Margaret's ghost just before they died – the way I did on the bus?'

'He had some undeveloped ability, though not as strong as yours or Rose's. But given that it was a moment of terror, there's a good chance he would have.'

'Perhaps that is the real reason why he keeps seeking fear? As if he somehow knows that is what he needs to understand what happened. If only we could get Margaret and Echo in the same place and time, seeing her might make him remember.'

'But he never saw her at the graveyard.'

'No. Well, I guess all I can do is try again next year, at his anniversary – to explain all of this and hope he can understand. That Rose didn't mean to kill herself, or him.'

'Wait.'

'What?'

'Be quiet. I'm thinking. Could we . . . no. Or maybe . . .'

'What?'

'Sssssh.' She holds up a hand. I stay silent. Minutes tick by. Finally she nods. 'Yes, I think it would be worth a try.'

'What would be worth a try? Tell me!'

'To bring Margaret and Echo together. If he sees her, it may bring back his memory. If he understands what really happened, he should be able to rest.'

'How?'

'Summoning Echo shouldn't be difficult if we pick the right time and place. The problem is getting Margaret where we want her to be. There could be a way, someone who knows how.'

'What way? Who? Tell me!'

'No. Not now. I have to think.'

Kashina calls me late that night, says she has something to tell me but not over the phone – to come in the morning. I agree, but after I put the phone down I can't wait. It needs to be now.

I slip out of the house quietly, apologising silently to Mum on the way and hoping she doesn't wake and notice I'm gone.

A quick walk in the dark to Kashina's front door. I knock. When she opens it she doesn't seem surprised to see me, and stands aside so I can come in.

'There is an organisation that researches psychic abilities,' she says. 'Rose was in the process of joining them when she died – not something I want to do. But I've called in some favours with them to borrow a trap.'

She reaches into a pocket and holds up what looks to be an oversized locket, and begins to explain what is involved.

98

Liv/Anna

I haven't been back to this graveyard since the last time I faced Margaret. I'm scared. She was horrible and I'm going to deliberately make her angry? And Kashina said she couldn't come with me – that she would if she could, but if Margaret could sense two psychics, she might be suspicious and either hide or be harder to trap. Which all made sense until I arrived on my own.

Well, not completely on my own – just lacking psychic backup. Bowie is here with Tina and Zahra – the latter to drive, and Tina, because she wanted to see me 'nail that bitch'. Even though I told her she wouldn't be able to see anything.

The sun is shining but I shiver when we get to the gate.

'Are you OK?' Bowie says.

'Ish. Yes. Fine. Remember what I said?'

'Stay out of the way until it's over. Got it. We'll stay by the gate until told otherwise.'

I walk on, leaving them behind. Through the gate, the sense of chill increases. Margaret is watching me; I can feel it.

The locket is around my neck on a long silver chain; I hold it in my hand.

I find the headstone: 'Devoted Mother, Margaret Fernsby'. What was it about these words that convinced me this was the grave that held the mother of Tina's kidnapper? I know the reasoning I used, but I also recognise, now, that wasn't the real reason. It's just something I felt in my gut. I feel it again now: Margaret is near. Watching me.

'Margaret, are you listening?' I say. 'Of course you are. I just wanted to thank you.' A pause. 'You really helped me find my friend Tina. Actually, if it wasn't for you, Oliver would still be alive.'

Now the sun is gone, obscured by darkness. There is a roaring in my ears – sounds that I hear inside not outside.

Margaret stands in front of me now. Kashina told me that if hostile ghosts have a weakness, it's curiosity.

You're lying. You must be.

'I'm not. Elsie – you remember her, don't you? The girl you imprisoned and forced to be your servant? The reason why your own son killed you? Anyhow, Elsie helped me find Tina. Elsie spoke through me to Olly, as she called him. Told him it had to stop. The police came, but before they got in, Oliver shot himself.'

Nooooo! A cry of anguish. *I don't believe you. You're lying. Why are you lying?*

'You'd know what happened if you'd been there. You've kept away from him – what kind of devoted mother does that?'

A shriek tears into me and through me and she's rushing at me now, and Molly isn't here this time to help me hold her back. It's all about timing. The moment Margaret tries to force her way inside me, I'm to open the locket. I throw up images of Oliver, the violence of his death – she's trying to crush me now, it's time—

But there is another voice, a small one. Crying and thrust between us just as the locket is in my fingers, poised to open.

It's that child ghost, the one that followed and giggled – then

325

vanished in fright at Margaret. Margaret is gripping her hard, holding her between us even as Margaret is trying to attack me.

'Let me help you,' I whisper to the girl and show her how. Pull her inside me, like I did Elsie, to shelter her from Margaret, and then I open the locket.

Margaret is clawing, struggling, to get away – she's swirling all around me now. Then like the locket is the plug pulled out of a bath, Margaret is sucked down into it all at once.

I close the locket.

The sun is shining again.

'I like being you. Breathing, feeling the sun.' Laughter is bubbling up inside me that isn't mine. She's squirming inside me, as if she is trying me on and liking the fit.

'Bowie! Help me. I— !' The words choke off. Anna is her name – she's filling me up inside.

We're fighting for control of my hands – Anna is reaching for the locket to let Margaret out.

Bowie comes running, Tina and Zahra at his heels.

'Liv?' Bowie says and I'm looking at him, wanting to ask for help even as my eyes and my voice are taken over. I'm pushed to a corner inside.

She sits up, and laughs. 'No, silly! I'm Anna.'

'What happened to Margaret?'

'She's in the locket,' she says, brandishes it, poised to open it, and I'm struggling to stop her but she's in control.

'Don't let her out,' Bowie says.

'Why? She set this up for me. I owe her a favour and . . . Oh. Actually, you're right. I don't want to owe her favours. Take it.' She pulls the necklace off our neck and throws it to Bowie.

Then there's another voice inside her – mine.

Anna! Listen to me, young lady. I use a sharp tone.

'What . . . ?'

I told you not to talk to strangers. Look at the trouble it has got you into! And how many times have I told you that it isn't right to take things that don't belong to you?

'But I want it!'

No buts. Give her back her body. It's not yours.

'Do I have to?'

Yes. Be a good girl.

A huge sigh. 'Fine.'

Anna slips away and I slump back into my body.

99

Liv

We meet Kashina near midnight by the cliff where Rose and Echo died – at the bottom of the cliff. She tells Bowie and the others to leave us now.

Bowie doesn't want to go. 'I'll be all right, I promise. Kashina won't do this with an audience.'

'Call as soon as you can, and we'll come get you.' He gives me back the locket with Margaret locked inside.

Once they're gone, I tell Kashina what happened with Margaret and Anna.

'You didn't mention Anna before. I would have warned you.'

'What was she – she seemed different to other ghosts? Not that I've come across that many.'

'Mischief, I call them. Restless spirits that want to mess with us a little, have fun at our expense. Not malicious exactly, just thoughtless – very like a young child. How did you know how to speak to her to make her leave?'

'Maybe because when I met her the first time she said she wasn't supposed to talk to strangers. And she sounded like a naughty child, so I spoke to her like one.'

'Just the right touch.'

'What next?'

'Now we call Echo. We are standing – as near as I can figure – where he and Rose died; this is the place with the strongest pull to him. Also, I have brought things that tie him to us and to Rose, things Rose owned that were important to her – that bind the two of them. We also need to make a circle Margaret can't easily cross, to make sure she doesn't just bugger off when we release her.'

'How do you do that?'

'With every ghost the answer is different. I've made some guesses. Margaret didn't want her son to be caught, yet it seemed that she never went near him after she died.'

'Which is weird, as it was kind of like everything centred on him.'

'Exactly. So I have made a rope.' She takes it out of her bag. 'It includes strands of his hair.'

'Oliver's hair?' She nods. 'How did you get that?'

'A friend in the morgue.'

'Yuck.'

'Yeah. But it should work.'

She twists the ends of the thin rope together and lays it down on the ground in a circle, half a metre or so in diameter. Then she takes out two lengths of string and threads one into one side of the locket and the other into the other, then places the locket in the circle, with the ends of string over opposite edges of the circle. This way we can release her by pulling the locket open with the string without any danger to ourselves.

'Now Liv, sit on the ground close to but not in the circle we've made.' She hands me a gold chain. 'This is Rose's necklace – Echo gave it to her. Wrap it around your hands. Here also are photos of the two of them. Rose's incense too – we will burn this.' She lights a match – it catches. 'And now, close your

329

eyes, focus on my words. Go back, in your mind. Think of Echo. And remember . . .'

Kashina's voice is hypnotic. At first I'm listening to her words, but then it fades away and I'm wandering in my memories of Echo, reliving them. His eyes – how they drew me towards him, as if I were falling into something dark that may never let me go. The fear I felt when he fell on that building site and I didn't know if he was hurt. The pain, too, when he told me he was in the car with Rose. I knelt, held him on the beach. He cried. And I can feel him in my arms, here, now . . .

He's here.

100

Echo

Someone holds me. I don't know where I am. I open my eyes.

It's dark, but I can see her in the moonlight – a girl. Pretty, tears on her face. One eye scarred. Like Kashina's.

'Echo,' the girl says. 'You came.' She reaches a hand to my face. But who is she? Where am I? I'm looking around, head spinning.

The cliff. The sea – so close. Are we? *That place.* No.

I scramble to my feet.

'What, you again?' A voice that I know: Kashina.

'Why am I here?'

The girl is standing now too. Her hand takes mine and it feels right, like my hand remembers how it feels to be held by hers. But I don't know her.

'Who are you?' I say.

'I'm Liv – your friend.'

I'm drowning in her eyes, her truth. But I don't know how we know each other.

'Listen to me,' she says. 'Please? There was a terrible accident – your mum was driving. The car went over the cliff. She died. You died too.'

'No. You're wrong. I didn't die. What is this nonsense?'

'Everyone thought she drove off the road and died on purpose. Took you with her. But it's not true.'

'She wouldn't do that—'

'Listen to me, Echo. You're right. She didn't. She wouldn't.'

'But then, how . . . ? What happened?'

'A hostile ghost, she caused the accident,' the girl says. Liv – she said her name was Liv – and Kashina look at each other. Kashina nods.

'It's time,' Kashina says. Each of them picks up a piece of string on the ground, pulls it—

A rush of anger and darkness fill a circle on the ground: a woman, long dead. The look of her, the feel, too – I know her somehow, but I don't want to remember, I want to run—

As if they know, Liv takes my hand, Kashina the other.

'Echo, you have to face her,' Kashina says. 'You have to face what happened.'

'He's a coward,' Margaret – somehow I know her name – spits out. 'Like all of his snivelling kind. His mother had more spirit but I still laughed when she died.'

And her words, her face – who and what she is and was – fill my mind. I drop to my knees, wrap my arms around my head, trying to make it stop . . .

Driving . . . too fast. Slow down a little, I said, and Mum eased off the accelerator, but then . . .

The road disappeared. A shriek of rage filled me with terror – the car, swerving, bouncing, flying through the air, twisting—

The impact far below – hard. Where we are now. On the road, the rocks, the sea.

Mummy – help me . . .

She loved me, but she couldn't save me, or herself. She couldn't . . .

But she didn't mean it. It was an accident.

And it was caused by *this* thing caught in the circle.

I'm weary. So weary of this world and this pain.

'Echo?' It's the girl, Liv. She cups my face in her hands. Tears stream down her face, and now I remember her too. How she almost died because of me. And she still did all of this, to help me?

'I . . . I remember,' I say. 'Everything. You, too. Thank you.'

She smiles. Sorrow grips me inside at what she could have been to me, if we'd been born at the same time. If I'd lived.

There's light shimmering all around me now. It's time — isn't it? At last.

'I think . . . I have to go.'

'I know.'

But there is one more thing I have to do.

101

Liv

Echo reaches for me. He smiles, and I see and feel what he could have been – if he'd had a life to live. He leans forward, closer. A feather-light kiss of starlight that tastes of my tears and forever, and no time at all.

Light shines through him more and more. He's radiant.

And then he's gone. He's gone, for ever.

Some part of me is aware that Kashina is drawing in the circle holding Margaret, making it smaller and smaller until Margaret disappears. But all I can feel are my empty arms.

Echo is finally at peace.

I am broken.

Epilogue

'Happy birthday, Molly,' I say.

And still I hold my breath, and wait. For her to rise out of the ground at her grave like she does every birthday. But nothing.

'How does it feel to be seventeen?' I say, and bend down, place the flowers I brought, and sit there on the ground next to her.

Funny how even though she never answers any more, I can't get out of the habit of talking to her.

A year is a long time.

A lot has happened. I give Molly a quick summary to mark the day.

Rod surprised me, and Mum too: he is still around. If having me in the family isn't enough to scare him off, he just might be a keeper. He has even moved in and brought the world's cutest puppy and her mum along with him. That puppy got me through a lot late at night.

Kashina still insists that she isn't training me, but she answers my questions now and then. She's not drinking, not so much, now that the burden of the guilt she carried for Rose and Echo has eased.

I've started to come to terms with what I have become, and how much I've gained from it: being able to save Tina and help Elsie. Freeing Echo too. These were things only I could do.

Molly was right about Bowie. A smile plays across my lips. It took me a while after that last dark night with Echo to process everything, to know what was right. I needed to mourn Echo, and Molly too. Bowie was amazing; he gave me the space and time that I needed. But ultimately everything that happened made me realise how much he meant to me. And that we waited to get together made it even more perfect when we did.

A year on, it gets harder to believe what happened. That Echo ever popped up behind that headstone on my sixteenth birthday and started the whole thing off. That he convinced me, somehow, to join him in doing all those crazy things.

That Molly was ever in my life. I run my fingers across the headstone.

It took me a while to realise that by trapping Molly in this world, it wasn't just her who couldn't move on. It was me too.

'Happy birthday, Molly,' I whisper again.

'Teri Terry is a master of the thriller'
Scotsman

THE *DARK MATTER* TRILOGY

THE *SLATED* TRILOGY

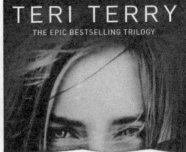

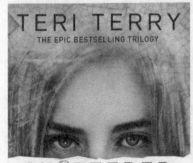

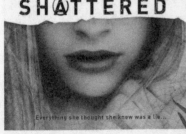

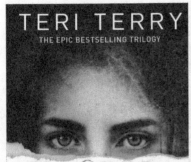TERI TERRY
THE EPIC BESTSELLING TRILOGY
SLATED
Can you know the truth if your mind has been wiped?

TERI TERRY
THE EPIC BESTSELLING TRILOGY
FRACTURED
In a world full of danger, who can you trust?

TERI TERRY
THE EPIC BESTSELLING TRILOGY
SHATTERED
Everything she thought she knew was a lie...

THE PREQUEL
TERI TERRY
MULTI AWARD-WINNING AUTHOR OF *SLATED*
FATED
One girl. One deadly choice.

AVAILABLE IN PAPERBACK, EBOOK AND AUDIO

photo by Debra Hurford Brown

TERI TERRY

is the bestselling author of the *Slated* trilogy and prequel, *Fated*, the *Dark Matter* and *The Circle* trilogies, as well as standalone titles *Mind Games, Dangerous Games, Book of Lies* and her most recent work, *Scare Me*. Her books have been translated into seventeen languages and won prizes at home and abroad.

Teri hates broccoli, loves all animals – especially her dog, Scooby – and has finally worked out what she wants to do when she grows up.

STAY UP-TO-DATE WITH TERI

🅯 @TeriTerryAuthor

🐦 @TeriTerryWrites

📷 @teriterrywrites

teriterry.jimdo.com